THE DUCHESS OF CASTILE

Also by Julian Fane

Morning
A Letter
Memoir in the Middle of the Journey
Gabriel Young
Tug-of-War
Hounds of Spring
Happy Endings
Revolution Island
Gentleman's Gentleman
Memories of my Mother
Rules of Life
Cautionary Tales for Women
Hope Cottage
Best Friends
Small Change
Eleanor

THE
DUCHESS OF CASTILE

——— ◆ ———

JULIAN FANE

CONSTABLE · LONDON

First published in Great Britain 1994
by Constable and Company Limited
3 The Lanchesters, 162 Fulham Palace Road
London W6 9ER
Copyright © 1994 Julian Fane
The right of Julian Fane to be
identified as the author of this work
has been asserted by him in accordance with
the Copyright, Designs and Patents Act 1988
ISBN 0 09 473630 8
Set in Monophoto Poliphilus 12pt by
Servis Filmsetting Ltd, Manchester
Printed in Great Britain by
St Edmundsbury Press Ltd,
Bury St Edmunds, Suffolk

A CIP catalogue record of this book
is available from the British Library

1

The overnight train from London pulled into Inverness Station in the early morning of the 11th of August 1908. The weather was dry, bright without being sunny, and the sharp air smelt of coal smoke, steam and hot metal. Porters in the uniform of the Highland Railway, operating from Perth northwards, lined the platform, standing by or leaning on their upturned barrows. As the train ground and squeaked to a halt against the buffers, most of them gravitated towards the extra number of sleeping-cars or coaches hitched on in consideration of the opening of the grouse shooting season on the following day.

Then all was bustle and confusion. Sleeping-car attendants hailed and instructed some porters – 'Lady and gent in number 30 . . . Single gent in 18 . . .' – while other porters offered their services in Scottish accents. Passengers alighted on the platform in varying states of exhaustion: ones without sleepers looking more bleary-eyed than ones with, and stiff joints and paper bags full of the remains of picnics especially distinguishing those who had travelled second and third class. A few extravagant local people, having invested in the luxury of platform tickets in order to be able to assist their relatives and friends off the train and with luggage, were waving their arms and barging through the crowd. Shooting-dogs barked and whined in the luggage van or were being handed over to their owners by the guard; labradors and spaniels wagged tails with pleasure and made messes on the platform. Ladies' maids and gentlemen's gentlemen supervised the unloading of cabin trunks, hatboxes, pigskin suitcases, soft leather cases for pillows, and flat gun-cases with brass corners. Their masters and mistresses emerged: the former tipped the relevant sleeping-car attendant, the latter extended gloved hands to pat dogs and followed in the footsteps of tweedy husbands. Porters with barrows piled high shepherded such groups towards the barrier. Tickets were fumbled for and surrendered, and the stationmaster in black braided frock-coat and bowler hat dispensed polite good-mornings or discriminatory nods of his head. In the so-called Booking Hall, the exchange of noisy greetings clashed with the shouts of cabbies seeking fares and the sounds of horses' hooves and vehicles' wheels on cobbled roadways. Grander travellers progressed to the Station Hotel.

When the platform was empty except for two railway employees stacking mailbags on a trolley, a man dodged through the barrier and bustled along to the first sleeping-car. He had been on the train, and in fact had obtained permission from the stationmaster to pass the ticket-collector in both directions; yet he seemed to be doing something illegal with a certain brash challenging air. He was not so young as he looked from a distance: he was a stunted and positively gnarled forty-five-year-old. Notwithstanding his third-class night on the train he managed to present a smartish appearance, although his brown bowler and cavalry twill overcoat gave a slight impression of not belonging to him. His legs were bowed, even visibly through his trousers, but limber enough to enable him to jump from the platform into the train without using the step.

Five minutes elapsed. The trolley of mailbags had been wheeled away, and now the guard walked down the platform to pass the time of day with the driver and his mate, who were still in the cab of their engine. The stationmaster and ticket-collector remained at their posts by the barrier, as if waiting for something or somebody.

A piercing whistle by the man in the brown bowler, reappearing in the open doorway of the sleeping-car, was apparently the signal for a renewal of activity. The stationmaster ushered a pair of porters through the barrier. The guard preceding them, they pushed their barrows briskly towards the luggage van. One porter collected four large suitcases there. The other was hailed and entrusted with what must have been a double-sided gun-case and a second case containing ammunition by the man in the bowler, who warned unsmilingly that both were fragile as eggshells and heavy as lead. The guard meanwhile had stepped from the van with a black labrador in tow: guard, dog, porters, plus the stationmaster in the distance and no doubt the driver, all stood as if to attention. They were joined by the authoritative manikin, carrying an initialled and crested dressing-case, and by the sleeping-car attendant, extending an arm in case his last and probably best-paying customer should need support.

The gentleman ignored this offer of help. Having stood for a moment in the doorway of the sleeping-car, perhaps while he checked that not too many people would see him with black stubble on his cheeks and chin, he descended or condescended on to the platform, producing from the pocket of his almost ankle-length tweed greatcoat as he did so an unfolded 'flimsy' a crisp white paper five pound note, and stuffing it into the hand of the attendant.

'Thank you,' he intoned in an impersonal manner and with the merest shadow of a smile.

'Oh thank you, milord,' the attendant exclaimed, bowing. 'Most generous, milord, and much appreciated, I'm sure. I wish you good sport, milord.'

But the gentleman was already striding along the platform, gold-banded thick walking-stick in hand, and enunciating the single syllable 'Zeals,' to which the man in the brown bowler, hurrying to keep up with him, answered, 'Present, milord!'

'Is my room in order?'

'It is, milord.'

The black labrador was showing signs of recognition and excitement, and straining at his leash held by the guard.

The gentleman spoke to it.

'All right, Topper.' He ordered raspingly: 'Steady, boy!' To Zeals he said: 'You take charge of him,' then to the guard, who received another fiver: 'Thank you for your trouble.'

'No trouble, milord. I hope your lordship had a comfortable journey.'

'Everything was satisfactory.'

'Thank you, milord.'

He swept on, followed by Topper, Zeals and the two porters with barrows. His black boots, 'boned' and polished to shine mellowly, and over which his tweed trousers 'broke' – in tailor's jargon – to perfection, had steel quarters in the heels: they caused his footsteps to ring and echo. He interrupted his progess to distribute more lavish gratuities to the driver of the train and the station-master, bowler hat in hand. His ticket was neither forthcoming nor asked for.

The procession entered the Station Hotel.

[7]

An obsequious uniformed commissionaire and a gang of bellboys took over from the railway porters in the hotel's foyer. The gentleman unbuttoned his overcoat, reached into his trouser pocket, emptied a clutch of coins into the hand of Zeals together with the instruction: 'See to it.' He added by way of an afterthought: 'And run me a bath.' His pieces of luggage were carried through a door marked Service, Zeals in pursuit, leading or being led by Topper.

The hotel manager made a respectful approach.

'Good morning, my lord.' He accentuated the 'my' instead of subsuming it into the single word 'milord'. 'A morning like this bodes well for tomorrow.'

The gentleman cleared his throat or grunted impatiently and made for the reception desk.

'Oh yes, my lord, if you'd be so good as to sign and register.'

The book was open, a pen and ink-well within reach, a semicircular blotter handy.

He clumsily scratched and scrawled the two words: Ivo Grevill. In the column for addresses he put: Brougham, Cumberland. He did not bother with dates.

'Have I my usual room?' he asked.

'Yes, my lord. I'll be pleased to escort you to it.'

'No need – I'll find my own way.'

'Very good, my lord – number three on the first floor.'

Lord Ivo Grevill, the vowels of whose Christian name were pronounced so as to rhyme with hi-ho, mounted the stairs. He was the younger son of the late Duke of Brougham and Castile, and the younger brother of the present Duke. He was thirty years of age and lived in bachelor quarters in Greenbury Street, Mayfair: that is to say he kept his clothes there, and slept under that roof during the London social season and in between his visits to country houses and to keep sporting engagements. He had achieved a measure of fame as a good shot, not to mention a certain notoriety for other reasons, and his ultimate destination today was Sweirdale Lodge, a house with grouse moor attached, or rather in order of importance a grouse moor with house attached, rented by Mr Jack Haspell, the owner of the successful fashion emporium Frère Jacques. Brougham, the address he had written in the hotel register, was either the home of his childhood or his brother's principal residence, depending on which way you looked at it.

The commissionaire and the bellboys waited in the passage outside his room. Ivo with an inclination of his head acknowledged thanks for the largesse already dished out by Zeals. Water was running into the bath in his bedroom's adjoining bathroom, from which Zeals now appeared, empty dressing-case in hand, and, having closed the door of the suite, helped his lordship divest himself of his specially shaped version of a black bowler, greatcoat, jacket, waistcoat, boots and socks, trousers, tie-pin, tie, stiff collar and shirt.

Their conversation during this routine was terse and minimal.

Zeals asked: 'What will you be wearing?'

The answer was: 'My brown suit.'

As his lordship headed for the bathroom in his vest and pants he said: 'Tell them I'll be down for breakfast in half an hour.'

The bath he took was leisurely and perfumed with essence of jasmine. It included washing his black hair. Then at the washbasin, on the glass shelves alongside which were arranged the contents of his dressing-case, he cleaned his strong teeth, applied shaving soap and brushed it into a suitable lather and scraped off his beard with a sharpened cut-throat razor, shook astringent lotion from a metal flask on to his hands and applied it stingingly to his face, rubbed hair tonic from another metal flask into his scalp, dabbed some talcum powder under his arms, and having donned fresh underwear re-entered the bedroom. A complete change of clothes was laid out on the bed, likewise what had been in his pockets. Zeals in attendance fastened his collar to the back-collar-stud in the neckband of his shirt, and his cuff-links; proffered his tie-pin and his shoehorn; and held the waistcoat and jacket of the brown suit for him to get into. Ivo threaded his gold chain through the vertical security buttonhole in his waistcoat, and clipping his gold half-hunter watch to one end he stowed it in the left-hand lower pocket, and the mother-of-pearl fruit knife clipped to the other end in the right-hand pocket. The upper pockets of the waistcoat were for his curved gold cigarette case and his match-case. In the top pocket of his jacket he flaunted a yellow silk handkerchief; his wallet occupied the inside pocket on the right, his diary one on the left. He had a special sheath-shaped pocket in the lining of his jacket for his fountain-pen; and in his trouser pockets he kept keys left, loose change right, and a second smaller wallet at the back. When dressed and accoutred he returned to the bathroom and parted his soft hair and brushed it flat with silver monogrammed brushes. Zeals inspected the finished article, so to speak, and in due course opened the bedroom door for his master to pass through.

[9]

During this familiar rigmarole they had spoken at intervals as follows.

'Our transport – have you checked it?'

'I have, milord – three o'clock on the dot to get you to Sweirdale Lodge by five . . .'

'Guns safe?'

'As ever, milord . . .'

'Topper must want water.'

'He's had it – I've given him a drink.'

'Good – I'll take him for a stroll later on.'

'He heard that, milord.'

'Later, I said, Topper – lie down, boy . . . Did you order my papers?'

'*Scotsman* and *Horse and Jockey* – they'll be on your breakfast table . . .'

'Many people in the dining-room?'

'The usual crush – but they'll have cleared off by the time you're down-stairs.'

'Anyone we know'

'Mr Max Kirby, and Mr and Mrs Staincross. I saw Mr Kirby's valet on the train. They're going to Sweirdale, and he told me the Staincrosses would be there too. He said Mr Haspell was sending a carriage to pick them up at ten.'

'That means they'll be at Sweirdale by twelve, and have a damn long after-noon with nothing to do . . .'

An afterthought struck Ivo as he was ushered out.

'Try to find out who else is shooting at Sweirdale. Mr Kirby never accepts an invitation to shoot unless he thinks he's got enough competition.'

'I'll do my best, milord.'

'Meet me here at two-thirty.'

'Right!'

'And when you've packed and locked this door, bring me the key.'

'I will. Milord, I'd be pleased to have your copy of *Horse and Jockey* when you've finished with it.'

Zeals shared his master's interest in horse-racing not only because they were both gamblers in their different degrees, but also because he had been a jockey. He was the son of a Cambridgeshire smallholder and the runt of a large family. Thanks to his size or lack of size he became a Newmarket stable lad at the age of twelve, then an apprentice. He was riding races at seventeen under the name Sam Zeals, had good money in the bank in his later twenties, but then suffered accidents and broken bones, was laid up and fell on harder times. At thirty-five he still got an occasional ride, he rode two more losers for an aristocratic young owner, Lord Ivo Grevill by name, before he was forced by ill health to call it a day. He thereupon approached Lord Ivo and begged him for a job and a living wage. He obtained his first objective at any rate.

And in the last ten years he had learned his trade: how to look after clothes, how to 'load' guns at shoots, how to curb his disrespectful impulses, how to extract monetary dues from his employer. The high-handed toff and the hard-bitten crock of a jockey suited each other. Ivo relied on his 'man', who was not too superior, while the man in question was diligent and protective from motives of self-interest.

Zeals in the Station Hotel in Inverness, having rung for the housekeeper and warned her not to allow any member of her staff to 'muck about' in room number three, locked the door and delivered the key as instructed.

Ivo in the dining-room read his racing news-sheet, which was propped against the coffee and hot milk pots. His breakfast consisted of a kipper, a plateful of eggs, bacon and tomato, a rack of toast and two baps with marmalade, and several cups of white coffee, each sweetened by four lumps of sugar. There were no other guests in the dining-room, and impatient waiters were surreptitiously re-laying a few tables for lunch: but he did not hurry. He might not have noticed that he was in the way – he scarcely noticed the delivery of the key of his room. He made his meal, reached for his cigarette case, selected one of the sixteen flat Turkish cigarettes with which Zeals had filled it, fished his match-case out of the opposite waistcoat pocket, struck a red-topped match, lit his cigarette, waved the match widely to extinguish the flame, puffed out and inhaled smoke, causing a brighter glow at the cigarette's lighted end. He exhaled smoke through his nose and mouth simultaneously, extended a hand backed with stiff black hairs for his copy of *The Scotsman*, opened the paper and flicked through the pages until he came to the obituaries. However, they – or the deceased – failed to catch his attention. He dropped the paper on the floor without reading the headline or any news item – he particularly wished not to strain his eyes unnecessarily before the serious shooting season began; smoked the rest of his cigarette in a meditative manner; stood, tossed some coins on to the breakfast table, collected his copy of *Horse and Jockey*, and strode past waiters and out of the dining-room.

Half an hour later he again descended the hotel stairs, but now leading

[11]

Topper. He had on his long tweed greatcoat and, instead of his bowler, a tweed cap. His stride was purposeful, suggesting he was urgently required elsewhere: he was accustomed to walking fast and far. His destination was the Post Office, where he wrote out on a telegram form the following message in irregular capital letters: Solomon 103 Bow Rd London E 3 stop Flintlock 4 pm Croxley stop Grevill. He had obviously sent such telegrams before and by arrangement with his bookmaker: he had no need to inform Barney Solomon that he was betting his usual hundred guineas that Flinklock would win the four o'clock race at Croxley in Northamptonshire.

He proceeded to the public park arranged on islands in the River Ness and reached by a bridge. Here he loosed Topper, and for the next ninety minutes by his half-hunter they took exercise in preparation for days to come on the hill. Ivo wore thicker clothing than the weather justified in order to work up a sweat and lose a superfluous pound or two, although he kept himself pretty fit year in and year out.

At twelve forty-five he was back in his room in the hotel. He washed and changed into the clean underwear and shirt with back collar-stud in place left ready on the bed; partook of a prolonged lunch downstairs; paid his bill at the reception desk; pressed money into various outstretched hands; checked that his luggage was safely stowed in the hackney coach drawn by two horses waiting at the door; climbed in and was joined by Zeals.

They drove for some fifteen miles in a south-easterly direction.

Their conversation was confined to two snatches.

At about three-fifteen Lord Ivo remarked: 'I wonder if Flintlock did any good at Croxley.'

Zeals tapped his forehead and said: 'Flintlock – Flintlock by Blunderbuss out of Keyring – should get the trip, milord.'

'I damn well hope so,' was his lordship's comment.

The other snatch was inaugurated by Zeals.

'I had words with Mr Kirby's valet, milord.'

'Oh yes?'

'He said the guns are going to be yourself, Mr Kirby, Mr Staincross, Mr McDonald, that's Mr Buck McDonald, and Mr Haspell and a gent called du Sten – Lord du Sten, is it?'

'Who the hell is he?'

'Don't ask me, milord.'

'Can he shoot straight? Mr Haspell can't – he's a dressmaker.'

'Mr Langthwaite senior and Mr Langthwaite junior might make up the party.'

'They should know what they're doing, they own Sweirdale after all. Who are the women?'

'Mrs McDonald and Mrs Staincross, and Miss Paull.'

'Oh God,' Ivo groaned. 'But there must be more women to balance the men.'

'Not that I know of, milord.'

'Well – let's hope the sport's worthwhile.'

'You ought to see some sport indoors in that company.' Zeals was referring to cards and card-players. 'And you've Gelts Abbey to look forward to on the seventeenth.' His encouraging reflections eliciting no response, he pursued: 'By the bye, did you remember your *Horse and Jockey*, milord?'

'No, I forgot, sorry.'

For the rest of the journey Ivo Grevill drowsed, his black head nodding on his chest, watched over by the cold eyes of his manservant.

Sweirdale Lodge was the second Scottish property of an old and previously wealthy family by the name of Langthwaite, whose main residence was Castle Drumm on the southern shore of the Moray Firth. The usual combination of bad luck and bad judgment over the years had forced the Langthwaites to sell most of the Drumm lands, and they now eked out a livelihood by managing and letting Sweirdale's seventeen thousand barren acres of moorland in the foothills of the Grampians for grouse shooting and deer-stalking, plus the Lodge itself.

For the last few seasons fortune had relented and persuaded the precious birds to breed at the right time, survive summer storms, fly strongly towards the lines of butts, and die in their hundreds; consequently sportsmen had been prepared to pay ever larger sums for the right to shoot them. A regrettable side-effect of this situation was that presumptuous types with nothing but their money to recommend them were apt to be successful in the Dutch auction for the shooting at Sweirdale, people in fact like Jack Haspell. On the other hand, Jack was following a general rule in that he felt obliged by the reputation of the place to beg the best shots of his acquaintance to be his guests.

He hardly knew Lord Ivo Grevill, and Ivo might have sworn that he thanked God he had never come across his would-be host. But Jack had once succeeded in shaking the hand of his lordship at a private gambling establishment they both belonged to, the Club of Clubs. He therefore wrote a flattering and tempting letter, claiming the honour of having met his fellow club-member, explaining that he had bought the two best days at Sweirdale, giving the numbers of grouse shot on those days in previous years, and expressing the far-fetched hope that the famous sportsman would come and show him how everything should be done, adding in a postscript that games of cards and billiards were also on offer.

Ivo's reply was affirmative for more than sporting reasons. Notwithstanding his responsibilities at Gelts Abbey, part of the Brougham estate where he was meant to be in charge of the shooting and entertainment, he was pleased to be able to tell his brother that he was otherwise engaged for the start of the grouse-shooting season, and Gelts would have to wait for him. The implications of this statement were manifold: he was asserting that he was not the Duke's servant, that he was not paid enough for the work he put in at Gelts, that the shooting there was rotten because the Duke was too mean to make it better, and that he was fed up with wasting his time on a lost cause, and his skills were in demand on the best moor in the country, and he was still a popular fellow, even if no longer asked to darken the doors of the stuffier sort of stately home. In short, and in a mix of metaphors, his lordship's visit to Sweirdale was rather one in the eye for the Duke of Brougham and Castile than a feather in the cap of Jack Haspell.

Jack, of course, saw only his own advantage. His origins were lower middle-class, and he had begun his career on the wrong side of the counter in his father's draper's shop in Cheltenham. He was an energetic youth with a good head for figures: he took over from his father and turned one shop into a chain of shops, then moved into premises in London, and eventually opened his salon in Berkeley Square. He had not married, and in his later forties found himself with the time as well as the resources to indulge his social aspirations.

He bought memberships of clubs; his donations to charities got his name on to lists of patrons and even seats on their boards of usually titled directors; he was courted by some ladies seeking contributions to their good causes, and by others wanting dresses at reduced prices; he was asked to lunches in smart houses at which stiff-necked mothers swallowed mainly their principles for the sake of daughters' trousseaux; and he gambled with gentlemen.

Sport came next. Jack was averse from squandering his hard-earned money on the ownership of racehorses; then he was a bit old, and too self-preservative, to start hunting; and the privacy of fishing would not further his interests. So he purchased his pair of Purdeys, took lessons, ordered plus-four suits and fore-and-aft hats to match, and rented odd days shooting here and there, pheasants in Buckinghamshire, partridges in Norfolk, inviting the participation of nobody more practised than himself.

Sweirdale was as it were the full-dress outcome of such rehearsals. He had paid more money than anyone else to rent the place; and Lord Ivo Grevill having stooped in theory to sample his hospitality, other dead-eyed notabilities, informed of Ivo's intentions, followed suit. Possibly Mr Philip Staincross and Mr McDonald, for whose wives Frère Jacques provided apparel, and Mr Maximilian Kirby, another Club of Clubs acquaintance, were not out of the topmost social drawer, and Lord du Sten was too young to count. But with luck all the gentlemen would have a good time, and broadcast news of it; consequently ever more gentlemanly gentlemen would agree to be Jack's guests in years to come and repay him with invitations to stay in their splendid houses and shoot their game.

That was the plan, and the main chance Jack had his eye on; and to make sure that nothing went wrong in the meanwhile he had arrived at Sweirdale Lodge with a small army of household staff, grooms, loaders and potential beaters, a few days before Lord Ivo rolled up the drive just on five o'clock.

The white-painted two-storeyed building with a low-pitched slate roof stood on a shelf of rising ground. Steep steps led from a pot-holed turning circle at the end of the drive to a narrow terrace and an insignificant front door. Behind the Lodge, and away to right and left, hills coloured with purple heather rose towards the clouded sky; and the chill currents of afternoon air carried the wild echoing rattle or cluck of the call of the red grouse. The extensive back parts of the house, providing staff accommodation, domestic offices, gunroom, game larders and so on, were invisible from the front, and the stable block and some cottages were at a distance and hidden by the lie of the land. Vegetation of the decorative sort was conspicuous by its absence, not a flower or creeper or shrub or indeed tree grew in the vicinity of the dour main edifice; but granite walls alongside the drive enclosed a square of kitchen garden, which looked more like a fort.

[15]

A butler and a wasp-waistcoated footman hurried out to attend to Ivo and his luggage. Jack Haspell, now a neat slight fifty-three-year-old, his perfectly parted brown hair greying at the temples, timed his arrival on the scene to coincide with his guest of honour reaching the terrace. He shook Ivo's hand with both of his and remonstrated on being addressed as Haspell.

'Please call me Jack!'

'As you say,' Ivo vouchsafed, without asking to be called by his own Christian name minus title.

Jack hoped that the journey had not been too uncomfortable, adding: 'But you really could have availed yourself of my transport – my people would willingly have returned to Inverness to fetch you.'

Ivo replied: 'I like to be independent.'

In the stony hall, where a peat fire smouldered and smoked, another footman took Ivo's stick and cap, helped to remove his greatcoat and escorted him to the cloakroom.

When he reappeared in the hall Jack led him along a passage and into a severe dining-room with antlers on the walls. The house-party, which he completed, were seated on oak chairs at the rectangular table laid for tea. He followed Jack round it, greeting those he already knew and being introduced to the strangers, and ended up in the place between Agatha McDonald, Buck's wife, sixty-ish and red-faced, and a certain Mrs Smythe, Beatrice Smythe, a beautiful young woman.

The female group included Marian McDonald, Buck and Agatha's daughter, single, plain and all too conscious of her twenty-three years. Betty Paull, a more determined spinster, was middle-aged and well-connected and looked like a man and behaved like one inasmuch as she hunted in Leicestershire and was an ambitious rifle shot. Also present were Judy Staincross, only about forty-five although she could have been sixty, judging by appearances and owing to her dropsical bulk, and Mrs Mason, Jack Haspell's secretary.

Mrs Smythe had the transitory black hair of youth, vivid shiny black, and large strange amber-coloured eyes and a pale complexion, and was smartly dressed.

Jack apologised to Ivo for not waiting to serve tea until he arrived, and received the snubbing rejoinder: 'I believe I told you not to.'

Max Kirby, a self-indulgent bachelor in his fifties, who maintained his

[16]

status on the fringes of society by virtue of his sporting prowess and speculative inclinations, called down the table in his fruity voice: 'Anyway we haven't
started — nobody's won or lost a penny so far.'

Ivo summoned a grim smile, and, when a footman asked him which tea he
preferred and how he liked it, replied: 'Indian without milk or sugar.'

Philip Staincross, a bald man in his fifties prone to meaningless nervy
smiles, spoke up: 'Have you heard the grouse? The moors must be crawling
with them.'

And Lord du Sten chimed in, spluttering slightly: 'We saw masses this
afternoon — they were even in the walled garden — we should have terrific sport
tomorrow.'

Gregory du Sten resembled a poor specimen of white rabbit. He was
twenty-something, had a little pallid hair, red-rimmed eyes and two pro-
truding teeth. His speech caused Marian McDonald to blush and cast at him
a congratulatory glance: she had spent the afternoon trudging round in his
company and was already bowled over by his charms.

Betty Paull boomed: 'You can all have your grouse — I'll be stalking on the
high ground — isn't that so, Mr Haspell?'

'It is indeed,' Jack replied smoothly. 'Miss Paull's going after the monarch
of the glen, and we chaps will be joined by Henry Langthwaite and his son
Michael, so there'll be eight of us shooting.'

'Did you invite the Langthwaites, or are they poking their noses in?' Max
Kirby inquired.

'It's a term of the tenancy — they reserve two places on every shoot — I expect
they'll try to tell me off — and I'll definitely be telling them if we don't bag a
couple of hundred brace and I get my money's worth.'

Ivo's knowing susceptibilities were jarred by Jack's telltale choice of words,
'chaps' for instance, and his jargon and vulgar reference to money; also by the
service of tea by a flunkey instead of by the hostess or senior lady present.

Mr McDonald, christened Brian but answering to Buck, seized his chance
to ask: 'I hope you're prepared for battle, Ivo?'

Mr McDonald's nickname, which hinted at libidinous spryness, did not
describe him: he was fifty and flabby, and looked unfit for any kind of battle.

But Ivo retorted with unmerciful relish: 'I'm prepared to give you a good
thrashing' — a threat that merely tickled Buck, and extracted a crusty chuckle
from Max Kirby.

[17]

The ladies expressed varying degrees of disapproval of such fighting talk and, while plates of sandwiches of beef, fish paste, egg with mayonnaise and cucumber marinated in vinegar, or scones with cream and strawberry jam, or chocolate or fruit cake were handed round, they began to chat with one another and their neighbours, to laugh and to scold their host for keeping altogether too good a table, meaning the irresistible but excessively rich food upon it.

Mrs Smythe pushed a plate an inch or two in the direction of Ivo.

'Nothing to eat, thank you,' he said.

Without comment she languidly selected a sandwich and took a tiny nibble, gazing not in his direction.

He cleared his throat and made the effort to address her: 'Do you know Scotland well?'

She turned towards him, stared at him almost, disconcerted him with her silence, then opened her eyes wide and replied with force that also startled: 'No.'

After pausing nonplussed, he was sufficiently intrigued to try again.

He observed: 'It's a mistake to arrive at a country house in the morning — there's never anything to do on the first afternoon.'

She repeated the stare and the silence, and returned with even more finality: 'I arrived yesterday. We went for a walk this afternoon.'

She was not impolite: it was more her unyouthful composure, her steely composure, that disconcerted. Her beauty compensated to some extent for her manner or her mannerisms. Her face was heart-shaped, her neck slender. Her cheek-bones were high, her amber eyes slanting, her nose was subtly chiselled and tip-tilted, her teeth white enough but rather recessed, and her lustrous wavy black hair piled on top of her head was held in place by combs. She wore an elaborate tea-gown, and stood out from the other women not least because her appearance was the opposite of countrified. She was peculiar too, somehow apart, not exactly charming, a sophisticated changeling who had strayed into a remote Scottish lodge.

Agatha McDonald claimed Ivo's attention with a question about his nephew Billy, his brother's son, the eight-year-old Marquess of Medringham, whose mother had died tragically young of tuberculosis.

By the time he had responded to her interrogation, which was more inquisitive than sympathetic, and pretentious into the bargain, for she did not know the ducal family and even managed to mispronounce Medringham, sounding the d, Jack Haspell was on his feet and marshalling the four belligerent card-players, Buck McDonald, Max Kirby, Philip Staincross and then Ivo himself, out of the dining-room and along passages to a small so-called smoking-room.

The curtains had already been drawn here and the oil lamps lit. There were leather-covered armchairs and a sofa around a peat fire; convenient tables at hand equipped with silver match-holders and ashtrays; a larger table on which were arrayed decanters of whisky and brandy, bottles of Malvern water and selzer, cut-glass tumblers, luxurious shagreen humidors containing cigars and tobacco, a silver cigarette-box with a partitioned interior, Virginia cigarettes on one side and Turkish on the other, and a little pyramidal contraption sport-ing a wick and naked flame; and under a pendant lamp yet another table, square and green-baize-topped, on which were packs of cards, scoring sheets, pencils and a box of coloured counters, and from which extended at each of its corners a flat wooden holder for a glass of refreshment. Four upright folding wood and canvas chairs were in position by this card table.

Jack Haspell having closed the smoking-room door and departed, Max Kirby remarked; 'Well – not a bad place to lose your shirt in.'

Buck McDonald, making for the drinks, queried: 'Can I help anyone to a tot?'

'Whisky, please – but I'll pour my own,' Philip Staincross said.

'Brandy neat,' said Max, asking: 'Any cigars there? How do they smell?'

Buck called across: 'Ivo?'

'I never touch alcohol till six, and it's still ten to.'

'Have a cigar instead,' Max suggested: 'they could be worse.'

'I don't smoke till six either, apart from one cigarette after breakfast.'

Buck said: 'That's discipline for you,' and Max, lighting a cigar with the flaming pyramid: 'He has no vices, you know.'

Ivo's bark of laughter was contradictory.

Philip Staincross drank some of the dark brown mixture in his glass and inquired: 'What's it to be?'

They settled on poker with five-pound counters, Philip agreeing to such high play nervously, and they sat down. A packet of cards was broken open and the cards were shuffled.

'Who's the dark girl?' Ivo wished to know.

Somebody named her.

[19]

'I meant what's she doing at Sweirdale Lodge?'

'Our host's property, no doubt,' Max puffed out with a cloud of cigar smoke.

'For sale, do you think?' Buck asked.

'I shouldn't wonder — he's a shopkeeper, isn't he? — though personally I'd pay to steer clear of her — she gives me the jimjams.'

'She's handsome enough,' Ivo said.

'More like a handful,' Max continued; 'too much for du Sten to handle — ditto yours truly — so that makes you into the only legitimate buyer, Ivo — unless you've got a wife and five children hidden away somewhere.'

Ivo ignored this sally.

Philip Staincross changed the subject, smirking: 'At any rate our host seems to be doing us proud.'

Buck's ungrateful comment was: 'He reminds me of the manager of a hotel.'

Max said: 'I'm reminded of an old-fashioned term — counter-jumper. He jumped from the wrong side of his counter, did he not?'

'And we're rungs on the social ladder he's climbing,' Buck put in.

Ivo, good-humouredly yet sternly, recalled the others as if to their duties, and play began.

After a quarter of an hour he rose and helped himself to whisky and water, and he was soon replenishing his glass. In the next sixty-odd minutes he drank three more whiskies, smoked ten of the fifteen cigarettes in his case, and lost ninety pounds.

He was not downcast. His measures of whisky were on the small side, and much diluted; he managed to consume a good deal of alcohol nonetheless, and it obviously relaxed him. He began to join in the racy backchat, and permitted himself sudden fits of loud laughter. At the conclusion of the session he rallied Philip Staincross, who had also lost a considerable sum of money and kept on mopping his brow and begging his companions to swear not to tell his wife, by saying: 'Never fear — we'll win it back at billiards.'

At seven-thirty Jack Haspell returned and escorted Ivo upstairs and to his bedroom at the end of the long passage on the upper floor.

The room was typical of shooting lodges seldom occupied. It had one window, two built-in corner cupboards, respectively for clothes and with a wash-hand-stand, a lumpy double bed, a square of carpet, and struck chill in spite of the peat fire. Zeals was in attendance, and had laid out his master's evening clothes on the bed, white shirt with starched front and cuffs, stick-up collar, satin bow-tie, black trousers with satin side-stripe, double-breasted black waistcoat, and the unusual dinner-jacket in the colours of the erstwhile Brougham Hunt – dark blue, green velvet collar and lapels and the Brougham brass livery buttons showing in relief the family crest of a tiger's head.

Ivo shed his brown suit, shaved again and washed in the rest of the water that he poured into the wash-basin from a white tin can. He then allowed Zeals to help him into his finery, and eventually to ease his feet into his slippers with the aid of a shoehorn: the slippers were blue velvet, and embroidered on the toe-caps in golden thread was the tiger's head under a ducal coronet, to which the wearer was not strictly entitled.

Meanwhile his abbreviated exchanges with Zeals ran thus: 'Have I got the best room?'

'One of them, milord . . .'

'Who's nextdoor?'

'Mrs Smythe.'

'And on this side?'

'Mr and Mrs McDonald . . .'

'Where's Mr Haspell?'

'He's got a room round in our part of the house, milord – it's a rambling old place . . .'

'Who's Mrs Smythe?'

'She's from South Africa. Her husband was one of those white hunters – he died in a shooting accident a year back. She's been helping at Frère Jacques.'

Zeals pronounced the French words: frear jakes.

'How do you know, Zeals?'

'Mr Haspell's got his London staff here, plus extras . . .'

'Has Topper settled in the kennels – has he been fed?'

'Yes, milord.'

'Don't wait up for me this evening, Zeals.'

'Thank you, milord.'

'What time's breakfast?'

'Eight-thirty onwards.'

'Call me at seven.'

Ivo checked that his cigarette and match cases had been refilled, had a last look at his half-hunter watch, decided he could go downstairs with dignity

[21]

since it was now ten past eight and he had been asked to be ready at eight sharp, and strode along the passage, an upright commanding figure, strikingly dark-visaged.

In the crowded sitting-room, to which he was attracted by the sound of raised voices and into which he was ushered by a footman, the company was intrigued by his attire. Questions and compliments were called forth by his evening coat. Jack Haspell remarked that he would very much like to have one just the same.

Ivo said, showing displeasure: 'You couldn't wear it. You'd not be allowed to. The Brougham Hunt colours were in the gift of the last Master, who was my father. My brother abolished all that. As for the Brougham button, again it's in the exclusive gift of the head of my family.'

He made a single syllable of Brougham, rhyming it with room, and took a glass of sherry from a proffered silver salver.

Jack apologised for having presumed to think he was worthy of wearing such a coat, and asked: 'May I have a private word?'

Ivo signalled forgiveness with a dismissive gesture of his hand, and deigned to step towards the less crowded part of the room behind a sofa.

Jack, having waited for him, spoke in an undertone: 'I've seated you again next to my relative Beatrice Smythe – between Beatrice and Miss Paull – will that be acceptable?'

'You're related, are you?'

'Distantly. She's had a hard time, and I happen to know she's looked forward to making your acquaintance.'

'I'm pleased to make hers.'

'Thank you, Lord Ivo. I hope you were as comfortable as possible upstairs?'

Their confabulation was interrupted by the butler's announcement: 'Dinner is served.'

Etiquette was informal in these rustic circumstances, therefore the ladies simply grouped together and moved in the direction of the dining-room without the aid of gentlemen's arms. The bare mahogany of the tea table had been covered and concealed by a white damask linen tablecloth, and transformed further by the soft radiance shed by candles in branching candelabra on silver cutlery, cut glass, napkins folded to resemble water-lilies, and fine china centre-piece dishes of hot-house muscat grapes, apricots and furry peaches.

Dinner consisted of courses of clear soup, fish in a sauce with grapes, vol-au-vents of chicken, roast beef, crème brûlée, fruit, accompanied by the following liquid refreshments, more sherry, dry white wine, claret, sweet dessert wine, coffee, crème de menthe, port and brandy.

Ivo talked to his friendly old acquaintance Betty Paull. He was aware that according to the rules of precedence he should have been sitting between the married ladies, Agatha McDonald and Judy Staincross, especially the latter since she was the daughter of a baronet; but, in vew of Agatha's purple complexion and snobbery and Judy's corpulence and anti-gambling attitude, he was not sorry that Jack — in his ignorance no doubt — had placed him between what might be called the pick of the female bunch. Betty had a corncrake voice, mannish features and the suspicion of a moustache. On the other hand she knew the social ropes and she was a fellow-punter.

Ivo got things going by telling her he had had a flutter on Flintlock at Croxley. They discussed the racehorses he had once owned, racehorses past, present and future, their breeding, and the money lost and won by betting on them, also other types of horses and how to buy them at the bottom and sell at the top.

Betty regretted the fact that the Brougham Hunt was no more. Ivo expatiated on his theory that the Duke, his brother Walter, was the meanest man in the world, a wet blanket, a spoilsport, and had refused to support the Brougham Foxhounds in order to prevent himself — Ivo — from stepping into their father's hunting boots and becoming the new Master.

He spoke freely because his tongue was loosened by wine, and because he and Betty were two of a kind inasmuch as they had rich tastes and poor bank balances, and lived above their stations, economically at any rate.

'Anyway,' Betty boomed as the beef came round, 'we aren't half lucky to be acquainted with a character who can afford to lash out on this sort of slap-up junket.'

Ivo turned to Mrs Smythe, and, when she continued to talk to Max Kirby, cleared his throat loudly.

Without haste she concluded her conversation with Max and swivelled round and let her light brown eyes, uncommunicative to the point of blankness, rest upon him. She was wearing another becoming dress, close-fitting, revealing almost, and with those piquant bows at the shoulder which were almost a trade mark of Frère Jacques. The girlishness of the slender white pillar of her neck was contradicted by her poise. She cut her meat deliberately and asked Ivo if he had won at cards.

'No. I live to win on another occasion.'

'You're not deterred by losing?'

'No – no, unfortunately, some would say.'

'I only play games I can win.'

'Indeed!' His comment was patronizing rather than interrogative, and combined amusement, scepticism and a touch of heavy flirtatiousness.

'Believe me!' She was ramming home her point with conviction.

'If you need to win, you can't ever play games of chance.'

'Precisely,' she said. 'I don't take chances.'

'In that case, what games are left for you to play?'

'Some,' she replied seriously, quelling possible innuendoes, and changing the subject. 'May I ask you a question? Why doesn't your brother use his full title?'

'Do you know my brother?'

'I know he has a wonderful name, or would have if he chose to use it.'

'Brougham and Castile, you mean?'

'Yes.'

'A bit of a mouthful, isn't it?'

She shrugged her shoulders.

He continued: 'He calls himself Brougham. He could just as well call himself Castile – he has the double dukedom. But no duke to my knowledge, none of my forefathers, has ever used the two titles together or Castile on its own.'

'What a pity!'

'Can I ask a question in my turn?'

'Please.'

'I feel rude for asking it – you're too good-looking to forget – but have we met before?'

'I've seen you – you've been pointed out to me – we weren't introduced.'

'When was that?'

'Some weeks back.'

'Where?'

'At a club I was taken to by Jack.'

Ivo frowned and inquired: 'Was it a card club?'

[24]

'Yes – you were pointed out – and your name impressed me.'

'I must have been in the middle of a game – if I'd spotted you I would have received the impression. You're related to our host, I understand.'

Mrs Smythe paused.

'Have you been discussing me with him?'

'I wouldn't say that. He merely mentioned the fact that you and he were related.'

'Oh.'

'The Club of Clubs isn't quite the place for a lady. I'm surprised Jack should have taken you there.'

She dismissed his stricture thus: 'Worse things happen in the land I come from.'

A silence fell between them. She loaded her fork with precision, and dispatched each mouthful briskly. She seemed relaxed, and not to suffer from the social obligation to converse and make herself agreeable. He munched his food in a ruminant fashion: he had always been a slow eater, and now appeared to be taking his time to digest their exchanges as well as the meat course.

Max Kirby leant forward and talked across Mrs Smythe to Ivo in the rallying accents of a superannuated ladies' man, saying that he was hoping to lure the delicious young person sitting between them into his butt on the moors tomorrow, and warning that by having asked her he at least had a prior claim on her company, which would improve his shooting no end.

She smiled at such gallantry, and kept quiet while Ivo entered into a discussion with Max and then with most of the other sportsmen about the prospects for the following day, likely weather and so on.

She spoke, interrupting and reclaiming his interest – she had finished her helping of crème brûlée.

'You're a very good shot, aren't you?'

'Passable.'

'What am I expected to do while you're shooting?'

'Join us for lunch on the hill, and stay for the two or three afternoon drives. You haven't been to Scotland before?'

'No.'

'You lived in South Africa?'

'I was born and brought up there.'

'And married?'

[25]

She inclined her head affirmatively.

'And lost your husband, I believe?'

Her pudding plate had been replaced by a fruit plate and finger-bowl, and she now selected two grapes from the bunch that was served and began to peel them and remove the pips with surgically accurate movements of her fruit knife and fork.

He watched her, and resumed: 'Seeing grouse driven is an experience. They fly like no other birds. I'd say they were the aristocrats amongst game birds. I like to listen to them, to that rattling call of theirs, you know. You're not afraid of gunfire, and not squeamish, I hope?'

She regarded him in a scoffing or snubbing sort of way and countered his inquiry with hers: 'Is anyone gun-shy in South Africa?'

He found it difficult to meet her strange eyes, averted his own, remembered that her husband's trade had been big-game shooting and that he had somehow died of it, and said: 'Forgive me if I've been tactless.'

'Will you help me to do the right thing during the shoot?'

'I'm sure everybody will want to do that.'

The table-talk again became general, and soon afterwards Mrs Mason, Jack Haspell's secretary who was acting as his hostess, responded to his signal by standing up and leading the other ladies out of the dining-room.

Ivo filled his glass with the port in the decanter that was passed round the table, lit one of his Turkish cigarettes and helped himself to a long cigar from the brown wooden box that was also circulating, inhaled smoke and imbibed the sweet sharp alcohol.

He had found it a strain, having to talk to Mrs Smythe. She had been called a delicious young person; but she was not delicious by Ivo's standards, she was too prickly in spite of her looks, and for that matter he could not think of her as young although she was certainly not old. Some force in her alarmed even as it excited him; and the ambiguity of her approaches, oncoming at one moment, stand-offish the next, made him glad to be rid of her for the time being.

The gentlemen in the dining-room smoked and drank and chatted for half an hour or so, then Ivo addressed their host: 'Where's our billiard-table, Jack?'

Jack so far forgot himself as to exclaim in shocked accents: 'You're surely not thinking of playing billiards now?'

'Why not?'

'The ladies would miss you, Lord Ivo. We all would.'

'You flatter me. There's money at stake, and some of us are impatient to recoup our losses.'

'Would it not be impolite to desert the ladies?'

'Impolite? No! My brother Brougham never sees the ladies again after they've left the dining-room. He does not consort with them socially, nor did my father. It's not done in our house. Of course you're at liberty to follow your own rules. But perhaps you'd be good enough to show me into the billiard-room?' He rose, turned to the three other prospective billiard-players, Philip Staincross, Max Kirby and Buck McDonald, who had sat looking sheepish during the subjugation of their host, and summoned them in his thick imperious voice: 'Are you ready for the fray?'

Jack made a virtue of necessity: he stood up smiling, accustomed as he was to dealing with difficult customers, and said, 'Who am I to quarrel with ducal precedents? This way, Lord Ivo. Would any of you gentlemen like more port?'

They trooped after him, Lord du Sten saying as he followed the others: 'May I watch the game? I wouldn't feel comfortable with all those ladies in the drawing-room – being the only man, I mean. I'd feel like Daniel in the lions' or rather the lionesses' den.'

Lamps were lit in the billiard-room and the cover removed from the table, cues were chosen and chalked, a coin was tossed and the first of half a dozen games of fifty-up began. Jack Haspell departed to break the news to the ladies that the gentlemen had decided to play billiards – or truant – for the rest of the evening; Gregory du Sten congratulated or sympathized with the shirt-sleeved players, and obediently slid the ivory markers to and fro on the scoreboard; tobacco smoke mingled with the smell of alcohol, and Ivo with much assistance from his querulous partner Philip Staincross managed to lose another fifty guineas.

At eleven o'clock they adjourned until the next evening: wishes to play on were subordinated to the need to give eyes a rest before tomorrow's test of marksmanship.

Having said good night to Jack and abandoned him to check that lamps and fires were not going to burn the house down, they drifted up the stairs and parted at the top.

Ivo reached his room where the bed was prepared for his occupation, and his black silk pyjamas and his red dressing-gown were laid out on it, and his

[27]

bedroom slippers placed on the floor underneath. He undressed, washed and cleaned his teeth at the wash-hand-stand, poured liquid from a blue bottle into an eyebath and carefully rinsed each of his eyes, then crossed the room, drew the curtains and raised the lower sash of the window.

The grouse were calling in the dark and mercifully dry night. But another sound caught his attention. Mrs Smythe had coughed. It was a small short cough, yet might have been construed as a reminder of her propinquity or even possibly a summons.

He permitted himself a cynical smile, and was pleased to climb into bed alone. He suspected that Jack Haspell had provided Mrs Smythe for his entertainment at Sweirdale, and perhaps that he – Jack – hoped thus to be extricated from her toils. He had been seated next to her twice at meals, and put into the bedroom next to hers; he had been told by Jack that he was the object of her interest, and by herself that he impressed her. Whether or not she was privy to the plot, or if with Jack's assistance she was simply and of her own volition setting her cap at him – these were moot points. The fact of the matter was that Ivo smelt danger in the form of the female of the species, and determined for the umpteenth time not to fall into a booby-trap. He was well aware of the attractions of the lady – or almost the lady – in question. But he was afraid of involvement and the misalliance it might lead to. He was content to make do with intermittent adulterous episodes in the safely married arms of Lady Dorothy Yealms, as he had for the last four years, and with the consolations in emergency of the professional girls of Greenbury Street.

Anyway, now, in consideration of having to be at his competitive best in a few hours, he banished thoughts of women, and untroubled by the monetary misfortunes of his day fell asleep.

The next morning, by seven forty-five, three-quarters of an hour after being called by Zeals, he had bathed and shaved and was attired in his thick tweed suit with plus-fours, a collar and tie soft and loose enough to facilitate movements of the neck and head, and brown brogue shoes with steel-studded heels and soles.

He followed Zeals downstairs and through a green baize door and via domestic offices to a room at the rear of the lodge. The window was barred. The walls were lined with floor to waist-high cupboards and, above, glass cases containing a variety of upstanding firearms fixed in slots. Two men with their jackets off and aprons on were cleaning a rifle at the central table: namely

[28]

the head-keeper Mr Macgregor, and a gillie called Barton, to whom his lord-ship was introduced by Zeals. Macgregor explained that the rifle was to be used by Miss Paull and that Barton had been appointed to take her stalking. He admitted dourly that the weather could be worse, Barton meanwhile clear-ing space on the table for Lord Ivo's double-sided gun-case, which Zeals unlocked and opened.

It held in shaped compartments the disconnected bits and pieces of four exquisite guns, a pair of twelve-bores, a rifle and a four-ten, all double-bar-relled, hammerless, their breech-blocks tooled and inlaid with gold, their stocks of matched burr walnut.

Macgregor observed: 'You've a great armoury there, milord. I've never set eyes on finer guns – and I've heard tell you know how to use them.'

Ivo replied, as Zeals put the little four-ten, the children's gun, together: 'I like to get my eye in before a day's shooting, and remind the dog of his duties.'

Macgregor emitted an expression of approval that sounded like: 'Oh ay?'

Zeals handed the four-ten to his master, placed the travelling cartridge-case on the table and unlocked it. Ivo grasped and pocketed a handful of four-ten cartridges lying horizontally in a section between the twelve-bore cartridges and a couple of boxes of rifle ammunition. The cartridge-case and the gun-case were then closed, locked and re-stowed in one of the cupboards.

Ivo said: 'I'll walk round for half an hour. When will you want us all to be ready, Macgregor?'

'Ten-thirty sharp, milord, the waggons'll be at the door.'

'Good.' He turned to Zeals. 'You lead the way to the kennels.'

Master and man crossed a sequence of yards formed by stables and barns, cow-houses and dairies, sheep-pens and coops for chicken, geese and ducks, and approached a shed at the far end of a paddock from which whining howls and barking emanated: dogs were kept so far from the house in order not to disturb the residents.

Topper, released by Zeals to an accompaniment of envious barks from the other dogs, bounded out, grovelled fawningly at Ivo's feet, and in due course came to heel.

The trio walked along a hedgerow towards some haystacks. A flock of spar-rows fluttered up from the ground in the vicinity of these haystacks, now at a distance of forty yards. Ivo raised his gun and fired both barrels. Two sparrows fell dead or dying. Topper responded to a command to rush forward, find, lift, retrieve and surrender one into the hand of Zeals, then was ordered to fetch the other. Ivo stalked on with the labrador, while Zeals tossed the corpses of the sparrows into the hedgerow.

They arrived at the wall of the kitchen garden. Zeals clapped his hands, a frightened blackbird flew over the wall, was shot and retrieved. Ivo also shot a couple of starlings, a great tit, a moorhen and an unidentified warbler before, having patted and praised Topper and passed the four-ten as well as the dog over to Zeals, he re-entered the house to partake of breakfast.

At ten-fifteen the shooting party assembled in the turning circle of the drive in front of the house. The weather was still promisingly dry and clear – mist, through which grouse could spring surprises on sportsmen, did not hang on the hills. One woman mingled with the twenty-odd men and half as many dogs: Betty Paull in breeches and boots, collar and tie, and, as if to advertise her reason for being there, deerstalker hat. She was smoking a cigarette and chatting with a group of five of the eight guns: the other three, Jack Haspell and Henry Langthwaite, the owner of Sweirdale, and Henry's son Michael Langthwaite, were engaged in earnest conversation with Macgregor and the larger group of loaders and dog-handlers. Transport up to the moors, vehicles for the men, a pony for the lady, would soon arrive.

There were two gentlemen's gentlemen who loaded for their employers, other than Zeals: Mr Kirby's and Mr McDonald's. The Langthwaites had brought their own menservants, and, as landlords with ultimate responsibility for satisfying their tenant and his guests, had provided loaders for Jack Haspell, Philip Staincross and Gregory du Sten, plus half a dozen dogs, labradors black and yellow, a springer spaniel and a mongrel spaniel. Macgregor, in charge of the sport on the Langthwaites' Sweirdale estate, also had a vested interest in making a success of what was the most important day of his profes-sional calendar: whence his deigning to discuss strategy and tactics with Mr Haspell, who knew nothing of grouse and how to shoot them.

The eight loaders were either gillies or had experience of the art of taking the used gun of a sportsman while handing him the primed one, of rapidly re-loading and being ready to repeat the exchange. All carried the cartridges that might be required during the day either in cartridge bags slung over their shoulders, or in belts of cartridges round their waists, or in the bulging side-

[30]

pockets of their jackets. Each of them was in charge of one or both of the guns that they would be loading: guns tucked under a forearm in the conventional manner, or shouldered military-style, or held horizontally straight-armed, or vertically with double-barrels resting on the toe-cap of a boot.

Pipes were in evidence here, and strong tobacco as well as cigarette smoke mingled with the steamy breath of the panting dogs and lingered in the mostly still atmosphere. The good dogs sat shivering with excitement at their masters' feet and trying not to whine, the bad or less good ones snarled at their fellows or made impulsive dashes in various directions and were recalled with harsh words of command and sometimes with the blow of a big hand or a swipe with the end of a leather lead. But the general mood was happily or at any rate tensely anticipatory. Much depended on the day for everyone concerned, credit for the host, reputation for the sportsmen, income and employment for staff, not to mention vocational pleasures for the canine participants. The two farm waggons drawn by cart-horses which rolled into the drive were greeted with restrained cheering.

The waggons had been adapted to carry loads of people. Central benches ran from the front of each to the backboard, and were separated by a raised plank of wood to lean against. Jack Haspell helped his guests to climb the steps into the first waggon, while staff used the second. Macgregor caught and bundled in any dogs unwilling or unable to jump. Betty Paull wished everyone luck, and vice versa. The leading carter cracked his whip and the horse with ponderous knowledgeability moved towards the walled garden and on to the track that led uphill.

Two drives were fitted in before luncheon. They were mainly manoeuvres designed to herd the game into position for the better afternoon drives, notwithstanding the fact that they accounted for fifty brace of grouse. Some twenty beaters helped to carry the birds and five hares to the shores of a little hill-loch, where the game was transferred into one of the waggons. This waggon, earlier on, had returned to Sweirdale Lodge to fetch the picnic, a chef and three footmen; the other waggon had fetched the ladies.

The scene was the more picturesque because the sun had now come out. Brown burn water trickled and sparkled as it fell downhill and splashed into the loch, the surface of the black deeps of which dazzlingly mirrored the light. A white cloth had been laid on part of the almost sandy shore, and open picnic baskets round the edge tethered it there – a breeze blew at this altitude. The baskets offered china, cutlery, glasses, napkins, and every kind of liquid refreshment — wines, beer, ginger beer in stone bottles, port, cherry brandy. On the white cloth were edibles galore, pies, plates of chicken wings, sausage rolls, patties, sandwiches, and sweet things, tarts, plum cake, chocolate cake, and cheeses and biscuits, and bowls of fruit. The mixed company, the ladies in their becoming sporting costumes, hats with feathers, graceful cloaks, were seated on tartan rugs in a rough semicircle on the hillside, looking at a twenty-mile view of shimmering landscape. The gentlemen removed their tweed caps, the chef pleaded with them to have second helpings, the footmen in their wasp-waistcoats replenished glasses, and from over a shoulder of the hill came the sound of the talk and laughter of the invisible army of servants of one sort and another.

Ivo sat alone: Topper was with Zeals. It was his practice not to socialize in the middle of a shoot — he took his shooting too seriously to permit the opposite sex to distract him. Besides, he was determined not to disgrace himself in front of his competitive cronies and that ignoramus Jack Haspell. He had discouraged the ladies with his brusque greetings, especially — he hoped — Mrs Smythe who might be getting presumptuous ideas in her head; and he had eaten little and drunk nothing alcoholic.

'Who's going to shoot the most grouse this afternoon?' Max Kirby called across to him.

And Buck McDonald followed up: 'Anyone feeling like a flutter?'

But Ivo resisted temptation: for one thing he had not shot as well as he could in the morning, despite his rehearsal; for another he remembered that yesterday had cost him a packet, or would have done so if Flintlock had disappointed him at Croxley. He would risk nothing more for the moment, and merely smiled and made a negative gesture by way of reply.

At half-past one Macgregor reappeared with pocket watch in hand, and Jack Haspell approached Ivo.

'I've been wondering how to disperse the ladies,' he said.

'Oh yes?'

'Mrs Staincross has decided to return to the lodge in the picnic waggon.'

Ivo, referring to Judy Staincross's immobility, said he was not surprised.

'And Mrs McDonald wishes to stay with Buck. I was thinking that Mrs Mason might start off with Max and then perhaps go with one of the Langthwaites, and Marian McDonald seems to be happy with Gregory.

[32]

Would you let Beatrice Smythe sit in your butt and watch the expert in action?'

'I'm sorry, no – I won't have females getting in my light.'

'But I can assure you she wouldn't do that – she's promised to do exactly as told, Lord Ivo.'

'Please offer her my apologies,' his lordship replied, rising to his feet and striding off in search of Zeals, his guns and his dog.

The sportsmen and ladies and loaders had parted company with the beaters at the picnic site, and each group hiked in different directions to be in position and prepared for action. The butts, open-ended pens with peat walls about four and a half feet high, on the outer sides of which camouflaging heather grew, were some forty yards apart and placed in line sixty or seventy yards back from the brow of a hill. The strategy here was that the grouse in an area of half a square mile or so would be forced by the advancing beaters to fly towards the sportsmen concealed in their respective butts, who would have to be quick enough to see and to shoot them coming and again going.

Ivo was between Philip Staincross on his left and Max Kirby on his right. Beyond Max were young Michael Langthwaite, then Jack Haspell, then at the end of the line Henry Langthwaite, who had sufficient experience to shoot at escaping grouse and by so doing to encourage others to fly towards the centre. On the other side of Philip Staincross were Buck McDonald and Gregory du Sten.

Ivo could not complain of the butt allotted to him. He realized that, owing to where it was and how the land lay, he should get the best of the sport. He accepted a loaded gun from Zeals and laid it on top of the wall. The other gun was loaded and laid with equal care on the part of the wall curving round to the right: his lordship was right-handed and therefore the exchanges of guns would take place on that side. Zeals pulled the cartridge-bag slung over his shoulders from his back to his front, tucked the flap out of the way so that the bag was open, and arranged a score of cartridges on an accessible sort of shelf in the peat wall. Ivo meanwhile was dealing with Topper, making the dog sit now outside the butt, now behind it, now on different sides of the entrance, and trying to judge where it would be less visible to grouse and at the same time safest from gunshot. Having settled these questions, he held out his hand and received from Zeals the gadget for canine control in such circumstances, a pocket-size telescopic spike, which he extended to its full length of eighteen inches, stabbed into the earth and attached the dog's lead to. Topper seemed

[33]

to understand this routine completely, and that he would not yet be called upon to perform. He lay down, pink tongue dangling, tail wagging, and gazed at his master with bright and confident eyes.

Ivo removed his heather-coloured tweed cap, mopped his brow with a silk handkerchief, replaced the cap and checked that it was firmly fixed. The afternoon was getting hotter. The waves of heat blurred the outlines of hills. Grouse were calling far and wide; and a muted chorus of laughter rang out – Max Kirby and his man and Mrs Mason were laughing at something – followed by more sinister sounds, the plop of cartridges dropped into breeches, one and then the other, and the oiled click of a gun being closed. A match struck to light a cigarette was audible in the humming silence.

Macgregor's distant whistle signalled the start of the drive. The shouts of the beaters and their tapping of sticks reached the ears of the sportsmen. Ivo lifted his gun off the wall of the butt, slid the safety-catch forwards and back a couple of times, and assumed a slightly crouching stance for the sake of concealment; and Zeals, who did not need to crouch, reached into the cartridge bag, clipped two cartridges between the index, second and third fingers of his left hand, and lifted and held the other gun vertically to facilitate a rapid transfer as soon as needed. A dog whined along the line and was ordered to shut up.

A gun fired. It was on the left, a single shot fired probably by Gregory du Sten, sounding more like a pop than a bang. But Ivo, and Zeals for that matter, kept looking straight ahead.

Two grouse swung low and diagonally over the brow of the hill, appearing in front of Philip Staincross who was too late to get in a shot, winging across the field of fire of Ivo, who let off both barrels, and hitting the ground in a flurry of feathers near Max Kirby, whose raised finger indicated that he thought he had shot one of them.

Ivo muttered: 'Hell of an angle,' as he swapped guns with Zeals.

The latter broke open the gun in his hands, which ejected the spent and smoking cartridges, slipped the two clipped in his fingers into the breech, snapped the gun shut and was ready for the next exchange. While waiting for it, he surreptitiously fiddled another pair of the cartridges in the cartridge-bag between his fingers.

A pack of grouse, semicircular wings momentarily black against blue sky, then almost lost against a background of heather, sailed towards the butt and

[34]

over it. Ivo downed one out of a dozen in front, and, taking his second gun and turning, two on the other side.

More grouse were flying towards, across, over and even at low level between the line of butts, larger packs twenty or thirty strong; and guns were going off everywhere and without stopping, and their barrels as well as sportsmen and loaders were growing hotter; and birds were falling out of the sky like confetti.

Five minutes of hectic activity ensued. Then a commotion on the right was followed by Max Kirby bellowing through cupped hands: 'Don't shoot, hold your fire!' Ivo and Zeals had to pause and pay attention.

A woman was walking in front of the line – Mrs Smythe – she must have walked out of Jack Haspell's butt – but how had she not got shot or at least peppered by Max or someone? She marched through the heather as if along Bond Street in the direction of the butt of Ivo, who scowled and shouted in his turn at Philip Staincross: 'Hold your fire!'

She approached smiling.

'What the hell do you think you're doing?' he demanded.

'May I join you?'

'What? For God's sake . . .' They were still shooting up and down the line. 'You might have been killed.'

Inconsequently, coolly rather than flirtatiously, she remarked: 'I won't bother you.'

'But I told Jack . . . Didn't Jack tell you?'

She very slightly shrugged her shoulders.

'You can't stand there,' he bawled at her. 'You'll be killed.'

Max was shooting again – he had just shot at a grouse.

Zeals addressed his master in an undertone: 'There's good sport going begging, milord.'

'Sit with the dog!'

Ivo's order was reasonable for all its rudeness, since there really was no room for three within the confines of the butt, and after all Topper had been considered to be out of harm's way.

She obeyed immediately and without demur.

He loosed both barrels at a pack of grouse. But he was shaking with anger, almost blinded by it, he had not clearly seen or steadily aimed at particular birds, and he missed and cursed, and missed again with three of his next six shots. He slammed his gun down on top of the wall, turned to tell the woman

[35]

what he thought of her, changed his mind, picked up his gun, missed more grouse, and kept on missing and cursing until the beaters hove into view and eventually walked through the line of butts and on to their starting-point for the next drive.

Ivo confronted Beatrice Smythe — she was standing and picking bits of heather off her skirt with her slow-moving long-fingered hands.

'You can't stay with me while I'm shooting, I won't have it, I told Jack Haspell — you'll have to go elsewhere,' he said.

'You wouldn't force me to do that,' she replied.

The coolness of her tone, as of her previous behaviour, astonished him, and eclipsed his sense of outrage for a moment. She had not even raised her eyes to his, she continued to pick at the heather on her skirt, sure of herself, or of the effect of the intimacy she was introducing into their relations.

He brushed past her, he was not going to have a row with her in public, and strode down towards where Jack Haspell had been shooting, leaving Zeals with his guns and to work Topper and recover the grouse he had shot.

His temper was not improved by Max saying to him as he passed: 'You seem to inspire a willingness to take risks, Ivo.'

He ignored it; but it served to warn him not to compromise himself further than he had been compromised.

Jack met him half-way in more senses than one, hurrying across to apologise: he said his cousin was a headstrong girl, and that he trusted she had not wrecked the sport.

'Can't you control her?' Ivo asked, more cautiously, with more outward tolerance, than might have been the case.

'Would you like me to try to walk her back to the Lodge?'

'Is that the alternative?'

Jack explained that one waggon had returned to base and the other was reserved for the collection of game; but he offered not to take part in the next two drives in order to escort the lady to the Lodge, provided she was agreeable.

'No — no need to wreck things for you too,' Ivo said, as if with some grinding of teeth, and turned towards his butt.

Mrs Mason buttonholed him with more apologies.

'I'm so sorry,' she began.

He cut her short: 'That's perfectly all right.'

To Mrs Smythe herself, who had pretended not to be aware that he was

[36]

approaching her, he said after clearing his throat: 'Will you do as I say?'

She stared at him with widely opened eyes, and he averted his.

'Naturally,' she replied.

He went to help Zeals and Topper to pick up dead grouse.

The other drives of the afternoon proceeded successfully from a sporting point of view. But Ivo Grevill did not shoot as straight as usual. He could not concentrate on his favourite occupation: he was unaccustomed to having his wishes disregarded, he was disturbed by having to submit to anyone else's will, especially that of a young nobody, and more especially because that nobody had confirmed his suspicion that she had designs on him.

He hardly talked to her, but derived scant comfort from the fact that she appeared not to notice his punitive silence. That she was content in his company neither to talk nor be talked to aggravated and even alarmed. He gave additional expression to his feelings at the end of the sporting day by waiting until she was seated with the others in the waggon bound for Sweirdale Lodge, then by indicating that he would walk home.

A small consolation to his lordship was his refusal to place a bet, which he would have lost, on the number of grouse he had shot. Again, at the Lodge, he was pleased to read in *The Times* that Flintlock had done its bit and won him more than enough to defray all the costs of this probably ill-advised visit.

The best of a bad job was that after two more days and three nights he would be at Gelts Abbey, on familiar territory and with people who knew how to behave.

Ivo Grevill spoke to Jack Haspell after tea on that day, and as a result had a dull time at dinner sitting between Agatha McDonald and Judy Staincross. He again played cards before and billiards after dining, and was annoyed to run up more gambling debts. And having been thankful to steer clear of Mrs Smythe, and taken care not to catch her amber eye or to give her any encouragement, he was then contrarily disappointed in his bedroom not to be greeted by a titillating little cough from nextdoor.

The following morning he rose at eight; consumed a substantial breakfast, a later daintier version of which was served to the ladies in their bedrooms; and met Zeals, Macgregor and Barton by appointment in the gunroom at nine-thirty. He left the lodge carrying his double-barrelled .30 rifle in their company, and at the back of the house fired half a dozen practice rounds at a wooden cut-out of a stag; handed the rifle over to Barton, who slipped it into a canvas and leather sleeve and slung it over his shoulder, the strap criss-crossing on his chest with that of the leather case of his spy-glass; was wished good luck by Zeals and a better result than Miss Paull's clean misses by Macgregor, followed Barton round to the front of the house, where a saddled and bridled pony was held by a lad named Archie, proudly refused the offer of a ride on it and set off on an uphill pathway.

The size of the Sweirdale estate did not allow grouse shooting on every day of its season. The biggest bags were achieved by letting the surviving birds rest and re-group, while sportsmen and the odd sportswoman stalked the deer on the higher ground above the heather-line.

Four to six thousand grouse not only could be, but actually had to be shot in an average Sweirdale year, in order to leave enough natural food to see the rest through the winter; and the same applied to the essential cull of deer in the so-called Sweirdale Forest.

Ivo had the pleasure of shooting not one but two fine stags, while Philip Staincross and Gregory du Sten made do with a spot of duck flighting, and Max and Buck elected to put their tired feet up. Having walked at least twenty miles, he returned to Sweirdale Lodge nearer seven than six o'clock. He sank into the bath that Zeals prepared for him, just stopped himself falling to sleep therein, ate dinner in a sort of trance seated between Marian McDonald, whose uneasy chatter and giggles spared him the effort of having to make conversation, and Mrs Mason, to whom he did not feel obliged to talk, and when the ladies had left the dining-room excused himself and retired to bed.

The next day dawned overcast and windy. Most of the guns had great difficulty in shooting the grouse, which flew at twice their normal speed with the wind behind them, and could scarcely be seen against a background of charcoal-coloured cloud. The exception was Ivo Grevill: he killed a bird with every shot he fired during the morning drives. He was so pleased with his marksmanship and indeed with himself that at lunch he accepted bets as well as congratulations, and raised no objection to having Mrs Smythe in tow for the afternoon.

After the picnic she had asked him: 'Can I come with you?'

She wore a pretty tartan beret, and her cheeks glowed pink from exposure to the wild weather.

[38]

'Why not?' he replied.

At the end of the third and last drive of the afternoon, during which he had merely given her orders and she had obeyed them, they swapped compliments.

'You do shoot well,' she murmured as they walked towards the waggon that would carry the party back to the Lodge.

'You weren't in my way,' he returned.

But he immediately regretted the unwarranted intimacy of her manner of talking to him, which he for some reason and against his better judgment had begun to imitate.

He avoided her throughout his final evening at Sweirdale, once more playing cards after tea and billiards after dinner, at which he sat between Betty Paull again and the wife of Henry Langthwaite, who had been invited to dine. He said goodnight and goodbye only to the Langthwaites; the whole house-party, ladies included, were to breakfast downstairs on the morrow before leaving to catch trains.

At eleven-thirty he reached his bedroom. He had enjoyed top-class sport, made money on the day, drunk a few weak whiskies and water too many, and listened for and duly heard that seductive cough from next door.

He prepared for bed, donned pyjamas, parted his curtains and looked out at the black night. A sudden roaring gust of wind shook the sashes of his window and large drops of rain splashed on the panes. The moon peeped through racing storm-clouds, and was obscured; but a flash of sheet lightning illuminated the landscape, followed a minute later by a rumble of thunder. The storm that had threatened since morning was breaking and clearing the air.

He would resist temptation, always supposing that a little cough at bedtime was meant to tempt him. It might mean nothing; to respond to it in any way would be certain to complicate his existence. He got into bed. He remembered that he disliked the Smythe woman, an adventuress if ever he saw one, a gold-digger, and weird with it, notwithstanding her fetching appearance. From another closer flash of lightning and clap of thunder he drew the conclusion that if he were to venture into the passage on pleasure bent, he might meet somebody who had been disturbed by the storm going to or coming from the bathroom.

He extinguished his candle, yet felt far from sleep. At shorter intervals the whole room was lit up by flickering lighning, which penetrated his closed eyelids, and thunder followed the flashes more closely. He opened his eyes to

[39]

see in the sky a great jagged dangerous gash of lightning that was forked. It crookedly rooted in the earth, and he was startled in spite of himself by an almost immediate sharp and brutal clap of thunder.

The next thing he heard, above the battering of wind and rain against his window, was a door quietly opening somewhere, but not the door of his room, as he fancied at first. Then lightning and thunder apparently overhead, reverberating thunder that seemed to shake the house to its foundations, was succeeded by an unusual sound, like an echo or obbligato, like the yelp of a dog or the cry of an animal in pain, and at close quarters.

His assumption was that one of the sporting dogs was in the passage, that the McDonalds perhaps had brought their dog indoors and kept it in their bedroom in case it was frightened by the storm, and it had panicked and escaped. He got up and threw on his red dressing-gown. But, as he was about to open his door and look out, thunder and again that cry which seemed to emanate from the other side of the room arrested him. He crossed to the window. Thunder rumbled, and the yelping cry of terror was repeated. He pulled open the door of the adjacent corner cupboard from which it seemed to issue.

Lightning showed him the white bundle on the floor – Beatrice Smythe crouching there and pleading with him to shut the cupboard door.

'Please – I can't stand thunderstorms – please!'

He was dumbfounded. It took him a moment to realize what that bundle was, and who, and why it or she wanted the door shut and the storm excluded, and how she happened to be where she was. He began to understand that his room and hers were connected by means of a door in the back of their respec-tive corner cupboards, and, according to her explanation, that she was so scared by the storm, scared almost out of her wits, that she had crept into the darkest and quietest place available.

The unanswered questions that he was too taken aback to ask – why had she opened the inner connecting door, and was her intrusion virtually into his room a part of her plot hatched in collusion with Jack Haspell? – were brushed aside by the aphrodisiac effects upon him of their situation in the dark. She had sensed and responded, as it were, to his repressed inclinations of a little while ago; and the ambiguity of her behaviour now inflamed him further.

'You can't stay there,' he said thickly.

'No – please shut the door – I didn't mean to disturb you – forgive me,' she mumbled.

But lightning flashed and she cried out: 'Oh no – you haven't even closed your curtains – go away, go away – you mustn't see me like this!'

He retreated as requested, or rather recoiled from her near-hysteria and hushed her, while in the darkness deepened after lightning she – without his knowing it – instead of retiring into her room entered his to close the curtains. But thunder clapped and new lightning flashed and flickered and revealed her in her transparent nightdress framed between his curtains, arms raised and holding the curtains, immobilized by her terror maybe, and emitting a stifled version of her prolonged yelping.

'Come here,' he said.

'No,' she protested.

He went and laid hands on her.

'No, no,' she said, struggling to close the curtains at last.

Thunder made her cling to him. He had to drag her towards the bed nonetheless.

They wrestled blindly. He panted, her cries turned into moaning as the storm waxed and waned over Sweirdale Lodge. Her continued verbal resistance was contradicted by the ingenuity with which she achieved postponement and prolongation and repetition. The physical compliments he paid her were like punishment, and his occasional curses replaced terms of endearment. Passion finally subsided in the small hours, as did the weather.

He said: 'You can go back to your room now.'

After a pause, during which he feared that she might not agree to do so, she replied without noticeable irony: 'Thank you' – and departed.

Nothing more was said.

Later that morning they joined the house-party for breakfast, not looking much more tired than others who had been kept awake by the storm. Mrs Smythe was not leaving for the railway station with the crowd that included Ivo and Zeals and Topper. Her lover of a few hours before consequently felt obliged to bid her goodbye.

She was in the sitting-room, idly turning the pages of a magazine. She looked up but did not smile at him as he approached her. On a conciliatory impulse, and because he had reason to be sure that she could not threaten him with fatherhood, he produced his wallet and extracted and offered her one of his visiting cards.

'You'll find me at this address,' he said.

She took the card, slowly tore it in half, let the two halves fall on the floor, and stared at him.

'I won't be finding you,' she replied.

He had to grovel on the floor at her feet to retrieve the two pieces of his visiting card.

2

BROUGHAM and Castile was known as the Double Dukedom, a nominal distinction not accorded to similar titular creations, Buccleuch and Queensberry, for instance, or Hamilton and Brandon. Although Brougham and Castile was not the premier dukedom of the realm, or the oldest, or the wealthiest, perhaps it was singled out in the popular imagination either by reason of the sheer luck of the acquisition of both titles, especially the second, or simply because of the euphony of the two together.

The Elizabethan Thomas Grevill of Brougham in Cumberland, son of a yeoman farmer, became a soldier and is said to have caught the eye of the queen as she reviewed her troops before they went to fight the Spanish Armada. He received a knighthood for the valiant part he played in that engagement, and was favoured by appointment to the command of the Queen's Bodyguard. Within a few years, and notwithstanding his youth, he was ennobled, becoming Lord Grevill of Brougham and being granted extensive formerly monastic lands in the north-western area of Cumberland. He was supposed to have the ear of the ageing queen, and not only her ear, was created duke, and sufficiently enriched to be able to commission a ducal residence on the site of the farmhouse of his forebears: whence the scurrilous doggerel of the day which rhymed Brougham with womb, and a palace having fifty room, and eventually 'dukedoom'.

The point of the latter misspelling was that in his mid-thirties he so far forgot himself as to propose to wed a maid of honour at court, thus infuriating Her Majesty, who ordered him to be impeached for malfeasance. But his luck held: before the queen could have him hung, drawn and quartered she expired.

The first Duke of Brougham flourished thereafter, consolidating his position, even to the extent of gaining a secondary title for the use of the eldest of his four sons, Marquess of Medringham, pronounced Meringham, and accumulating more property and treasure.

His descendants sank into the obscurity of the backwoods for two centuries. Then another Grevill soldier revived the fortunes of the family. The thirteenth Duke, nicknamed Black Brougham, probably in consideration of the colour of his hair and dark complexion, fought alongside Wellington in the Peninsular War, and seemed to be mortally wounded while commanding the British left flank at the battle of Burgos. His brilliant generalship and gallantry had helped to win the day, and he was recommended for the highest honour a grateful nation could bestow. Certain steps were taken which would make him think on his assumed deathbed that he was to receive the dukedom of Castile in addition to Brougham; whereupon he rose almost from the dead, those steps proved irreversible, and he became not only the Double Duke but also the Accidental Duke.

Black Brougham's son Baldwin differed from the family type in that he was a spendthrift and wastrel, and the luck of the family seemed to run through his fingers. His wife died young of being married to him, he burned his houses to the ground by mistake, his investments slumped, his racehorses never won, he mortgaged everything, and ended by borrowing from moneylenders.

Baldwin fathered Edward, fifteenth Duke of Brougham and third of Castile, who was a nonentity, except in name and in so far as he sired Walter and his younger brother Ivo Grevill.

The differences between the brothers, physical and moral, were marked; yet rumour was silenced by the darkness of visage, the complexion deriving from Black Brougham, which they shared.

Time, too, came between Walter and Ivo: the former was fifteen years older than the latter. Moreover only Walter had known their mother, who had urged him to restore the family finances virtually as she died giving birth to her second child.

This maternal injunction fell on fertile ground. Walter aged seventeen, while still Marquess of Medringham, wrested the reins of authority from the nerveless hands of his father and dedicated his adulthood to untangling the affairs of the estate. Later on he married Lady Lily Campbell-Davidge, no doubt he loved her in his cold-fish way, and they produced William, known as Billy. But having a wife to provide for, and then a son and heir, he seemed to regard as extra reasons to concentrate on the task in hand; and the death of Duchess Lily from tuberculosis, possibly complicated by the unhappiness of her marriage, enabled him to retire into mourning and not to have to bother about social obligations and distractions.

In his forty-sixth year in 1908, Walter Duke of Brougham and Castile might have decided that he had succeeded, and could relax and recreate himself. He had disposed of the Irish property, the racing stables in Newmarket, the stud-farm in Sussex, the Brougham Hunt, the villa in Nice and the steam yacht. He had got rid of large numbers of employees: men of business, agents, lawyers and other financial leeches; domestic servants mostly kicking their heels in the ducal residences; and the so-called work-force of gardeners, foresters, keepers, grooms, who had nothing much to do and did less. He gradually replaced bad tenants and repaid mortgages and cleared debt. After three decades of trying, he could reunite the dukedom with its estranged consort, fortune. When harvests were good, he or it was again rich, and he was no longer in danger of ever being poor.

On the other hand his possessions were still great, and always liable to cost him more in upkeep than he could easily afford; and they were the birthright of Billy and therefore not to be sold.

In addition, or, more graphically, in subtraction, he had to deal with Ivo, cough up for Ivo, be ready not to let his brother go broke and drag the family into disgrace, have enough money ready to rescue his brother from the next scrape and all the other scrapes that he was likely to get into.

His consequential attitude to the fraternal thorn in his flesh, his shyness with the man who had bitten into his bank balance not once before but repeatedly, and threatened never to stop doing so, was illustrated when the brothers dined alone at Gelts Abbey eight days after Ivo was relieved to see the last of Sweirdale Lodge and especially Beatrice Smythe.

Gelts was one of the four remaining Brougham estates, the other three being Brougham itself, a large slice of the city of Carlisle, and Castile House and roughly a dozen satellite dwellings in London. Gelts Abbey, twenty miles distant from Brougham and also located on the westward flank of the Cumbrian mountains, was an almost sacrilegious misnomer: it was in fact a hunting lodge, built with the stones of a ruined religious edifice. Good Queen

[45]

Bess, for some extra service rendered by her Grevill favourite, had given him the former monastery and its twenty thousand acres of moorland, respectively destroyed and seized by her father Henry VIII. The lodge was sheltered to some extent by its attachment to a high old ivy-clad wall, a relic of the monastic chapel, and was about as big and as outwardly severe as Sweirdale. The interior, although comfortable enough, suffered from having always been a repository for Brougham cast-offs, second-rate portraits of obscure Grevills, and incongruous pieces of furniture from every epoch.

For the last eight years Ivo had been in charge of the place: that is to say Walter, as soon as he became the Duke, formally requested his brother to relieve him of the sporting and social duties it entailed. Thus Walter hoped to kill several birds, and not only avian game, with a single stone. He would be making work for the idle hands of his twenty-two-year-old sibling, keeping him out of mischief for at least a few weeks of the year, and creating a respectable method of paying him a sort of salary; at the same time he would have a means of dealing with guests that he needed to entertain but did not want at Brougham. Of course he retained ownership of Gelts, and ultimate responsibility for whatever happened there. The result was a typically ambiguous arrangement and a sure cause of the exacerbation of mutual resentment.

Ivo had reached Gelts from Sweirdale in time for tea, which, served by the resident butler Tempell and prepared by his wife, he consumed in solitary state. Then, as on previous occasions, he had to greet Saddlecombe, Walter's major-domo, loyal and efficient Saddlecombe with years of serving the Grevill family behind him, who had driven over from Brougham with a waggonload of housemaids, scullery maids, footmen, wines and foodstuffs; and see the Gelts head-gamekeeper Thark and discuss sporting matters. He drank his usual weak whiskies and water and changed for dinner, after which he studied and amended Mrs Tempell's menus for the coming week.

The next day he put on a show of welcoming the people invited by Walter: Sir Arthur Bullinger, who had shot at Gelts for donkey's years, and his arthritic wife Mildred; Baron Janse, a Belgian agriculturalist who had done Walter some favour, and animated Baroness Janse; the Earl and Countess of Hazzlewood, Henry and Constance, who had rented Castile House when they had a daughter coming out; Lord and Lady Deveraux – Valentine Deveraux was a House of Lords crony; Brigadier Ronald Dimmick, the

[46]

retired commanding officer of the Grevill Rifles; and the High Sheriff of Cumberland Sir Cedric Byrch and Louisa, his wife.

The party's average age was fifty-seven. It was duller than Jack Haspell's, but indeed better behaved – bridge was played in the evening for matchsticks; the food was less copious and showy, but probably healthier; and the shooting was not so good as to put undue pressure on the guns.

Ivo considered that he worked pretty hard for the pittance he was paid for acting as host on behalf of his brother. He was not rude to anyone. He repressed his gambling instincts. He invariably chose the worst position to shoot from. Yet as usual, when the Duke arrived at Gelts to dine with his guests on the last evening of their stay and to bid them goodbye in the morning, he was the recipient of their thanks.

The brothers did not see much of each other during the day of departure of that first party of grouse-shooters. Walter had to inspect some of his lowland farms, Ivo went rabbiting with Thark. They changed into evening clothes and met at seven-forty-five in the parlour of Gelts Abbey.

Walter was shorter than Ivo, a spare tense worried sort of man, not at all flamboyant, not expansive. His face was thinner, his features were aquiline or sharper, than Ivo's, and his black hair was going grey at the temples, and he had still darker skin under his dark eyes. His looks were not the outdoor sort; his habitual uniform in the country was a blue serge suit; and his charm, such as it was, for those who recognized it, lay in his quiet self-assurance, not to say pride, and his aristocratic dignity.

He wore a conventional dinner-jacket, stiff shirt and stick-up collar, and stood in front of the fire, a small glass of sherry held in his right hand, and his left behind his back and extended to the blaze; while Ivo, similarly dressed, having decided it would not be diplomatic to wear the evening coat of the Brougham Hunt which Walter in his wisdom had swept off the face of the earth, helped himself to another weak whisky and lit a Turkish cigarette.

Diplomacy fared badly from then on.

Walter began by asking in a dry and disapproving tone of voice: 'Who was it you were staying with in Scotland?'

'A fellow called Haspell – you wouldn't know him.'

'Not the dressmaker Haspell?'

'I told you weeks ago that he runs an establishment called Frère Jacques, Walter.'

[47]

'Good gracious! Who else was there?'

Ivo mentioned Max Kirby and Philip Staincross.

'Say no more,' Walter commented. 'You certainly fish in muddy waters. I can't imagine why you mix with people like that. I suppose you like them because they're prepared to gamble with you and take your money.'

'Well, to start with, I took theirs, if you must know. Secondly, a friend of yours was there, Betty Paull, so the water wasn't all that muddy by your standards. And the party was a damn sight more amusing than the one I've just had to put up with, and the shooting was top-hole.'

'You touch a sore spot.'

'What?'

'You say your shooting in Scotland was top-hole – what do you mean?'

'I believe we shot seven hundred brace in two days – and Sweirdale has another six days to offer.'

'The total bag for twice as many days at Gelts was less than half as many grouse.'

'I'm well aware of it.'

'Would you say the poor sport was due to bad luck or bad management?'

'I'd say what I'm sick and tired of saying to you, Walter. I'd say the trouble here is money, the lack of it, your refusal to invest and bring the shoot up to scratch.'

'It's always come easy for you to spend my money. I warned you when I offered you this post that the shoot would have to be more or less self-supporting. It seems to me to support itself less and less.'

'That's not my fault. I always understood that the Brougham Hunt funds would be directed into Gelts; but it hasn't happened, has it? You've kept the money, and expect me to run the shoot on a shoe-string. You can ask Thark: he's been on at me for years about the two extra gamekeepers that he says he needs and I've repeatedly told you we require. And another thing, Walter: you compare the bag after two days' shooting at Sweirdale with the bag here; but that's ridiculous, because you're comparing the efforts of some of the very best shots and some of the worst. Half of the old codgers you invite to shoot grouse can't see, and the other half couldn't hit a barn door if they tried. You stand there and grumble – well, I've got more cause to grumble than you have, and you know it!'

'May we skip the hard line story?'

[48]

'In other words I have to listen to your complaints but you'd rather not listen to mine.'

'Please stick to the point! What we both know is that if you were prepared to spend more time and energy on improving the Gelts shooting, I might be prepared to spend more money. I've told you often before – and the position remains the same. Frankly, I was extremely put out by your decision to postpone our grouse-shooting season from the 12th to the 17th of August – it was inconsiderate and, I'm sorry to say, typical. As a result of your preference for the sport and no doubt the gambling of your second-rate friends, I had to apologize to mine and beg this week's guests and next week's to reorganize all their plans. We've aways entertained here for the first two weeks of the season, and you undertook to stand in for me as host and run the sporting side. More frankly still, you are not paid to inconvenience me. Wait a moment! I'd like to remind you that your job didn't exist in Father's day; and I will not agree that it was mean of me to give you a good wage and a chance to salvage your self-respect, in addition to the pounds and pounds I've had to spend on rescuing you from bankruptcy over the years.'

At this point Tempell knocked and entered the room and announced: 'Dinner is served, your grace.'

'Thank you, Tempell,' Walter returned, moving away from the fire and addressing his seated brother in friendlier accents designed to stop gossip below stairs. 'Come along, Ivo.'

But Ivo delayed sulkily, sunk in a chair, smoking and sipping whisky. He was dark red in the face and he scowled. At length he stirred himself, rose, chucked the stub of his cigarette into the fire, and in the dining-room took the place to which he was relegated when his brother was in residence, at the lower end of the long table.

They sipped their soup.

Then Ivo broke the silence which was embarrassing in front of Tempell and a nameless footman: 'How's Billy?'

'All right, thank you.'

'His health all right?'

'I'm afraid not. But his spirit makes up for a lot.'

'Asthma still his problem?'

'Approximately, yes.'

'Brougham's not a healthy spot.'

'Where would you say was healthier?'

'Anywhere except Brougham.'

'That's helpful.'

'I was joking.'

'You seem to forget that we spent our early years there, and it's always been the family seat.'

'It didn't suit Billy's mother.'

The Duke directed a shocked and angry look at his brother, who busied himself with buttering a triangle of toast. The footman cleared away the empty soup plates. Tempell put hot dinner plates in their place, the footman then served the fish course and Tempell replenished the glasses of white wine.

At length this silence was brought to an end.

'What would you do with Billy?' Walter inquired.

'You should have brought him here.'

'Oh – why?'

'I'd have taken him out shooting, got him fitter and made a sportsman of him.'

'He's much too young for that, setting aside other considerations.'

'He's eight, isn't he? I was shooting with a four-ten at his age. I went to board at St Asaph's when I was eight.'

'He's certainly too young and delicate for a boarding-school. I myself didn't go to St Asaph's till I was ten. You were a robust boy.'

'Of course, if you want to mollycoddle him you could send him down south. You could send him down to Nanny Cormack. Nanny is still alive, isn't she?'

'Alive and living in the nurseries at Castile House. I let her stay on there, which is not to say that I ever wanted her to have any hand in Billy's upbringing. Apart from the fact that Nanny must be getting on for ninety, she was always a spoiler, she spoilt you in particular. No! Billy's safely in the nursery at Brougham with Nurse Tucker, who was chosen and appointed by Lily, and is highly qualified and capable. I'm hoping to get him into the swing of things as soon as possible, and find him a decent tutor, although I'm not at all sure about forcing sport down his throat. Meanwhile, as he's so sensitive and susceptible, I intend to exercise care over the influences he's exposed to.'

Ivo in his turn glared along the table, having taken his brother's last remark personally. He emptied his glass of wine and growled: 'Billy would be fine if

[50]

he was treated right.' An afterthought struck him and he suggested with a malicious glint in his eyes: 'Perhaps you shouldn't have sold up in Nice. You could have packed Billy off to the Villa Grevill and turned him into a proper hot-house plant.'

The fish plates were removed, and the next course of young grouse roasted and on toast with bread sauce and fried potato flakes and vegetables, complemented by a silky smooth claret, was served.

The Duke summoned Tempell, handed him a piece of paper and instructed him to bear it to his brother. On the paper were written lists of the guests who would be arriving tomorrow afternoon to stay for the second week's grouse shooting, also of possible house-parties for various pheasant shoots later in the year – the estate had some lower-lying woodland suited to pheasants and to shooting them. A practical discussion ensued: lists were amended, questions of protocol settled, plans made, Tempell's opinion sought.

The armistice lasted until the pudding and savoury courses, a lemon mousse and hot cheese wafers, had been consumed.

An order was then given to Tempell to bring coffee and port into the parlour, where his grace, having preceded his lordship into that room and waited until they were alone, resumed his stance in front of the fire, coffee-cup in hand, and uttered the following reproach: 'I must ask you not to be rude to me in front of my servants.'

'What are you talking about? You were ruder to me than I was to you.'

'I shall bring up my son as I please and without your interference.'

'Well, I wish you a bit more success than you seem to have had so far.'

'Thank you. Speaking of success, I wish and hope you'll start to do better in a general sense.'

'If you're afraid you'll be ruined by not having a few more grouse to sell in Carlisle, I repeat for the last time, Walter, that your remedy's in your own hands, not mine. Put money in, and you'll take grouse and money and probably profit out. That's been my contention all along and my advice, though I can't for the life of me think why you're so damn keen on profits. You're not a shopkeeper, for God's sake. As for your implying that I could do better, I won't let you sit back and criticize me. You're beginning to sound like a schoolmaster.'

'The trouble with Gelts isn't confined to grouse, Ivo.'

'Oh? What else is wrong?'

'You beg for money, but you're already getting it or taking it.'

'What do you mean?'

'There's no need whatsoever for you to run the place in such a luxurious manner.'

'I won't serve bread and water at any table I preside over, if that's what you're getting at.'

'You serve much more elaborate fare than I do at Brougham.'

'But you're noted for penny-pinching. My wish is that you'd behave more like a duke, Walter. You should have seen the table kept by my acquaintance the dressmaker at Sweirdale. I can assure you that generous hosts in your financial league would make you look an inhospitable skinflint.'

'I'm not in any league with dressmakers. And I marvel at your nerve in telling me I'm less than generous. You'd have gone to prison long ago if I hadn't been generous.'

'Maybe. But I never would have needed to call upon your generosity if you hadn't been so selfish over the inheritance.'

'Since you choose to speak hypothetically, I'll follow your bad example for once and say that if Father had split the inheritance between us, or I'd shared it out, every single family possession would either be sold, or so run down and depleted by your extravagance as to be no longer viable. There's nothing left of all you've had, and it would have been the same story if you'd had more or if you'd had everything.'

'You'll be surprised to hear that I agree with you, Walter. There certainly is nothing left of the little I have had.'

'Oh?'

'My bank manager tells me my account is looking sick.'

'What's become of the money I forked out only months ago?'

'It reduced my overdraft.'

'Why do you never really and truly surprise me, Ivo?'

'Spare me your sarcasm, please! And I won't be patronized. You've got Brougham and Gelts and Castile House – what Mother and then Father left me was petty cash, which I'd spent on essentials within a year or two of receiving it. Admittedly, since then, I've had to turn to you for help just to tide me over until I get back on my feet. But you've never forked out much more than you must spend daily, and you've never given me enough to make my bank manager crack a smile.'

'Ivo, I'm not going to argue with you yet again about the law or the convention of primogeniture. And I would strongly advise you not to be quite so aggressive towards the person you hope to touch for money. What's the damage this time round?'

'Twenty thousand would come in handy.'

'Be serious, please.'

'Twenty thousand would leave me with a mite of capital after all expenses were paid.'

'Debts, you mean – and debts run up for inessentials – I know! Well, I'm not giving you money to gamble with, or money that would spare you the necessity of doing a stroke of proper work.'

'That's rich – idle rich, I might say – coming from you. What proper work have you ever done? Why don't you shoot, why didn't you bother to learn? I'm one of the many people who relieve you of work – by working at entertaining the bores you're too damn lazy to entertain yourself.'

'You'd better not complain of being paid for wasting my money with your grand ideas.'

'My pay from you buys my cartridges and my cigarettes.'

'Would you prefer to do without it? Would you rather not have the job?'

'I've a damn good mind to chuck it in – I obviously don't give satisfaction, and I get no thanks.'

'Take care, Ivo! I'll accept your resignation with relief if you're not careful. Now, to conclude this unpleasant and repetitive conversation, and in a spirit of friendship, I ask you: isn't it high time for you to settle down? I realize that you weren't brought up to work at a humdrum job any more than I was. I see that it might be difficult for you at your age and with your tastes to find congenial employment. But I'm sure there must be a niche where your accomplishments and experience would be appreciated and remunerated, and I can't help feeling you'd find it a lot more quickly if you had a wife and family to consider. Again, a wife might have the resources to back you. Rumours of your involvement with Dorothy Yealms have reached me: wild oats scattered in that direction can yield nothing good. A nice respectable girl with a dowry would be the making of you, Ivo, I do believe. Meanwhile, try to understand that my duty, at least from my point of view, seems to be to put maximum pressure on you to come to your senses. Let me have a written account of your indebtedness before I leave Gelts in the morning. One further

[53]

word: I won't give you any more than a percentage of the sum you've asked for. Good night.'

'Walter, wait! You ought to know by now that your preaching at me drives me wild.'

'Good night, Ivo.'

'Good riddance,' the other, smoking and scowling in his deep armchair, muttered under his breath.

The Duke left Gelts and did not honour his second group of guests with his company. At the end of the week in which the seven guns he had invited to shoot grouse, plus their spouses, were entertained by Ivo, his grace, instead of coming over from Brougham to act the host on the last evening of their visit, as was his customary practice, sent letters via Saddlecombe, who was reclaiming loaned members of the ducal staff. These letters, two in number, were addressed to his brother, and received and opened in the course of the final picnic luncheon on the hill.

Ivo read and stuffed them in a pocket, muttered an excuse and abandoned the party in order to go and march about, kicking at clumps of heather angrily, out of sight of prying eyes.

But he recovered himself and, rejoining the picnickers, conveyed his brother's apologies.

It was the other letter that had upset him

'Dear Ivo,' it ran. 'The cheque enclosed represents the best I can do for you in present circumstances. You will guess the real reason why I'm having to neglect my friends and the claims of hospitality, and steer clear of Gelts: yes, because I cannot face another pointless row with you. I'm afraid it does not seem right to me that I should be paying you to keep me out of my property and frustrate my wishes; and I would be pleased to have your comments on the situation, rapidly becoming unacceptable to me, created by your bitter jealousy and resentment. I would just add that were you inclined or able to heed my counsel, and to control your extravagant impulses and regularize your existence, I'm sure my approval and means of expressing it would not disappoint. A good woman might well be the making of you. Yours, Walter.'

The cheque was for £3,750.

Twenty-four hours elapsed. The guests had dispersed; Saddlecombe and supernumerary servants departed; and Thark rendered his account for paying beaters and pencilled in the prospective dates of pheasant shoots. Mrs Tempell, having cooked lunch for one, and Tempell, having served it, waited in the hallway of Gelts Abbey; and now Ivo appeared, shook their hands, thanked them and brushed aside their polite objections to the receipt of princely gratuities, was helped into his greatcoat and presented with his gloves and bowler hat, and bowed out of the house and into the carriage, the door of which was held open by Zeals.

His lordship with his manservant and his dog travelled to Carlisle, to the Grevill Arms, and after dinner to the railway station, where he caught the night train to London.

He re-occupied his quarters in Greenbury Street. Zeals' permanent lodgings were round the corner in Mayfair Mews East. Topper, in London, lived in kennels in a stableyard on the other side of Hyde Park.

Ivo resumed his daily metropolitan round: spending time in his clubs, reading the racing papers at the Turf, lunching at White's, playing cards at the St James's, gambling when he had nothing better to do in the evenings at the Club of Clubs. He had his hair trimmed and his nails manicured at Wilson's, he ordered a suit from Robinson in Savile Row and half a dozen shirts from Higgins and Hill in Jermyn Street. He took trains to Lewes races, to Melton Mowbray to buy a new hunter and trade in an old one, to Stockbridge for a day's fishing. He tore up bills, placed bets with Barney Solomon, frittered away more money, and eventually remembered to pay into his bank account his brother's cheque. He did so with haughty disdain, and, when the cashier said that he believed the manager wished to speak to his lordship, replied that he was too busy and walked out.

Lady Dorothy Yealms was in Scotland, staying in various renowned sporting establishments with her husband: she had not been available for getting on for six weeks, which partly accounted for the restlessness of her lover.

Ivo, notwithstanding the confident exterior he presented to the world, also writhed inwardly and vengefully when he remembered his latest fraternal grievances.

One evening, before going out to dinner, as he changed into his white waistcoat and tailcoat, he inquired of Zeals, who was fastening his shirt and collar studs and his cuff-links: 'Do you keep in touch with Mr Haspell's staff?'

'Not specially, milord.'

'I'd like to know Mrs Smythe's address. Can you get it for me?'

'Very good, milord.'

Two days later Zeals supplied the information on a scrap of paper.

His master's reaction was not thanks but an ungrateful question: 'Where did this come from?'

'A little bird, milord.'

'You didn't tell the whole world that I wanted her address?'

'I did not.'

'Was my name mentioned at all?'

'No milord.'

The following afternoon, Ivo overcame his caution to the extent of walking to one end of the backstreet of small terrace houses in the Paddington area, Monamy Buildings so-called, where Beatrice Smythe resided. He soon retraced his steps: he was aware of attracting possibly perilous attention in his smart clothes, and he recoiled from further non-commercial involvement with a woman in more humble, not to say squalid, circumstances than he had imagined.

But the day after that, again in the afternoon, he was drawn back to Monamy Buildings for the very reasons which had frightened him off, in short by his favourite element of risk, reinforced by lust and by some contrary dim desire to punish his brother.

As he loudly banged the door-knocker down against the stop, the semi-formulated thought in his mind was: serve Walter right.

Nobody answered the door. He produced his wallet and his gold pencil, selected a visiting card and was about to write on it. But he changed his mind, put the wallet and the pencil back in their pockets, and turned to leave rather hastily.

The door behind him opened and Mrs Smythe said in an unenthusiastic tone of voice: 'Come in.'

'Thank you,' he replied, brushing past her into a narrow passageway.

'My sitting-room's on the first floor. I'll take your hat and coat.'

'Thank you.'

She laid his garments on a chair and led the way upstairs. The sitting-room was L-shaped and had a curtain drawn across the extension. It was prettily feminine.

'May I offer you a cup of tea?'

[56]

'Nothing, thank you.'

'Will you sit down?' she asked.

He did so. But the chair was uncomfortably small for him, and he was surprised and to some extent tongue-tied by several factors, for instance the difficulty of reconciling his memory of her sexual performance and her present manner, at once socially formal and oddly familiar. She was more composed than he was, and she was better-looking than he remembered.

'You weren't expecting to see me,' he observed heavily.

'Oh yes, I was. But I don't usually open my door to callers.'

She had rebuked him for not giving her notice of his visit, she was not showing him the deference he had counted on. He did not know quite how to treat her: she was out of his class, almost a stranger, and as near as nothing insolent. Her looks and her slim tensed figure were compensatory.

He tried another conversational tack: 'It was good at Sweirdale, wasn't it?'

'I regret things that happened there.'

'Really?'

She stared at him with her amber eyes that slanted, and, when he was unable to meet them, addressed him with force and even ferocity: 'I hope you do too.'

'What? No – I don't regret anything. I've nothing to regret.' He stood and approached her – she was standing in front of the fireplace. 'I said it was good at Sweirdale and I meant it. That's why I'm here.'

She commented drily without moving: 'I detest slobbery expressions on men's faces.' It stopped him. She embarrassed him. She sat down and continued: 'You take too much for granted. You've run away with the wrong idea. I'm owed a great deal of respect. Are you prepared to give it to me?'

He slumped into another chair and blustered: 'I don't understand you.'

'No. No, you wouldn't. But you'll do as I wish, I shouldn't wonder.'

'What's going on? You were hot enough in Scotland.'

'What's going on is that I won't be spoken to as you've just spoken, or treated as you seem to think you can treat me.'

'I haven't treated you badly.'

'You would if I let you. You turn up on my doorstep without any by-your-leave.'

'I thought you'd be pleased to see me.'

'I'm pleased on my terms, not on yours. I don't have to repeat my mistakes

[57]

for your benefit. It's a question of respect. It's up to you to choose.'

'Naturally I respect you.'

'Persuade me that you do.'

'What?'

'No – stay where you are! Let's get things straight. You're an aristocrat, I'm an unprotected colonial. You've got everything you want or can get it, I have not much more than my pride. You must bridge the gap between us if we're to be friends – I can't. When you've shown me respect, I'll respect you for what you are. Forget Scotland for a start. Shall we begin again?'

'I haven't got everything I want – I mean the necessary – far from it – you're wrong there.'

'Well, I said you could get it.'

'Younger sons wouldn't agree with that notion.'

'You could get more money or make more with your connections.'

'Not real money.'

'I don't follow.'

'A few people grab hold of money in worthwhile quantities. But they're brainy and they're lucky. It seems to me that the only way to get rich is to inherit the stuff.'

'Didn't you inherit it?'

'Not I!'

'But your family's supposed to be incredibly wealthy.'

'The family that's incredibly wealthy is my elder brother's.'

'Your brother inherited his wealth?'

'Yes – from my father.'

'Didn't your father share it between you?'

'No – it all belongs to the dukedom, that is the duke, by tradition.'

'But your brother could share with you?'

'Could.'

'He hasn't, he doesn't?'

'You don't know him.'

'I'm amazed. Haven't you and he talked the matter over? Hasn't it been possible for you to come to an arrangement?'

Instead of answering these questions, he stirred uneasily in his chair and said: 'What's passed between us – what I've told you – is in complete confidence, of course.'

'Of course,' she murmured. 'But may I ask you one other thing? You were going on from Sweirdale Lodge to Gelts Abbey, weren't you? I was under the impression that Gelts Abbey belonged to you.'

'No. I'm the hired hand there. I receive a wage for running my brother's shoots.'

'Jack Haspell doesn't know it.'

'Jack Haspell's an outsider.'

'But you gamble and lose and don't turn a hair.'

'Sometimes I win. Listen – you'll have to keep my secrets.'

'I'm not a gossip.'

'No – I didn't mean that – you're damn touchy.'

'Why have you confided in me?'

'God knows!'

'Are you sorry you have?'

'Not specially.'

'Perhaps you needn't be and won't be. Would you introduce me to your brother?'

'What? Why?'

'Why not?'

'That's difficult. He's never in London. And you wouldn't like him. I don't see the point.'

She stood up and said: 'Goodbye, Lord Ivo.'

'You play a bit rough, don't you?'

'No. I don't play. Goodbye.'

'Oh well – you can probably get away with it – you're damned attractive, I will say that.'

He rose grumpily and followed her downstairs.

She smiled at him as he was edging past her in the passage, but when he paused she turned her face away and repeated: 'Goodbye, Lord Ivo.'

'You're a cool customer and no mistake.'

'Listen,' she said. 'You can come here again. I'd like to help you. I'd like to see you. But write me a note beforehand. Now I've other things to do. Remember my suggestion.'

Ivo Grevill walked back to Mayfair in a pensive frame of mind. He was relieved, as before, to be out of range of the influence of Beatrice Smythe, and to feel he had regained control of his destiny; but his main sensation was disappointment.

[59]

He had wanted that woman, and been denied satisfaction. Instead of getting the prize he had thought he deserved for seeking her out in her slum, he had been kept at arm's length and given a lesson in prim middle-class etiquette.

And she had dared to talk of respect: she demanded to be treated as if she were some high-grade virgin, although she had deliberately and expertly seduced him at Sweirdale. The respect that was missing was hers for his masculine appetites, which she herself had sharpened. He was not willing to be teased by a cheap little semi-professional and social climber.

The active consequence of his indignation against her was the following communication, written on Turf Club paper two days after his first visit: 'I shall be with you at four-thirty on the Thursday of next week, unless you let me know at this address it won't suit. There are misunderstandings that need clearing up.'

In the interval he received a letter not from Beatrice Smythe but from Dorothy Yealms, who was back in London and keen to see him. He accepted her invitation to a luncheon party in the Yealms house in Charles Street, stayed on after the other guests had departed, made furtive love to his hostess on a chaise-longue behind the net curtains of her drawing-room, and was surprised to catch himself thinking of and wishing for a different partner.

Impatience vied with his other motives as time dragged on towards Thursday. At last he was knocking on the door of 9 Monamy Buildings.

She stood before him, erect, unflinching, smiling reservedly, her politeness not giving much away.

'Good afternoon,' she said.

'You got my letter?'

'Obviously. Come in.'

He removed his coat in the passage with her assistance, and was duly tantalized by her subtly scented proximity, especially as he followed her upstairs.

In the sitting-room a coal fire in the grate and a tea-tray on an occasional table showed willingness to please him.

They stood facing each other, she with her back to the fire.

'I'm glad you wrote, I'm glad you're here again.'

Her level gaze and her directness robbed him of the initiative.

He could not bring himself to lay a finger on her.

He said lamely and tamely, 'Good,' and sat down.

[60]

'What are these misunderstandings?'

'Oh yes.' Her stare made him uncomfortable. 'Let's leave all that to later.'

'Will you take tea?'

'I'll have a cup if it's there.'

She bent down to light a gas ring under a kettle in the fireplace. Soft strands of her black hair had escaped and curled over the back of her white neck. He had never looked at her properly before: when she straightened up he noted the delicate modelling of the tip of her nose and the charming slight protrusion of her white eye-teeth as if for the first time.

'I don't suppose you've ever seen tea made like this,' she said.

'Oh yes, I have. My nanny made it in the nursery when I was a boy at Brougham. We've our own gas plant at Brougham with a miniature gas-ometer.'

'Is Brougham called Brougham House or Brougham Castle – what's its full address?'

'Brougham, near Carlisle.'

'No more?'

'Brougham without Carlisle finds it, I believe.'

'That's grand.'

'It's a big place.'

'When was it built?'

'The present house was built in seventeen hundred and something after the old Elizabethan pile burned down.'

'How many rooms has it?'

'God knows.'

'Well, how many bedrooms?'

'A hundred and twenty, they say.'

'Aren't you sure?'

'A few one way or the other doesn't signify.'

'And your brother lives there in state?'

'Yes.'

'But he's married.'

'He was. His wife died seven years ago – he's a widower. Her name was Lily and she had TB. My brother never would admit the Cumberland climate was bad for her health – he won't entertain ideas that don't suit his book. Anyway, he still lives there, and the same applies to his son, my

[61]

nephew Billy, though he's like his mother and not strong.'

'What's Billy's name?'

'Medringham, do you mean?'

'How's that spelt?'

He told her, and she asked, emphasizing the first of the two words: 'Lord Medringham?'

'Marquess of.'

'How old is he?'

'Eight, getting on for nine.'

'And who looks after him?'

'A nurse.'

'Like a nanny?'

'Yes.'

'Your nanny?'

'No – my nanny's old, she's retired and living in London, hidden away in our family house in town – Castile House, it's called.'

The kettle boiled. Beatrice Smythe, having infused the tea and poured it, asked: 'With milk and sugar, Lord Ivo?'

'Neither, thanks – and drop the Lord.'

She inclined her head in order to convey readiness to obey his order and gratitude for the compliment he had paid her by issuing it.

Ivo Grevill sipped his tea. He could no longer identify the wanton accomplice of Sweirdale with the proper housewife of Monamy Buildings. Superimposed upon his memory of those tempestuous embraces in the dark was the fresher memory of Beatrice Smythe's face, her expression of curiosity and wonder as he spoke of ducal matters, telling what no doubt seemed to her a fairy-tale of privilege. He was attracted anew and at once to her various charms and to the dangers with which she ringed them round. And her imitation of ladylike behaviour amused him: she was more carefully polite than any lady born and bred.

'What has been misunderstood?' she inquired.

He was even excited by the terrors of interrogation.

'I believe you misled me.'

'How was that?'

'Last week – between Scotland and last week, you changed your tune.'

'What did you think of me in Scotland?'

[62]

'I'm not answering that question.'

'You assumed I was setting my cap at you, didn't you?'

'I won't answer.'

'Oh — haven't you changed your tune? In your letter you wrote that you wanted to clear up misunderstandings.'

'All right.'

'What does all right mean?'

'You say I assumed you were making a dead set at me.'

'That's correct, isn't it?'

'Very well — yes — you were willing to sleep with me.'

She stared at him.

He retracted to the extent of saying: 'We slept together.'

Still with her eyes fixed on him, she related: 'I arrived in England a year ago. I had very little money, but an introduction to my cousin Jack Haspell. He employed and befriended me. I was able to rent this house. One evening he took me to the Club of Clubs. I saw you there, and your invitation to Sweirdale and mine followed on from there.'

'Were you Jack's mistress?'

'I certainly won't answer your question, which you shouldn't have asked.'

'But are you?'

'Are you the lover of Lady Dorothy Yealms?'

'How do you think you know about that?'

'Shall I continue? At Sweirdale I tried not to be scared by you. What happened in the thunderstorm was involuntary on my side. I can't control my fear of thunder and lightning — it's always driven me half-mad. You benefited from my weakness — no trap was set — you made me swear I can't have children, and explain how I was injured as a result of my husband's accident. But what I gave you then, or what you took from me, was not a commitment. I demanded nothing. I didn't pursue you. You pursued me. You turned up on my doorstep of your own free will, expecting something for nothing. Now tell me who did the misleading and who was misled.'

'I can't compete with such speechifying.' She shrugged her shoulders scornfully, and provoked him to add: 'You know what I'm talking about — you led me on and then choked me off.'

She subjected him to another stare, then said: 'You haven't listened to me. I asked you to forget Scotland and start again. I've hinted at how you could

[63]

please me, and incidentally help yourself.'

'Oh yes?'

'Your memory's very selective. Invite me to Brougham.'

'I can't do that.'

'What a pity.'

'It's my brother's place – and he never has a cat there if he can help it. That's why I'm paid to do a lot of his entertaining at Gelts Abbey.'

'I know.'

'What are you thinking you'll get out of meeting my brother and so on? He may be a widower, but he won't marry you. And I'm not making a commitment any more than you are.'

'You insult me. Goodbye.'

Although she had not altered the tone of her voice, and did not look particularly angry, she alarmed him. Besides, he was reluctant to let her cut short another visit, and unwilling to be deprived of her company.

'What have I said now?'

'I won't be misjudged as well as misled.'

'For heaven's sake!'

'Goodbye,' she repeated, rising and heading for the door.

'Oh, very well, I'll try to extract an invitation from Walter.'

'Thank you.'

'I'm not promising to succeed.'

'Will he approve of me, do you think?'

'You ask devilishly awkward questions.'

'I'll answer this one for you. I imagine he's much too hidebound to approve of me. But I'm at my best with enemies. And I'd be your friend and ally.'

'Would you? That's different. That's not such a bad idea.'

Ivo Grevill was allowed to remain in the house of Beatrice Smythe for another quarter of an hour, and to that extent rewarded for undertaking to attempt to make her inappropriate wish come true.

Two noteworthy events occurred in those fifteen minutes. She drew aside the curtain across the extension of the sitting-room to show him where she made hats for Frère Jacques. And downstairs, when she had her hand on the interior doorknob preparatory to letting him out, she unexpectedly reached up and brushed his lips with hers, opened the door, pushed him through and banged it shut behind him.

He was all the keener to tackle Walter as arranged because of his impression that she would be bound to give herself to him again under the ducal roof.

Yet his overriding motive was neither lust nor the extra value he placed on what he could not have. He was bewildered by the contrariness of the lucky object of his attentions, and by the unaccustomed strain of the verbal sparring with which she kept him at bay. Through his bewilderment, or perhaps because of it, he saw and was determined not to lose sight of the chance of annoying his brother.

Walter would object to Beatrice's breeding, and rule her out of order and beyond the pale. But Ivo had his reasons to champion her cause, not the least of which was her offer to back him up and fight his battle.

Therefore, at his desk in Greenbury Street, he concocted the following letter: 'Dear Walter, As usual I have taken your advice and formed a close tie with an excellent young woman. I believe she is what you have in mind, and that she will also be your friend. May I bring her to Brougham for the three nights of the second weekend in October? I hope that after meeting her you will not deny me the means to improve my personal prospects. Yours etc.'

Ivo's tie to Beatrice was not so close that he returned to Monamy Buildings in the three and a half weeks between writing to and hearing from his brother. He had other fish to fry in the interval. He visited Lady Dorothy Yealms and her stockbroker husband Sidney at their country house near Maidenhead, Tallow Court, where he pleased his mistress with his ardour, and his interest in other women subsided. He kept long-standing engagements to spend time with old friends and new acquaintances, and registered the fact that Beatrice would have embarrassed him with her ignorance of smart society and its usages, and her slight but peculiar accent. He cub-hunted in Leicestershire. He attended sporting fixtures and participated in indoor and outdoor games, on the results of which he could stake money. And he had a worrying number of second thoughts. He began to appreciate that by using Beatrice as a stick to beat Walter he might be pickling a rod for his own back. He liked nothing more than gambling, nor was he deterred by narrow odds; but Beatrice was a darker horse than those he put money on. In most ways she was an unknown quantity. He recalled her menacing personality and wondered if, on the strength of a spot of casual sex

[65]

and a butterfly kiss, he was storing up a hell of a lot of trouble for himself.

Walter's reply to his letter rekindled resentment and obliged him, willingly again, to pursue his plan.

'Dear Ivo,' it ran. 'Those dates suit. I shall have the London train met on the Friday. Please jump to no foolishly optimistic conclusions in the meanwhile. I hope you are not playing one of your tricks on me. B.'

Ivo now repaired to Beatrice's sitting-room, where they spoke of their impending journey north.

Although she had neither reproached him for neglecting her, nor expressed much gratitude for the invitation he had obtained, reacting with equally cool detachment to his reappearance and his news, she took warm exception to his offer to buy tickets.

'I shall buy my own,' she said.

'You might as well let me pay,' he urged in a tone between complaint and exasperation.

'No, sir! That's exactly what I shall not let you do. You miss the point. You don't have the right. And I won't be travelling in your company.'

'Oh? That's an interesting idea. How do you propose to travel to Carlisle in that case, if I may ask?'

'By rail.'

'Well, I'm sorry to have to tell you there's only one train a day, and I intend to be on it on the Friday we're expected to arrive.'

'Isn't there a night train?'

'I'm not taking that, I'm not altering all my arrangements.'

'I see.'

'Anyhow, isn't it a bit late to be so damn strict?'

'Please refuse your brother's invitation on my behalf.'

'What? I won't do it. Write to him yourself.'

'Why should I? He hasn't written to me. I don't care to be another piece of your luggage. I'll treat you as properly as you treat me. Otherwise, nothing doing. Suit yourself.'

'Oh my God! I can't think why I bother.'

She smiled at him, showing her somewhat animalic eye-teeth, and rallied him almost coquettishly: 'You know perfectly well why you have bothered and why you will.'

'All right – how do you want to play your hand?'

[66]

'I'll travel independently or not at all.'

'What about me?'

She shrugged her shoulders and concentrated on making and pouring out tea, which he drank hurriedly before departing earlier than intended.

But he did as he was told, or rather, he decided to think, as he chose: he was prepared to give away points in order to win the game. He informed his brother that he would be on the train arriving in Carlisle on the relevant Friday morning and Mrs Smythe on the Friday evening train, and that both would have to be met.

Most of that weekend disappointed Ivo. Setting aside the satisfaction of imposing extra duties on the staff of the duke's stables, he found Beatrice's door locked on the first night of their visit. They were the only guests in the house, and, no doubt with malice aforethought, she had been allotted the Duchess Lily Suite in the East Wing, which was some two hundred yards from the bedroom Ivo had had since boyhood and about fifteen yards from Walter's. When Ivo could not quietly gain the admission he had looked forward to, he refrained from knocking louder or raising his voice for fear of creating a scene and involving Walter in it, and retreated on tiptoe, candle in hand, to his narrow bachelor bed. He decided to assume that Beatrice had locked her door by accident or something, that she must have been in the closet or asleep while he turned her door-handle and scratched on her door. He did not demean himself so far as to mention his exclusion on the following day. But that night, the Saturday night, the same experience tried his temper too highly and he determined not to swallow this latest snub.

The next morning, unsuitably as the two of them traipsed through the house in the wake of Walter and Billy on the way to Matins in the Chapel, he growled at her in an undertone: 'I want to talk to you tonight.'

She showed no sign of registering his statement.

'I'll make trouble if you try to keep me out,' he warned her a little louder. 'Do you understand?'

Her response was a gesture which might have been half a nod, and he was forced to leave it at that for the time being.

Why he mixed sex with religion – to put it in exaggerated terminology, since he was denied the sex and would have denied the religion if he had ever given it a thought – was that he had not exchanged private words with Beatrice since her arrival, and feared there would be even less chance of such an exchange today. He had been shadowed everywhere by Billy, who was bound to be the more attentive the larger his uncle's departure loomed.

He was hero-worshipped by his nephew – Billy's attitude to Ivo was the opposite of his father's. He had been woken, watched while he shaved and dressed, escorted down to breakfast, cross-questioned, begged for favours, listened to wide-eyed by Billy, and hardly left alone for a single moment in which he might have had words with Beatrice.

Eight-year-old William Augustus Sylvester Grevill, Marquess of Medringham, was a clever gallant weakling, dark-haired and dark-eyed with thick dark eyelashes. He obviously missed his late lamented mother; he was probably scared by his preoccupied undemonstrative father; he wheezed bravely in a sort of limbo between starchy and stern Nurse Tucker in the nursery, gentry down the stairs and servants below; and yearned to be strong and dashing like his Uncle Ivo. The promises of favours he extracted from the latter were all sporting: a proper long ride off the leading-rein, fishing on the lake, shooting with their four-tens, billiards and bagatelle. Ivo, for his part, liked the boy, and was encouraged to please him by the consequential displeasure, the noticeably sour smiles, of his parent.

Besides, Billy kept him busy while he otherwise would have had to guide tours of the house and grounds for Beatrice, and bear her paeans of praise of all that was once his home. The Friday evening when she arrived at Brougham had been fine, still sunny, and she had spoken at dinner of the marvel of the view from the last bend in the drive, of the palatial edifice with its colonnades and pavilions, its domes and myriad windows catching the sunset light, and its setting behind the formal garden, backed by woods of great trees, flanked by the lake that reflected the architectural follies on the islands, and facing the subtle man-made undulations of the park where the deer grazed. He had heard it before, he had heard it too often. The result was, on the Saturday morning, that he instructed Saddlecombe to show Mrs Smythe around the place when she had put in an appearance in the reception rooms, and to make appointments for her to see the Library with assistance from the librarian Mr Leckwith and the Muniment Room with the archivist Mr Roofe: he explained that he himself was trying to give Lord Medringham a bit of fun for a change.

Admittedly he had met Beatrice at meals. But Walter was using the small Chinese dining-room, so-called because of its hand-painted Chinese wallpaper, where the table was circular, conversation almost had to be general, and

[68]

every utterance was overheard by Cox, the Brougham butler, and his team of footmen either serving the food or standing behind the chairs of diners. Ivo could not dicuss his love life and what was wrong with it virtually in public. Moreover on Sundays, traditionally, the duke's Chaplain and his spouse – namely at present Mr and Mrs Pibbs – were invited to lunch, and his Agent – Ian Macmurrary – to dinner. In front of such people, not to mention his brother, how was he to persuade Beatrice to grant him access to her bedroom?

The rest of Sunday, following his edict and his threat before the morning service, passed. He was never alone with Beatrice, and he fished with Billy in the afternoon and taught him how to play billiards until they parted respec-tively to dress for dinner and to go to bed.

Ian and Mrs Macmurray duly arrived at eight and took their leave at ten o'clock, when Beatrice also said goodnight. Walter seemed to be disposed to talk, he even offered a nightcap of whisky although he had often complained that his brother drank too much. But Ivo said no, he was dog-tired, and pre-tending to yawn hurried upstairs.

He washed, changed into his night things, left his room and stole along the passages towards the Duchess Lily Suite. He checked that lamps still burned downstairs, he could see the glow in stairwells and courtyard windows, and realized that he was in no danger of running into anybody provided he could get into Beatrice's room without delay. He turned the door-handle and was able to open the door.

She was fully clothed: she had not removed the elaborate evening dress worn earlier, surely designed by and borrowed from Frère Jacques, like the rest of her weekend wardrobe. They were in an ante-room, a small sitting-hall with two armchairs, almost a passage, beyond which was the bedroom door, firmly closed.

He said: 'I thought you'd be ready for bed.'

She returned in a low voice: 'Did anyone see you come in here dressed like that?' – referring with a glance to his red dressing-gown, visible pyjama trousers and slippers.

As he shook his head she added: 'Not that it makes much difference – you shouldn't be here at all.'

'Let's go into the bedroom,' he said.

She stared at him, then asked: 'What did you want to talk to me about?'

'Don't be stupid!'

'I'd like to be told, please.'

'Very well. Why are you keeping me at arm's length?'

'Nothing is settled between us.'

His face reddened and darkened as they stood and faced each other in the confined space.

'Oh,' he expostulated. 'Oh – is that it?' he huffed and puffed. 'You make all the running, and then it's touch me not. You led me on, you led me into this mess, then it's no more carrot, only stick. I know your sort. I see through you. You ask too much. You give too little to ask so much. I won't be teased any longer, I'm warning you.'

'Lower your voice.'

'My voice is my business. I'll do as I please in my house.'

'It's not your house.'

'Don't you dare contradict me.'

'But it's not your house. It belongs to your brother. You forget that, but I don't. I don't want your brother eavesdropping or coming to investigate the racket.'

'And I don't care what he does.'

'Please calm down and sit down.'

'Let me into your bedroom – I let you into mine at Sweirdale.'

'No. I'm not ready. I've got things to talk to you about – more important things. But I don't think you're prepared to be reasonable or listen.'

'I've listened long enough.'

'Yes, perhaps. Good-night.'

'What? I didn't bring you to Brougham to be fobbed off again.'

'Either you listen to me or I'll call the Duke.'

'That's blackmail.'

'You blackmailed me into not locking my door. I gave in, now it's your turn.'

'God, you're tough!'

'I live and I learn. You mentioned Sweirdale. You took advantage of me there. I'm not letting it happen twice.'

'Lies – you're telling me lies – you did the seducing at Sweirdale, not me – you can't walk into a man's room half-naked in the middle of the night and expect no reaction – you can't cling to a man who's damn near naked and fuss over your virtue – you can't pretend you were raped – you can't have it both ways!'

[70]

'Are you willing to listen to me? It would be in your interests to stop ranting and do so.'

'In my interests? You haven't considered my interests ever before.'

'Sit down.'

He obeyed her, subsiding into one of the armchairs and averting his head, rather like an overgrown sulky child.

She remained standing and said: 'First, thank you for arranging this visit. I've read about houses like Brougham, but I never believed they existed. I can see how hard it is for you, being just another guest in your old home.'

'Let's change the subject.'

'It'll change in a minute — wait and see. Your brother's a king, isn't he, living in his palace and reigning over his kingdom? The customs of your class are crueller than I imagined. He's entitled to sweep the board — because of a few years' difference in your ages he gets the houses and acres and pictures and books and money, and his brother lives in lodgings. Not fair, not cricket, I'd say.'

'I wish you'd stop rubbing it in.'

'But your brother wouldn't agree. He takes everything in his stride. Yes, he takes it. He isn't embarrassed, he doesn't suffer from guilt, and he can afford to be gracious to the common people.'

'When has he ever been gracious?'

'He's been polite to me.'

'I'm glad you think so. He was offhand, he sat you as far away from himself as he could at meals, he's treated you so as to cause me the maximum aggravation. I've told you before, my feelings for him or against him are fully reciprocated. He'd tell you that every action of mine is designed to ruffle his feathers. But the truth is that he hates me more than I hate him, or at least as much, he's always been jealous of me and wanted to do me down.'

'It's not the whole truth.'

'What? How do you know? How do you think you know?'

'Because I've discussed the matter with him.'

Ivo's face registered astonishment.

Beatrice, as if satisfied that she had finally engaged his rapt attention, sat down in the other chair.

They both perched tensely on the edges of their armchairs, not leaning back.

'When did the discussion take place?' he inquired.

[71]

'This afternoon.'

'When this afternoon?'

'Before tea, while you were fishing.'

'What did he say?'

'I said it to start with. I said I'd be grateful for some advice.'

'He fancies himself in the role of adviser.'

'Exactly.'

'Where were you?'

'In the library. We chatted for half an hour or so. He was polite enough.'

'What advice did you ask for?'

'Advice about your prospects.'

'Are you trying to be funny?'

'No.'

'But how could you? It's none of your business. How could he let you?'

'Instead of going off the deep end, wouldn't you like to hear what he had to say?'

'Go on.'

'He's prepared to help you.'

'I won't be helped by him. I'm after what's rightfully mine.'

'He'll give you money, or more money. You have no rights, so far as I can see.'

'How much money?'

'A fortune by my standards – money to buy a house in London and another in the country – money to live in them comfortably.'

'I bet a figure wasn't named?'

'No – but promises were made.'

'Oh? My brother's never promised me a thing. He's not to be trusted, you know.'

'I trust him. And I wouldn't let him break his promise.'

'I can't believe that. What was promised anyway?'

'To provide adequate funds for you for the rest of your life, and for your dependants.'

'My dependants? Do you mean my children? But Walter hates the idea of my producing children. He doesn't want me to produce sons and possible heirs until he's married again and has some more of his own to safeguard his very own line of succession. He'd be so put out by a son of mine breathing down Billy's neck that he probably wouldn't be able to do the trick with a second wife. Listen, I'm beginning to smell a rat. The advice Walter gave you smells all wrong to me. You said promises. What other promises were made? What conditions were tacked on to all this untypical generosity?'

'Our talk was frank. I think we understood each other.'

'I wish I understood.'

'All right – I promised to take you off his hands in return for a proper financial settlement.'

'So that's it! I suspected it all along as a matter of fact. My God, you've got a nerve!'

'The settlement would be final. You wouldn't get a penny more from your brother afterwards, and he'd have no further responsibilities whatever the circumstances.'

'Anything else?'

'Obviously the terms would have to be tempting to persuade everyone concerned to settle.'

'And you're one of the temptations?'

'Your brother believes a nice tame English débutante isn't likely to be able to help you break your bad habits.'

'Thank you very much. I've never heard such impudence.'

'You can't pretend your gambling's been good for anyone.'

'Thank you for warning me that you're on my brother's side.'

'That's not so. The offer merits investigation. It might be worth your while to think everything over calmly. Besides, I'm good at negotiations.'

'I suppose you got round Walter by saying you could control me. I suppose you got round him by explaining that you're barren. Why have you gone and embarrassed me? It's disgusting. So are you.'

'Is that why you're sitting there in your pyjamas?'

'Beatrice . . . You owe it to me after what you've done to let me sleep with you tonight. Will you, please?'

'I'll answer your question when you've answered mine.'

'No – don't you order me about – I've waited for you too long already.'

'If you touch me your brother will hear, and then I'll force the issue. I swear it, Ivo.'

'Good night, God damn you!'

* * *

Ivo Grevill slept badly that night at Brougham. In a small hour of the morning he went downstairs and drank two weak whisky and sodas and smoked five Turkish cigarettes. He tackled breakfast without his usual appetite.

Beatrice Smythe, on the other hand, coming downstairs in her pretty travelling clothes two minutes before she was due to be driven to Carlisle, looked rested and radiant.

He met her in the hall and escorted her out of doors, while Cox and several footmen held doors open and generally fluttered round.

'My brother asked me to say goodbye on his behalf. He was sorry he had business to see to. He wished you a good journey,' Ivo explained gruffly.

'Please thank the Duke for a most interesting visit,' Beatrice replied.

But then she took Ivo's arm, squeezed it and murmured: 'Come and see me. You know I could make up for everything.'

He disentangled himself and, without waiting for her to be driven away, without a word or a wave, strode indoors.

At eleven o'clock he sallied forth with a twenty-bore and a pocketful of cartridges borrowed from the gunroom and in the next hour and a half shot a couple of pigeons, a rook, a crow, a mallard, a grey squirrel and three rabbits.

He felt better at luncheon, although having to share it with his brother and his brother's bailiff and to listen to their exclusive discussion of agricultural matters did not improve his temper.

After lunch he announced that he wished to have a private word with the Duke, whereupon Mr Jones withdrew, leaving the brothers alone in the smoking room.

Walter said: 'In future, I'd prefer you to channel your requirements of my employees through me.'

'What's the matter now?'

'I'd rather you did not talk to Dan Jones so peremptorily.'

'Oh what the hell! I don't suppose I've got time to argue the point. I'm sorry. You know I'm going into Carlisle this afternoon, then catching the night train south? I just wanted to ask you about a talk you apparently had with Beatrice Smythe.'

'Like you, Ivo, I really haven't time to go into all that.'

'Oh but you'll have to tell me whatever you told her about me.'

'I don't have to tell you anything. However, for the record, she buttonholed me. She advanced certain ideas. She made certain claims.'

[74]

'For instance?'

'For instance that she could get you to marry her, and stop you frittering away your existence and my money.'

'And you said you'd loosen your purse-strings in return for her working these miracles?'

'I'd give quite a lot to conclude our financial dealings once and for ever.'

'In other words you're backing her to take me off your hands – she didn't exaggerate. Good God, Walter, you're trying to bribe me to make an idiot of myself! Beatrice Smythe's a penniless adventuress. She was one of Jack Haspell's girls and she's set on catching me, she's nothing but a social climber with a shady background, and not a good person, I'd say. You can't honestly wish me to marry her.'

'Do you think a good person would take you on, Ivo? Your reputation isn't encouraging. I don't believe a good family would willingly let you have an innocent daughter for a wife. And why should an heiress want you to spend her money instead of mine?'

'Thank you for being so damned encouraging.'

'Nobody could be keener than I am for you to marry and lead a sensible life.'

'And nobody would suit you better than a wife of mine who couldn't compete with the sort of little snob you're likely to wed second time around, and who couldn't breed possible heirs to family property.'

'Ivo, I can't keep Dan Jones waiting any longer, and I can't face another quarrel. At least Mrs Smythe seemed to me to have no dangerous illusions. That's my last word on the subject.'

'Hang on a minute! If you're in favour of a marriage of convenience, your convenience, I wouldn't mind knowing what might be in it for me.'

'Yes – well – I guessed the rustle of banknotes would flush you out. You never surprise me, Ivo. Go and see Horace Reed. Goodbye.'

The Duke made his escape.

Not long afterwards his brother and his brother's manservant were driven from Brougham to Carlisle.

During the journey they spoke as follows.

'Did Mrs Smythe leave any tip for staff in her bedroom?'

'No, milord – not a sou, as I understand.'

'She doesn't know what's expected of guests in a gentleman's house.'

[75]

'No, milord, that's a fact.'

A week elapsed. Ivo Grevill in Greenbury Street suffered changes of mind. He resolved more than once not to go cap in hand to the family solicitor. However, after an unfortunate evening at the Club of Clubs, he addressed a shaky line to Slater, Gregan and Reed at Bedford Terrace, Bloomsbury, and two days later kept the afternoon appointment he had asked for.

Horace Reed sat behind his desk in a dark office smelling of old legal papers and furnished mainly with piles of black tin boxes bearing the legends in white paint: Duke of Brougham and Castile, Marquess of Medringham, Lords and Ladies Grevill with bygone Christian names, Brougham Estate, Gelts Abbey Estate, and so on. He was a middle-aged man with coarse crinkly iron-grey hair and a perpetually stubbly chin.

'What can I do for you, Lord Ivo?' he inquired in cautious accents in his grating voice.

'My brother asked me to call on you, Horace.'

'Ah!'

'Have you heard from my brother?'

'In connection with what, Lord Ivo?'

'Can't you guess?'

'The Duke wrote to tell me that you were toying with the idea of marriage. Is it too soon to offer congratulations?'

'My marriage and your congratulations are not quite what I'm interested in.'

'I see. The Duke did ask me to look into the question of a type of marriage settlement.'

'Have you done so?'

'I have scribbled a few notes on the subject, and will be submitting my proposals to the Duke directly.'

'What are they, these proposals, Horace? There's no need to beat about the bush. My brother sent me here to discuss my future.'

'I remember getting into hot water for discussing such matters openly in the past, Lord Ivo.'

'Oh for God's sake, what's the figure? That's all I want to know.'

'The estate could probably find a hundred thousand pounds.'

'With which I'm expected to buy two houses and support a family and live like a gentleman? Listen to me, I'm not bowing out of the family,

[76]

financially speaking, for chicken-feed. Write and tell my brother that!'

'The sum is large by most standards, Lord Ivo. And a larger one, a larger gift, would not be a prudent use of the resources of the estate in my opinion.'

'What are you talking about, a gift? This money won't be a gift, it's a debt – the clearance of a debt. But you wouldn't agree, I suppose. You're paid to be as penny-pinching as my brother.'

'You have no cause to insult me, Lord Ivo. I've always done my level best for every member of your family.'

'Well, your best isn't good enough for me, it never has been, nor has my brother's. I'm looking for what's better than best for a change, I'm looking for justice.'

'Your income could be augmented without recourse to the Duke.'

'I know what you're getting at. Why the hell should I work when he doesn't? Why should I live in a hovel? Blame our parents: they didn't prepare either of us to be poor. I'm busy in my way as he is in his. And I couldn't afford to marry on a fraction of a percentage of family funds any more than he did.'

'You omit to mention the Duke's generosity over the years. But we've covered this ground before, repeatedly, even too frequently. Do you wish me to inform your brother that the offer at present on the table is not acceptable by yourself?'

'It definitely won't keep me quiet for the rest of my days, unless I die sooner than expected, which might solve every problem.'

'Come come, Lord Ivo. No doubt the Duke will reconsider, although I'm sorry to say a revised figure may not fulfil your aspirations. Shall I communi-cate with you when we have something more to talk over?'

'Please.'

Ivo Grevill was ushered out of the solicitor's offices and after walking a hundred yards hailed a cab and asked to be driven to 9 Monamy Buildings.

He knocked on Beatrice Smythe's door, waited, knocked again, and almost as he was turning away heard her footsteps within.

She must have seen him from a window, for she opened the door wide and said without surprise: 'Good afternoon.'

'I'm glad you're in,' he exclaimed in a voice expressive of angry satisfaction, pushing past her into the passageway. 'I've only come to tell you your plan's fallen flat and all bets are off between us.'

'Let me take your hat and coat.'

'What's the point?'

'Come upstairs and explain.'

He surrendered his coat and followed her to her sitting-room.

'I've talked to our solicitor and to my brother – their meanness beats the band – if I sign on the dotted line, and can never ask for another penny, I'll soon be ruined – and so would you be.'

'Sit down, won't you?' she asked, standing by the fireplace.

He ignored her and added: 'As things are I don't know where to turn, I've had a run of bad luck lately, I'll have to go back to Walter anyway – what a mess! You keep out of it!'

'I'll help you.'

'You can't help – that's nonsense!'

'Is it?'

She approached him, put her hands on his shoulders, pushed him towards a chair and applied pressure to make him sit, subsided on to the floor in front of him, and, kneeling, leaned forward slowly and deliberately to kiss his lips. She kissed him not as she had before in Monamy Buildings, with teasing friendliness, nor with the abandonment of their communion in the Sweirdale night; but rather to convince and to persuade by physical means, or as if by paying over a first instalment of the reward that could be his, provided he did not weaken and obeyed her instructions. She took charge of him in her own fashion, with her imperious clever kisses, by insinuating her body between his knees, by the expertise of her caresses and the heat of her embrace.

But she, or he, or they together stopped short of making love.

At a critical moment she murmured, 'Not yet,' and rose to her feet, while he was saying, 'This is getting it wrong, it's all over – I shouldn't be here.'

'When did you see your solicitor?' she asked with no trace of passion or excitement.

'Half an hour ago.'

'What was offered?'

'A hundred thousand.'

'How did you leave things?'

'I wouldn't wear it – the money's next to nothing in comparison with Walter's fortune – I told Horace to try again – but Walter won't budge, you can be sure – I might as well give up now, it's a wild-goose chase – and I wish

[78]

you hadn't started it and I hadn't listened to you – now I must go back to begging for pennies to tide me over.'

'On the contrary, you must let me finish what I started.'

'You take a hell of a lot on yourself.'

'Who's going to help you in every way if I'm not allowed to?'

'You just don't know how powerless you'll find you are against my brother and the army of people protecting him and family treasure.'

'Let me protect you.'

'How?'

'By talking to your solicitor.'

'Talk's worse than useless.'

'Do you agree?'

'Hold hard. Agree to what?'

'I'll pose as your fiancée and do the negotiating.'

'Marriage is not on the cards and never will be, Beatrice – I've told you.'

'You'll marry me if I win.'

'Don't bank on it – and you won't win. Oh well, I haven't much to lose. I promise nothing, understand? No promises! But I would dearly like to see you getting your teeth into Horace Reed.'

'Are you feeling better now?'

'A little. Thanks, my dear.'

'Go away before we do something silly.'

'I half agree with that at any rate.'

A week later Ivo received a brief letter from Horace Reed suggesting various appointments, and wrote back to say he would keep a particular one, which was again in the afternoon. He did not mention Beatrice Smythe. He had nearly decided to have nothing more to do with Beatrice: she was too danger-ous, she tied him in knots. She was not even his type, she was the opposite of a piece of fluff, and the excitement she aroused in him was damn near vicious. And he could not clearly remember what they had and had not discussed, or the plan of action he might have encouraged her to think they had arrived at. Far from loving her, he began to be aware of hating the strain of their relations, which boiled down to attempting to resist her demands and his own unwise impulses to supply them.

On the day before his appointment with Horace, he joined a luncheon party given by Lady Dorothy Yealms, with whom he afterwards fell out. Dorothy somehow knew he had taken Beatrice Smythe to Brougham, and taxed him with infidelity, with sleeping with a common trollop, with putting his brother in a horrible position and disgracing his family, and with proving himself unworthy of her favours. Whereupon he called her a jealous dog in the manger, or rather a bitch, who would not let him have what she was unable or unwilling to give him, who was wrong about his getting it elsewhere, and who should not talk of fidelity since she admitted to sleeping with her husband as well as her lover, ex-lover, or lovers in the plural.

He then walked out of the house in Charles Street and to the nearest Post Office, where he wrote and sent this wire to Smythe, 9 Monamy Buildings, London W.2: 'Please meet me at Slater Gregan and Reed in Bedford Terrace at 2.30 tomorrow stop Grevill.'

He regretted it, of course: a further characteristic of his dealings with Beatrice was that he seemed to be bound to regret each and every one. The telegram was not so much a summons to one woman as a gesture of revolt against another. He spent almost twenty-four uneasy hours hoping that Beatrice might have the tact not to turn up at the solicitor's.

She was in the waiting-room, elegantly dressed, ladylike even if she was not a lady, cool and collected. And to make matters worse for Ivo, when the two of them were ushered into Horace's office his brother was sitting there.

He attempted to explain Beatrice's presence by announcing lamely: 'I brought Mrs Smythe along.'

Walter, looking startled, rose to shake hands with her, then frowned at Ivo, who tried not to notice as he introduced her to Horace Reed.

Walter offered Beatrice his chair; Horace was dragging another chair from behind a pile of tin boxes into the semicircle around his desk; Ivo, as if overcome by the difficulty of the situation, sat down or collapsed into a third chair, and the others followed suit.

Horace opened the meeting by addressing Beatrice with ponderous gallantry: 'I hope, madam, your presence foreshadows a happy event in the future.'

She acknowledged his speech with a gesture of her head, and corrected it: 'I'm here only to speak for Lord Ivo.'

Horace cleared his throat, thus suggesting that Lord Ivo neither deserved nor needed a sort of defending counsel, and asked the Duke: 'Shall I proceed, your grace?'

[80]

'Go ahead,' Walter snapped.

Horace did so: 'Lord Ivo, is Mrs Smythe aware of the subject of our discussion?'

Beatrice interposed: 'Gentlemen, if you'd let me say my piece I would then leave you. I apologize for getting in your way, but I may have an interest in what you decide today.' She turned to the Duke, whose lowered eyes and bent head signified embarrassment and irritation but failed to deter her. 'I've already given you undertakings and promises which I would carry out and keep in the event of my becoming Ivo's wife. I would see to it that he was no more trouble to you provided he had received adequate assistance from yourself. I gather an offer has already been forthcoming, which makes me think that my idea of adequacy could have a bearing on all our decisions, yours and Ivo's and ultimately mine. Without your assistance to the extent I have in mind, I don't believe I could stop Ivo gambling, therefore marriage would not be a viable proposition from my point of view. The most modest sum that would be required is two hundred and fifty thousand pounds, placed in a legal trust fund, of which I would have to be a trustee. Thank you for listening to me, gentlemen. Goodbye, Duke. Goodbye, Mr Reed. Goodbye.'

She stood up and moved towards the door. As the brothers remained seated, apparently stunned, Horace hurried to bow her out.

Nothing was said until the latter had re-occupied his seat behind the desk. 'I fear the lady has set her sights higher than was anticipated,' he remarked.

'Oh God,' Ivo, mortified, growled or groaned.

'Would your grace care to comment?' Horace inquired.

The Duke pushed back his chair and stood, and, clearly irate, said to his brother: 'I've a good mind to agree – then you'd have to marry your woman – which would serve you right in my opinion,' and stalked out of the office through the door opened in a rush by Horace, who followed him into the hallway.

Ivo Grevill stayed put. He could hear his brother's and his solicitor's voices, but not what they were saying. He was angry too, he smouldered with characteristic comprehensive anger, because Beatrice had gone too far, pinned him down matrimonially, exposed him to Walter's exasperation, ruined everything, and because he was beset by the familiar feeling of having compounded many unrectifiable mistakes.

He said grudgingly, when Horace had rejoined him: 'I suppose I should

[81]

apologize, too. I had no idea Mrs Smythe was going to do that dictating.'

'Lord Ivo, may I ask you a straight question: are you engaged to the lady?'

'No – no, not formally.'

'Informally then? Do you intend to marry her?'

'That seems to depend.'

'But have you known her for long, Lord Ivo? Do you know her family and background?'

'What business is that of yours?'

'Excuse me – I must apologize now – I was hoping for answers to questions put to me by the Duke – yet indeed such considerations are nobody's business but your own.'

'My brother has absolutely no right to pry into my private life.'

'He was concerned, Lord Ivo. This type of marriage settlement for you, which has been mentioned, would be a final transfer of funds from the estate – and Mrs Smythe insists upon becoming a trustee of any such trust that might be set up. In other words, she would have some control over your expenditure, and no more money would be forthcoming if you or she were to get into financial trouble in future.'

'Who would be the other trustee?'

'Myself. And I must admit that Mrs Smythe struck me as a forceful personality.'

'Horace, do I get the impression that my brother may actually be contemplating a hand-over of a quarter of a million? Wonders will never cease!'

'I must reserve the right to confirm the Duke's views in writing. But he has spoken of improving on the hundred thousand.'

'Tell him I won't take less than a quarter of a mill.'

'As I see it, Lord Ivo, and as I believe I have to warn you, if such a sum were on offer, marriage to Mrs Smythe would be almost obligatory. I hope she would not stoop to bring breach of promise proceedings, although she has witnesses to compromising statements made in this office today, which you did not contradict.'

'You can leave Mrs Smythe to me. Have you any more to say?'

'I think not. Have you, Lord Ivo?'

'Yes. Let's get this business moving. Frankly, I'm not in a position to hang around. No further questions, Horace! Write to me soon. Goodbye.'

Outside in the street Ivo Grevill hailed a cab, as he had after his previous visit to Slater, Gregan and Reed, but now in a better frame of mind, and gave the address of Monamy Buildings.

He was in luck, perhaps in luck for a second time in the day, even if luck is notoriously difficult to recognize except in retrospect; Beatrice had come home and admitted him into her house, in the entrance passage of which he made as if to embrace her.

But she drew away and asked, her customary smile qualified by vocal asperity: 'What's this?'

'I think we swung it.'

'What did we swing?' She accentuated the 'we' sarcastically.

He was removing his coat and handing it to her, and he preceded her up the stairs.

'I think his grace is going to be really gracious at long last,' he said. 'And just in time so far as I'm concerned.'

They reached the sitting-room, and she asked in her sharper voice: 'Would you explain, please?'

'Explain what? Walter's good for the two hundred and fifty thousand unless I'm very much mistaken.'

'With no strings attached?'

'Oh – yes – I haven't got round to that side of things.'

'Ivo, why not start at the beginning? What happened after I left Mr Reed's office?'

'Walter flounced out with Horace Reed in pursuit, and when Horace came back he suggested all might be well. He was a bit cheeky. But who cares? You were terrific in there – I wanted to tell you and thank you.'

'What was Mr Reed cheeky about?'

'He tried to ask me personal questions, how well I knew you, and so forth.'

'What did you say?'

'I advised him to mind his own business.'

'Do you know me well enough, Ivo?'

'Horace asked me what your background was.'

'Oh? But you know I was born and brought up in South Africa, and I'm a widow who makes ladies' hats. I've concealed nothing from you.'

'I'm not saying you have. What's wrong, Beatrice? I imagined you'd be waiting to hear the result of our meeting and delighted by my rushing round to tell you.'

'Oh yes, I'm delighted. But I'm still waiting.'

'I see. So that's it. Well, we're both waiting if it comes to that. I'm waiting to see the small print tacked on to Walter's generous act.'

'How flattering!'

'It's not like that. I've thanked you, haven't I? I can't marry you if the money doesn't come through. I couldn't support you.'

'Are you proposing to me, Ivo?'

'My God, you drive a hard bargain.'

'Conditionally, are you proposing?'

'Yes. No – at this stage I refuse to commit myself.'

'Same here. So you'd better go.'

'I was hoping we'd celebrate. I hoped you'd stop teasing and we'd have a nice time together.'

'Leave me alone. Go!'

'Have it your own way – you always do!'

Ivo Grevill slammed out of the room and the house.

He returned to Greenbury Street, drank weak whisky and sodas and smoked Turkish ciagarettes, simmered down, brooded and remembered that he was dining with Max Kirby in Holland Park, and that cards would be played after dinner without any doubt. He also remembered that he was in debt, he was five hundred pounds overdrawn at the bank and owed another thousand or so, and could not afford to gamble – he could afford nothing. Then memory rammed home the point that he was going to have to marry Beatrice to escape bankruptcy and disgrace.

At seven o'clock Zeals entered the flat to run his bath and lay out his evening clothes.

The master as he dressed spoke to his man.

'I may be getting married, Zeals.'

The response was non-committal: 'Yes, milord.'

'To Mrs Smythe.'

'When would that be?'

'I can't say when – not yet. You don't sound particularly pleased, Zeals.'

'I shall be tendering my notice, milord.'

'What? Is this some sort of reflection on Mrs Smythe? I won't stand for impertinence.'

'No, milord.'

'Well, I'm not accepting your notice. If you let me down I won't give you a reference. You'd better not forget which side your bread's buttered.'

'I'm short of my wage as it is.'

'You'll get paid. I'll be better off if I marry Mrs Smythe.'

'Will you, milord?'

'Don't you take that tone with me, Zeals!'

'No, milord.'

3

THE engagement was announced, or the bargain struck, between Lord Ivo Grevill of Brougham, Cumberland, and Beatrice, widow of Robert Smythe of South Africa; and the wedding was celebrated in the chapel at Brougham in November.

Beatrice was given away by Jack Haspell, who happened also to be the one and only guest she invited to the ceremony. Ivo's best man was his brother Walter, and the congregation was composed almost entirely of tenants, staff and dependants of the ducal family.

Each member of the quartet that approached the richly decorated altar with its golden crucifix and candlesticks, before which stood the Reverend Pibbs meekly or deferentially smiling, was getting more or less, but at any rate something, out of the religious rite. Jack was ridding himself of the burden of a poor relation and possibly an ex-mistress. Walter was buying his freedom from being bled white – in his own estimation – by Ivo. The latter was hoping to become a wealthy man by most standards in the near future, and sexually satisfied to boot. And Beatrice in Frère Jacques wedding dress and tiara borrowed from the Brougham strong-room, her left hand flashing the solitaire diamond engagement ring that had belonged to the bridegroom's mother, had achieved a Cinderella-like transformation.

Yet the event could not be called happy. Even Jack Haspell, who had the least to lose from participating in it, was rendered uneasy by his equivocal position, part protector of the bride, part guest and part tradesman. Walter's resistance to happiness was founded in scepticism and suspicion: he could not believe that his brother would no longer demand money with menaces, and he suspected that Ivo and Beatrice – or Beatrice who had suborned Ivo with her feminine wiles – were making him the victim of a confidence trick. Ivo, while donning his grey morning suit in the hostelry in the village, the Brougham and Castile Arms, where he had stayed the night, felt he was probably cutting his own throat, and could not recall exactly how it had come about that he was doing so. Beatrice smiled, unblushing; but the grandeur of the setting for the marriage, the golden chapel, the jewels she had seen in the strong-room, in short the evidence of the wealth of the family of which she was almost a member, caused her eyes to glitter like two more diamonds and her countenance to assume a sharper hungrier look. As for the congregation, generally and naturally the majority were disappointed that their own Lord Ivo had not done better for himself than to marry a widow and an upstart from nowhere.

After the blessing, although the newly-weds cut stylish figures processing down the aisle arm-in-arm, her veil thrown back to reveal her pretty face, her hard-edged features and composed expression, and his bearing proud and dark, the consensus of opinion was not so sentimental as it might have been: on this sacred ground the men's thoughts about the bride were unusually profane, while the women pitied and despised the groom for having been hooked by such an artful minx.

Photographs were taken in the Chinese drawing-room and on the West Front terrace, and the wedding breakfast so-called, actually a sit-down four-course luncheon, was served in the Great Hall. Considerable quantities of alcohol were consumed in some quarters, particularly, for instance, by Zeals, who snatched the chance to have a word with his future mistress as she and her husband retired to change into their travelling clothes.

'You know me, milady – the name's Zeals – I'm his lordship's man – we met at that Sweirdale,' he slurred as he extended a horny hand and looked up at her.

'Oh yes. How do you do?'

'You're the lucky one, aren't you?' She stared at him. 'Come on, milady, you and me's got to make friends – we'll be seeing a lot of each other – and I understand you better than some.'

'Do you?' she remarked, and tried in vain to pull away her hand which he was holding.

Ivo, having concluded a conversation with a well-wisher, turned and demanded of his manservant: 'Are you drunk, Zeals?'

'No, milord – only congratulating her ladyship before I go to prepare your honeymoon bedroom.'

Ivo said irritably: 'All right!'

Beatrice, released, moved on, evincing no outward sign of having been embarrassed or annoyed.

The bedroom referred to was in the hotel where Ivo was accustomed to wait for the night train from Carlisle to London. Zeals was to go ahead with most of the luggage to check that all was and would be in order.

The Grevills said goodbye at four-thirty to Walter, to Billy, who had been considered too old to be a page, to neighbours, and to Horace Reed, Mr Leckwith and Mr Roofe, Ian Macmurray, Saddlecombe, Cox and innumerable other retainers. During the two-hour drive Beatrice managed with difficulty not to pay the price of honest womanhood, she persuaded her Ivo not to claim his reward for the benefits he had conferred upon her until they could lock the door of their room at the Grevill Arms. But she was as enthusiastic as he was pent up in this context, and in their double sleeping compartments in the train she repeatedly proved it.

Their destination was Castile House in Belgravia. That they would be spending their first nuptial weeks, or the brief period until they had found and bought their marital home or homes, in Walter's London residence was part of the deal negotiated before the wedding. The idea of honeymooning there derived from the simple fact that the means to go elsewhere, that is to say the cash, was not available. Ivo's trust documents could not be signed and sealed until the trustee-designate had become his wife, and funds would then be subject to the usual lawyer-like delay: therefore, since women were not permitted to live in the bachelor digs in Greenbury Street, and Ivo did not deign to squash into Monamy Buildings, Beatrice's suggestion that Castile House might provide temporary accommodation and a sort of bridging address was accepted by Horace Reed, speaking for his employer. Besides, where else would the Grevills be so comfortable, considering the full permanent staff and the infrequent visits of the Duke?

It was an architectural gem, a Regency villa pre-dating Cubitt, built for the family by a certain Winstone, stuccoed, having three floors plus basement, and standing in its own grounds behind railings which rivalled those protecting the property of the first Duke of Brougham and Castile's fellow-peer and former commanding officer, the Duke of Wellington at Apsley House. It had a portico and an in-and-out driveway, a small garden in front, a large one at the back, and a fine stable block with a number of cottages attached. It had a parapet and a pediment above, hiding the top floor and the various roofs, and curving spiked ironwork below, guarding the basement windows and the sub-terranean area.

The interior was spacious: even owners accustomed to the proportions of their main residence, Brougham, had no cause to complain of feeling cramped at Castile House. There were a dining-room, a library and a double drawing-room with twin fireplaces and chandeliers on the ground floor, a marble stair-case hall, a master suite and six other bedrooms on the first floor, and nurseries and servants' bedrooms on the second. In the basement were kitchens, pantries, brushing-room, laundry, coal-cellar, wine-cellar, servants' hall, and a room in which the housekeeper, Mrs Tighe, entertained the cook Mrs Lewis, the butler Graves, and visiting domestic dignitaries such as valets. Graves had his cottage down by the stableyard; the two footmen, Albert and Charles, and the pantry-boy shared a dark room in the basement, while senior female staff and an assortment of maids slept on the top floor. Nanny Campion retained her little empire of day-nursery and two night-nurseries with a bathroom behind the parapet of the front elevation.

The odd-job-man Fred, who stoked the boiler in an outhouse and carried coals, lodged with the grooms over the stables. The house-carpenter who was in charge of the oil and gas lamps, the head-gardener, the stud-groom, the coachman and retired employees lived in cottages that went with their present or past jobs close to the stables or in the mews.

The complete indoor staff was assembled in the front hall to greet Lord and Lady Ivo on the morning of their arrival in London. Coachman Harris stopped the old town carriage under the portico later than expected, Beatrice having taken her time in the train to dress and prepare for inspection by the reception committee. Graves opened the carriage door, the footman Albert unfolded the step, Ivo emerged, then helped out his bride and introduced her to the butler, who said, bending his grey head in half a bow: 'May I extend to your ladyship the warmest congratulations of everybody at Castile House?'

'Thank you,' Beatrice replied, and unlike Ivo did not offer Graves a hand to shake.

[89]

Graves ushered them into the house, where Mrs Tighe took over. Again Ivo shook the hands of the servants, most of whom he already knew, some since he was a boy, whereas Beatrice merely smiled and nodded. Mrs Tighe drew her attention to the maid called Mary, instructed to act as lady's maid for the duration of her visit.

Mary, twentyish and wearing a regulation black dress with white cambric pinafore and starched headgear with streamers, declared as she curtsied: 'Honoured, I'm sure, milady.'

Beatrice smiled at her in the same distant way.

Ivo asked Mrs Tighe: 'Is Nanny upstairs?'

'Yes, milord, and looking forward to seeing you at your convenience.'

'We'll go and say hullo at once.'

'You will,' Beatrice interposed; 'I shall take off my things.' She turned to Mrs Tighe. 'Please show me to my room.'

'Yes, milady – Mary will show you. I'll have your luggage sent up.'

Beatrice was already walking towards the stairs. Mary followed her, and Ivo hesitated.

He scowled and growled at Mrs Tighe: 'Where's Zeals to sleep?'

'In the valet's room, milord, we were thinking.'

'You mean that black hole down below? Well, he'll have to make the best of it. We shan't be here for long. Incidentally, he's taking my dog across to the stables – you remember Topper? There's a kennel in the stables, isn't there?' He added in an apologetic tone: 'It was a tiring day yesterday, and the train journey's not a rest cure. My wife's tired.'

'Yes, milord.'

'She'll talk to everybody later.' He called out to Mrs Lewis as he mounted the stairs two at a time. 'Her ladyship will talk to you about food later on.'

Mrs Lewis, a stout irascible widow swathed in white garments, muttered: 'Very good, milord,' and marched disapprovingly through the green baize door leading to the domestic offices in the basement.

Up in the nursery Ivo greeted Nanny Campion. They embraced. He received more congratulations, was asked what he had done with his wife, scolded for not giving his impatient old Nan a sight of his dear bride, scolded again for his neglect of herself in recent years, and smiled and nodded at and pressed to eat and drink things. The room had hardly changed since he first knew it. A french window opened on to the leads behind the parapet.

[90]

Another budgerigar squawked in the same cage. The guard round the low coal fire was high enough to stop a child falling into it.

'I know I should have come to see you ages ago,' he confessed.

'You had more important people to visit, dearie, that's the truth. And you've fallen in love and married a beautiful girl – just fancy! I expect you can guess what I'm hoping for.'

'Don't start on that, Nan.'

'What did you say, dearie? You mustn't mumble – my hearing isn't what it used to be.'

'Nothing, Nan. I'll have to leave you. We've only just arrived and I've business to attend to.'

'Oh it's always business with you and your brother! The Duke's scarcely through the door downstairs before he's off again. Won't you stay for a cup of tea? I want to have a proper account of your wedding, and news of little Billy.'

'Not now, Nan – and we had breakfast on the train not long ago – I'll bring Beatrice up to have tea with you at teatime – all right?'

He went downstairs and straight into the best bedroom. Beatrice was absent, in the bathroom, and Mary was on her knees, unpacking.

'Come back in ten minutes, will you?' he said.

'Yes, milord,' Mary replied, looking scared.

Beatrice emerged from the bathroom, and Mary on the way out closed the other door.

Beatrice inquired before he could speak: 'What are you doing here?' He was taken aback and obviously perplexed by her question, so she explained: 'You didn't knock, I didn't ask you to come in.'

'Don't be ridiculous – I can walk into your room when I feel like it. I'll be sleeping in that bed – it's more my room than yours as a matter of fact.'

'Wrong,' she said. 'You'll sleep in your dressing-room unless I indicate otherwise.'

'Are you serious? I can't believe you are, judging by what's gone on in the past twenty-four hours.'

'I won't be taken for granted. Nobody takes me for granted.'

'Oh for God's sake!'

She stared at him, he glared back momentarily, then averted his eyes and turned away from her in an exasperated gesture.

He was as tired as he had said she was. He had the drained look and the

[91]

shadowy black beard – despite its morning shave – of male lust over-indulged; while she had the glistening eyes and the somewhat hectic facial colouring of the female response to the same experience. Their attitudes to each other now were intolerant and verging on savage.

'What did you want anyway?' she asked.

'We're having tea with Nanny Campion today.'

'Are we?'

'Don't try to get out of it – I've made the arrangement and I'm telling you. Nanny looked after Walter and me, she made a favourite of me, and I won't have her ignored, or let you hurt her feelings.'

'Why should I hurt her? She's nothing to me. When did you see her last?'

'Too long ago, I know that, but now we're here it's different. I won't have you being hoity-toity with the servants.'

'And I won't be ordered about, Ivo. You march in and bark orders at me. I can judge by recent events too – why are you complaining?'

'You put me in such a damned difficult position when we arrived. Graves and Mrs Tighe aren't slaves, and they don't belong to us – couldn't you be more pleasant? I've known them for ever – they're friends of mine, and would be of yours. Offending them won't wash from any point of view. Next thing they'll be telling tales and getting us thrown out before we want to go.'

'Have you finished?'

'Yes – no – but you'll answer back whether or not I've more to say.'

'Of course! You find fault with my behaviour in this house – let me remind you that you wouldn't be here, you'd be nowhere, if it wasn't for me.'

'I'm grateful, Beatrice – I married you after all.'

'It's not enough. Listen, Ivo – I'm not being thrown out of Castile House – servants can be sacked for impoliteness but not me – I make the rules now, do you see?'

'Do I not!'

'Your friends, these servants, are going to have to do some work for a change. I intend to make them work for Walter's money. How many of them are there, twenty or thirty, all twiddling their thumbs? I shall be hoity-toity and preserve my authority, if you don't mind, even if you prefer not to keep your place.'

'Their work's no business of ours. I'm fed up with arguing. It's ten o'clock. When you see Mrs Lewis tell her I'll be out to lunch.'

'When will you be back?'

'I don't know – I've things to arrange at Greenbury Street – late afternoon.'

'Well, I'm not sitting by the fire and waiting for you to come home for the rest of my life.'

'My God, you're impatient! We only arrived in London an hour ago. I haven't forgotten that you want to meet my friends. I'll introduce you to them as soon as I can. I'll take you wherever we're invited.'

'Wrong again, Ivo: I'm meeting your sort of people on my ground and on my terms, I'm not being dragged round as the appendage you made the mistake of marrying. Society comes here, at my bidding, and without delay.'

'You can't entertain like that at Castile House.'

'Oh but I can! It's the perfect setting. The staff's on the spot. And we won't be paying.'

'There'll be a row. If we run up big bills, there'll be a big row.'

'We were lent Castile House and everything that goes with it until we find a home of our own and choose to move out.'

'The loan was never meant to include entertaining. We'll end by being dunned for payment of excessive expenses.'

'But your money will be ours in a day or two, and I'm to be one of the trustees of it. I wouldn't sanction any payment of expenses that Walter could well afford.'

'You've got it all worked out, haven't you?'

'I owe it to Walter to stop you gambling, or losing money that he would feel obliged to find. I promised him to stop you gambling, nothing else. And you've promised me, haven't you?'

'I know.'

'I hope you know that I'll be stricter than Walter was. I believe that as your trustee I can keep our money intact. I won't be reduced to penury.'

'I'm not doing any gambling, I've told you.'

'Ivo, better not, that's all.'

'And you'd better be in the nursery at teatime!'

He left the room, slamming the door, before she could get another word in. Downstairs in the hall he allowed the second footman, Charles by name, who was waiting there, to help him into his blue London overcoat and hand him his top-hat, gloves and stick. He then walked to his bachelor lodgings to discuss the termination of his lease, and to lunch and to read the papers at the Cumbria Club, where cards were not played. And in the afternoon he

[93]

refrained from popping into a Post Office to send a telegram to Barney Solomon.

He was already beginning to repent at leisure, as the saying goes. Since, for the time being, he no longer wanted Beatrice in one way, he realized that he did not want her, and perhaps never had, in any other way. He remembered something said to him at the wedding reception by Jack Haspell: 'I never believed you'd marry her, Lord Ivo.' He had not only fallen into a booby-trap, but had been observed in the undignified act of falling into it. He had made what was worse than just another mistake, to wit a fool of himself. And the agent of his folly, the cause of his misalliance, was a bossy shrew who was about to abuse the hospitality of his brother and grab more than she was given.

Yet she had obtained for him or for them more money than he had ever either possessed or dreamed of possessing. She had appealed for justice on his behalf, as no one else had, and won damages which were much better than nothing. Her militancy was for marriage and against his profligate existence: were those aims bad?

Moreover, despite his instinctive rallying to the family flag, as it were, and his shrinking from the quarrel that she seemed to be determined to pick with Walter, he was not averse from twisting his brother's tail. He had administered repeated minor tweaks in the past; he had never dared, had never had such a tempting opportunity, to assert himself in the major manner apparently envis-aged by Beatrice. The question was: were they to live like paupers in a land of plenty for Walker's sake, or, more logically, to eat, drink and be as merry as Walter's first and probably last generous action enabled them to be?

Ivo Grevill detested his new wife on that day, but admired her too. She had robbed him of his liberty and championed him. She had excited him sexually as no other woman had, introduced him to thrills that had seemed worth waiting for; also, in retrospect, refused and frustrated him, and from a replete point of view disgusted him too. She inspired ambivalence, a mixture of grat-itude and blame, a confusion of attraction and revulsion, a sense of rebellious dependence. The fact remained that her ruthlessness had proved its uses, and that entertaining at Castile House, if they could get away with it, would be a cut-price method of repaying those who had entertained him in his bachelor days.

* * *

Time passed, a week, a fortnight. Invitations had been issued and accepted, and no noticeable objections were raised by anybody to the unwonted social festivities at Castile House. The quarter of a million pounds of which Ivo Grevill was the beneficiary, and Beatrice Grevill and Horace Reed the trustees, was duly paid over.

One morning Ivo received an envelope postmarked Carlisle. It was from Walter, and ran: 'The tiara your wife wore at your wedding has not been returned. I understand that it was packed in her luggage here at Brougham, no doubt by accident. I hope it is safe, and that Beatrice understands it was only on loan. I should be grateful if you would give it into the keeping of Slater, Gregan and Reed without delay.'

Ivo's breakfast was spoilt. He was again angry with Beatrice, who had stirred up gratuitous strife. As soon as he thought she would be willing to receive him, he went upstairs, knocked on her bedroom door, was told to enter and tossed the letter on to her bed, where she breakfasted on black coffee.

He said: 'If we're going to annoy Walter, let's annoy him with one thing at a time. Where is this tiara?'

'I haven't got it,' she replied.

'You haven't lost it, for pity's sake?'

'No.'

'Well – let's do as he asks and keep him quiet until he discovers we're eating him out of house and home.'

She stared.

'Where is it, Beatrice?'

'At the jeweller's.'

'You're not selling it?'

'I'm having it made to fit me more comfortably.'

'But you can't – it doesn't belong to you – you knew it was lent.'

'Tell your brother I'm getting it mended.'

'What do you want it for?'

'For a ball – if we gave a ball – or when we give a ball.'

'No – that's going too far! Which jeweller's is it at?'

'Leave me alone, Ivo.'

'But Beatrice!'

'Go! Go!'

Ivo wrote back to Walter: 'Sorry about the tiara. A few bits of damage are being repaired at present. I'll let you know when it's ready, though I can't see that you'll be needing it for the foreseeable future.'

He did not like lying, and getting involved in what was uncomfortably close to theft; but, again, there was another side to the story. The dukedom had at least three tiaras to his knowledge. The best two were called the Brougham Jewel and the Spanish Fender: the poorer pretty one used by Beatrice really would not be missed. Despite being brought up to believe that the son and heir of a Duke of Brougham should conserve family property and transmit it to subsequent generations, and his consequent unthinking lip-service to the conventions of primogeniture, he had in fact devoted his adult life to righting the wrong of having been born after Walter, or, in more down-to-earth terms, to extracting money by hook or by crook from the ducal coffers: and what was the difference between pounds in cash and pounds in gold and diamonds? Beatrice was only better at doing what he had always done; and although he had reason to suspect that she would never surrender the tiara, he shelved the problem by telling himself that Walter neither needed nor deserved it.

Christmas was coming. The Grevills had by now established a routine. Ivo slept in his dressing-room on one side of their bathroom and Beatrice on the other: he had almost ceased to be embarrassed by this un-honeymoon-like practice which she insisted on. He was called by Zeals at eight, washed and shaved, using another bathroom for fear of disturbing his wife, and had break-fast alone at the small dining-table by the east-facing window of the dining-room, waited upon by a footman. Graves' absence was intentionally conspicuous; the butler was making the point that he was too old to burn the candle at both ends, he had to have peace in the morning if not at midday or in the evening, the sort of peace he was customarily left in by his esteemed real employer, the Duke, who, during his rare visits to London, hardly ever invited anyone to a meal.

Ivo glanced at the newspapers and magazines he had ordered – they were ranged on the big dining-table – and strolling over to the sideboard viewed the food in the silver entrée dishes, the lids having been lifted by Albert or Charles. The methylated spirit lamps heating these dishes added a nostalgic element to the aroma of food and coffee; he was reminded of the hungry breakfasts of his youth, and the present partial loss of his appetite. He refused eggs, bacon, sausages, kidneys, a kipper or breadcrumbed bits of Dover sole, and opted for a thin slice of Bradenham ham. He sat down with his copy of *Horse and Jockey*, which also caused him a pang of regret, and soon adjourned to the library on the other side of the hall, where he continued to think of the bets he was not permitted to place.

By about eleven o'clock he was ready to face Beatrice, and vice versa – she did not encourage him to visit her earlier. She might be in bed, one-sidedly discussing household matters with Mrs Tighe or menus with Mrs Lewis; or bathing behind a locked door; or having her hair done by Mary; or trying on still more Frère Jacques clothes; or dealing with correspondence.

The letters she wrote and received were a prime cause of dissension. She would assail him with questions: who else should she send invitations to, should she ask them to lunch or dinner, who would they like to meet and who would like to meet them, how was she to address the wives of knights, lords, earls, marquesses, and how was she to seat people, what was the protocol and the order of precedence, what was she to give them to eat, and would he be sure to see to the wine? More than likely she would express dissatisfaction with her past and future guests, who were his friends and acquaintances, and did not treat her with sufficient respect, and in her experience were arrogant, insolent and ungrateful.

With luck he would escape by eleven-thirty and hurriedly putting on outdoor clothes stride across the garden to the stables. He liked to reminisce and exchange racing gossip with old Harris, who had been his father's London coachman, and Langham the stud-groom, who tried to tempt him to ride some of the horses in Hyde Park. But Ivo had not been so keen on riding since he failed to become the Master of the Brougham Foxhounds, and he would release Topper from his kennel and take him for a longer or shorter walk.

The walks were short when he was required to put in an appearance at a smart lunch at Castile House. The long ones probably included a bite to eat at that quiet club of his, the Cumbria, where very few members dared approach him, followed by a trek to Hampstead Heath or Highgate. He as well as Topper needed the exercise. He had excused himself from his duties at Gelts Abbey during the period of his courtship; and although he had often been asked to shoot since marrying, he would agree to do so only at places within the easiest reach of London. He and his wife, together with Zeals and Topper, occasionally caught early trains to Essex and Buckinghamshire, and travelled back in the evening. Beatrice had ruled against their vacating Castile House for a single night: although he had told her not to worry, that Walter

[97]

would never evict them by the crude means of locking the doors while they were out, she would remind him of the effects of the cat being away, and, even at Christmas-time, refused to sleep in any bed except that which she called her own.

He therefore walked in town instead of shooting or hunting in the country, and, to start with, eyed possible future marital homes.

But Beatrice's response to his suggestions of property seen or advertised was to shrug her shoulders and declare: 'I'm not moving anywhere till I have to.'

Her attitude to and occupation of Castile House were definitely not what Walter had in mind when he offered to lend it to them on a temporary basis. Yet as in the case of the tiara there was another way of looking at their staying put. Beatrice harped on that point: for a man to keep one of the best London houses more or less empty year in and year out while his brother needed a roof over his head was unjustifiable. Besides, she said, Walter or Horace Reed representing him had given no deadline for getting out of Castile House and set no limit on their expenditure while they were in it.

Ivo saw the force of her logic. That is to say he excused her behaviour which he could not modify or change. He was nonetheless aware of an unwonted sense of unease. Living like a king or at least a duke, with money almost in his pocket and his debts paid, with a desirable wife and a chance to be happy ever after, he lacked the confidence or the arrogance of his penurious and unpromising bachelorhood. He could not abide the scenes that he was subjected to. The temperament that made Beatrice good at night – when she felt like it – made her bad by day. He squirmed to remember the interview at which Mrs Tighe, grey-haired, the soul of honour and honesty, shedding tears, had explained that she was afraid of being accused of embezzlement because the household accounts were so extraordinarily high, and Beatrice had answered the poor woman's request for guidance as to what she should do by saying: 'You're paid to obey my orders, not to upset me.' Horace Reed had fared no better. When he came to Castile House to draw attention to the escalating bills, Beatrice said to him: 'How we choose to live is not your business. I cannot believe the Duke would wish you to be rude to us.' Ivo had not minded quarrelling with his brother: he did not want to feel at odds with almost everyone, and exist in an atmosphere of resentment and unpleasantness. He was more apprehensive than he had been when he looked ruin in the face.

He was trying to keep the word repeatedly demanded by Beatrice and supplied by himself in respect of gambling. But one day he wrote a note to Barney Solomon, instructing the bookmaker to communicate with him in future at the Cumbria Club, marking letters: To await collection. And a couple of times in these last weeks Ivo had had flutters on horses – nothing to speak of – not a gamble by his standards – sure things, as proved by the bulging registered letters he duly picked up. These trifling transactions may have been his somewhat feeble substitute for the risks he was formerly pleased to run, including the narrow squeaks of his adulterous relationship with Lady Dorothy Yealms.

The Yealmses, Dorothy and Sidney, were amongst the first guests asked to lunch at Castile House by Beatrice. Ivo's ex-mistress's acceptance of what was more a challenge than a treat was no doubt partly due to Sidney's interest in the Duke's collection of pictures, combined of course with her own curiosity. They had joined a small party of ten, and Ivo and Dorothy were kept apart to the best of the hostess's ability. In fact their intercourse on this occasion was confined to an exchange of greetings and goodbyes, and, more intimately, to her passing a single sarcastic remark as he helped her into her overcoat. She said to him in an undertone: 'What a brave boy you are!' – a reference to the formidable personality of the woman who had superseded her in his affections and become his wife.

The jibe rankled. Ivo minded it the more because of his growing conviction that he was the opposite of brave. He could not, or did not, stand up to Beatrice. He was ashamed of things he had done and was doing in order to ease his matrimonial lot. It shamed him somehow to have to pay court to stuffy grandees he had never mixed with or bothered about in the old days. He supplied Beatrice with the names of potential guests whom he scarcely knew, and felt as if he were the social climber. He descended into the cellar and purloined the choicest wines and the most precious bottles of port and brandy, which were later used as weapons in Beatrice's campaign to subdue and defeat the snobs and the snobbery she believed she was up against. He ate and drank too much, and had to agree with the public opinion that his brother must be the most generous man in the world to let him have the run of Castile House and all its appurtenances. He could not quite stomach the false pretences of the entertainments he now presided over. In the evenings he would look along the extended dining-room table, past the famous set of Spanish silverware softly gleaming, and wish in vain that his better half at the far end, imperturbably

[99]

smiling as she received compliments on her looks and hospitality, was not a scheming cheat.

After a particular afternoon walk he returned to Castile House via the stables, entrusted Topper to Langham, crossed the garden in the wintry gloaming, entered by the tradesmen's door and mounted the backstairs, the servants' stairs, to the nursery.

He had not visited Nanny Campion since the tea-party for three many weeks ago, which Beatrice, at his insistence, had attended for a few sulky minutes.

'Oh my dearie!' Nanny exclaimed at the sight of him. 'Come in, do – this is an honour – but I know what you're after, a cup of tea and some of my homemade biscuits – you remember them, don't you? Come and sit yourself by the fire.'

He accepted the proffered chair and refused the biscuits, said he was putting on weight, which was why he had just walked for miles, and that he missed his shooting, would give a lot for a couple of days with a gun at Brougham or Gelts, and reminded her that he preferred his tea as black as pitch.

'You always were a one for strong tea, Ivo. And truth to tell, you look as if you do need a strong cup. Couldn't you slip away and get some fresh air in your lungs and enjoy yourself shooting for a few days, dearie? I know, I know, you're too busy, and you're a fine gentleman nowadays with a fine lady, and soon to be the father of a family, I'm hoping, and you can't call your time your own.'

Nanny's reference to potential issue was corrected with force: 'I've told you, Nan – leave that out – we won't have children – Beatrice can't – so that's that.'

'Oh I am sorry, dear. What a blow, what a sadness! And you that fond of children, too! But how was I to know, dearie? Don't you bite my head off.'

'Well – don't you go gossiping about it – I've told you in strict confidence, and I don't want to hear another word on the subject.'

'Oh I'll keep it to myself, I promise you – still tongue, wise head, that always has been my motto. But I must say, dear, for the first and last time, it's wonderful that you married her ladyship considering.'

'I was fully informed before I proposed to her, Nan.'

'That shows how much you loved her, and gives me an idea how much she must love you. All right, dear, I'll shut my trap, as you used to say to me when you were a boy. You weren't slow to bark, though you never did have much of a bite, thank goodness. How you barked at your brother! I'm glad you two have made it up at last, and the Duke's given you this house to start your married life in.'

'He hasn't given us Castile House, far from it. In fact he wants us to clear out.'

'Who'll be living here then?'

'He will for a couple of days a year.'

'What a pity! It does seem a waste, this great big place without any family in it, but I expect your brother has his reasons, not that I shall know them because I never do catch sight of him when he is about. Anyway, dearie, don't you fret – you'll be happier soon in a nice house of your very own.'

Ivo took tea on other afternoons with his erstwhile nanny, and seemed to derive comfort from her sympathetic scolding.

'You're tired, dearie, aren't you? I always could see when you were tired and run down because of your natural dark colouring. Why don't you pack a bag and get in a train and pop up to Gelts Abbey? You're in charge there – it's your right and duty to keep an eye on those grouse and pheasants – and I'm sure it'd do you a power of good.'

'I can't, Nan.'

'Never say can't, dear.'

'You don't understand, Nan.'

One day he gazed into the fire and grated out: 'Graves has become damned awkward, hasn't he?'

'He's getting on, like me, Ivo. And he's not used to having so many guests in the house, and the late nights and that.'

'We can't be expected to keep our friends out because Graves is feeling his age.'

'Oh no, you mustn't.'

'What he's not used to is work, and that's the trouble with the entire staff. They've had it too easy with Walter paying them for doing damn all.'

'Mr Graves and Mrs Tighe are devoted to your family and always have been. Everyone's trying hard to give satisfaction. It's the difficulties they're up against, dear.'

'They're not the only ones it's difficult for. Tell them we won't be here much longer. I can't say more.'

Round about six o'clock he would look at his half-hunter watch and

[101]

announce: 'I need a drink – I'd better go – I'll have to change pretty soon. Thanks for the tea. It reminds me of the old days.'

'Old and happy they were. You loved to be in Castile House when you were little. You'd climb about on the roof out there and ride your rocking-horse.'

'I'm afraid that rocking-horse got me too keen on the gee-gees altogether. Does it still exist?'

'Oh yes, dear, it's just in the night-nursery where your brother slept. Would you like to see it?'

'No, Nan – good heavens no, though a rocking-horse might be the one horse I'm allowed to take an interest in.'

When he stood up to leave she would say without fail: 'Please give my regards to her ladyship, and tell her she'd be most welcome if she should ever feel like climbing the stairs for the cup that cheers.'

And he would mutter: 'Yes, yes.'

He did not deliver these messages. He was loath to cause or to witness a second skirmish between Beatrice and Nanny. But Beatrice herself suffered from no such inhibition.

At five-thirty in the afternoon of his fourth or fifth visit the door of the nursery burst open and Beatrice entered.

'Oh so you are here,' she exclaimed, as if the sight of her husband allayed a suspicion.

'Where did you imagine I was?' he batted back equally sharply, not liking to be disturbed, let alone suspected.

Nanny intervened: 'Please take a chair, milady. I'm very glad to see you, if I may say so. Let me make you a fresh pot of tea.'

'I hate tea – we don't have tea.'

'Your husband likes his cup and always has.'

'What he does is his own affair. I haven't got long.'

'It won't take a minute, milady.'

'Oh very well.'

A chair was drawn towards the fire for the lady to sit on – 'Not too close – you'll make my face burn bright red!' – and another teapot was produced and a cup and saucer, and the kettle boiled and the tea was infused – 'I can't drink the nasty stuff my husband prefers' – and Nanny's chat smoothed over conversational hitches and filled silences.

'His lordship showed me the photographs of your wedding, milady,' she ran on. 'I did admire your dress – you looked elegant with the diamonds in your hair – I wish I could have seen my boy married to such a pretty lady. I specially liked the group photo – your lordship had his hand on Lord Medringham's shoulder – what a handsome pair! May I ask, milady, isn't our young Lord Medringham – Billy, as I have permission to call him – a most beautiful child? He quite stole my heart away, the few times I've set eyes on him, Billy did – and I'm sure you appreciated him all the more.'

Beatrice shrugged her shoulders and said: 'Maybe.'

'Oh but I pitied you, milady, for not having your people there to see you on your wedding day.'

Beatrice stared at Nanny, who inquired in anxious tones: 'Your parents are still living, aren't they, dear?'

'So far as I know.'

'Oh I am relieved, I was afraid for a moment I'd put my foot in it. Well – of course – news must take time to travel all the way from South Africa – and you must worry, never knowing quite how they are when you're thinking of them. Just fancy – you so far from your home – and your parents with too many miles to travel for your wedding! But perhaps you've brothers and sisters, milady?'

'You're very inquisitive.'

'Beg pardon, milady – I was only wondering if your parents had other children – I was hoping they'd have other children's weddings to go to.'

Ivo addressed his wife: 'There's no call to be short with Nanny. I'd like to know if you've got brothers and sisters. You've never told me.'

'You've never asked. Don't be boring, Ivo – drop the subject.'

Nanny resumed: 'It was my fault, milady – I was always curious – and I expect I'm silly and sentimental about weddings.'

'Well, if you want to know, I didn't invite my parents to mine.'

Nanny emitted a shocked exclamation, part puzzled question, part apology for having somehow annoyed her guest.

Beatrice rubbed it in: 'I didn't invite them, I didn't inform them of my engagement, I'd have nothing to do with them if they ever came to this country, and I neither know nor care if they're alive or dead. Does that answer your questions?'

The others spoke together. Ivo said repressively: 'Beatrice!' and Nanny, pinker in the face and with eyes that winced behind her spectacles: 'I'm sorry if I've caused offence, milady, I'm sure I never meant to.'

[103]

Beatrice stood up and held out her half-full teacup to Nanny, who had also risen to her feet.

'It's not important,' she said. 'Thank you for the tea. I must go and get ready for dinner. Are you coming with me, Ivo?'

'I'll follow you – I'm not in a hurry – I seem to spend my life getting ready for dinner.'

'Come with me now. I don't like to know I'm being discussed. And you shouldn't complain about having the chance to entertain and take your place in society.'

'We don't need to entertain day after day and night after night.'

'You mean I ought to depend on you to provide me with the resources of Castile House somewhere else in the future?'

'Thanks for the sarcasm. Anyway, I don't see the point of dining and wining half the population of London.'

'No – you wouldn't – it's different for you – but all the same you'll do as I say, won't you, Ivo?'

He addressed Nanny as he at last got up: 'Don't worry, Nan – her ladyship enjoys arguing – take no notice!' And he almost swore at his wife who was waiting by the door: 'All right, I'm coming!'

The feature that temporarily redeemed Ivo Grevill's marriage was sex. Love was not quite what he and Beatrice made; souls and true minds were not involved in the exchange; tenderness was trampled on in their selfish rush for satisfaction; violence roughly described the range of things they did to each other. Yet for Ivo their embraces, or rather hers, were a belated sensual education, worth a lot, if not worth the rising price he seemed to have to pay for it. Their arguing, their quarrelling, was like foreplay, and their coupling the nearest thing to reconciliation.

Her contrariness heightened his excitement. Her wishes teasingly seldom coincided with his. On the other hand her wishes overruled his reluctance and exhaustion.

They copulated without regard to convenience or comfort. If he was amorous at bedtime, she was not – but then she would rouse him from sleep in his dressing-room in the middle of the same night. They used, instead of the great four-poster in the bedroom she called her own, a chair by her fireside or the rug on the floor, or his narrow single bed or the bath between their rooms, or somewhere downstairs at hours fraught with possibilities of discovery behind doors she might forbid him to lock. She introduced danger into the equation. To maintain the drama and novelty of their first experiences of each other she would break more rules and cross more frontiers.

He learned to read the facial conveyance of her messages of lust, a certain relaxation of the musculature of her mouth which he might have mistaken for a half-smile once upon a time, a specialized glitter of her eye. That she could see what he was often thinking was borne out by her answering questions he no longer needed to ask aloud. For instance she would suddenly say to him: 'Sorry, Ivo, bad luck,' or 'Forget it!'

Yet words, although becoming superfluous as an overture to sex, played an increasingly important part in their actual sexual communing. She would implore and beseech him not to, as if he were raping her, or say she was being killed and urge him on to kill her, or issue incontestable orders, or swear at him until he obeyed her; while his passion took the verbal form of berating her for her materialism, hard-heartedness, mischief-making and present whore-like behaviour.

They quietened down and cooled off, and he was apt to laugh at their recent excesses. His laughter resembled a vaguely gentle rallentando at the conclusion of a piece of feverish clashing music; but she kept her own counsel. She would dismiss him, at any rate in an emotional sense, and, whatever the state of her clothing or lack of it, re-assume the mantle of her dignity. Initially, before leaving, before they parted, he would thank her; but since she did not thank him, he sometimes demanded, 'What did you make of that?' or 'When you're not hot, why do you have to be so damn cold?' Her responses were merely to pat his cheek or say she was sleepy or shoo him out of the room and her sight.

In spite of these not very happy endings to such sexual stories, he would at least be satisfied and gratified, proud of the performance which she provoked, glad that his wife put his former mistress in the contextual shade, and spent and relaxed as he also liked to be after a day's sport.

His post-coital mood was transient. Second thoughts took over. Where had Beatrice learnt her tricks? What else did he not know about her? She had just confirmed his suspicions that she was not ladylike. Where would their fun and games, which were more repellent than funny in retrospect, stop? Where was she misleading him?

[105]

He suffered from dread of the quarrel to end all quarrels with his brother that he and especially Beatrice were asking for by their prodigal behaviour at Castile House. He felt obscurely that, since he had now received enough money to live on, if not enough to live as he was living at his brother's expense, he did not have a leg to stand on in the forthcoming fight. He, or rather Beatrice, was turning his family row, in which he had had a degree of right on his side and Walter had had a degree of wrong on his conscience, into a crime against innocence. He sweated apprehensively in expectation of the reckoning. What defence had he? Should he, could he, put a brake on Beatrice's wilful-ness?

One rainy day he was soaked through on his walk and re-entered Castile House by the front door at three o'clock instead of via the garden at five or six, as usual. Having ordered Topper to sit under the portico, he handed his hat and stick to Albert, who was on duty in the hall, allowed the footman to peel off his overcoat and gave instructions that Zeals was to be summoned to dry the dog and take him across to the stables. He then heard voices in the library, unexpected as he understood that Beatrice would be lunching early and alone and afterwards going shopping. He investigated and found her there with a sleek young man whom she introduced as Mr Goldsworthy, an art historian.

'I was showing Mr Goldsworthy round,' she said, as if in explanation, but without explaining how Mr Goldsworthy came to be in the house and why he was being shown round it.

'Oh yes,' Ivo commented on a rising note of interrogation.

'I wanted him to see the Gainsborough painting of your ancestors,' Beatrice continued non-committally.

Mr Goldsworthy spouted praise of the picture which formed the library overmantel.

Beatrice addressed Ivo: 'But you're wet, you're dripping – go and change your clothes before you catch cold!'

Ivo said he was on his way to do so and bade Mr Goldsworthy good after-noon.

'Shall I write to you, sir, or to Lady Ivo?' Mr Goldsworthy inquired.

'Write to me about what?'

'No, no – write to me – it's nothing to do with my husband,' Beatrice inter-jected. 'Ivo, go and change, please! I'll see you later.'

He did as he was told.

When he came downstairs in the different suit that Zeals had laid out for him, he was informed by Albert that his wife and the gentleman had left the house. He waited for her and wondered if she was committing adultery with Mr Goldsworthy. He doubted it, therefore was not particularly incensed on that score; but he was sure he was being deceived in another sense, that trouble was somehow being stirred and stored up for him, and he grew generally angry.

She arrived at a quarter to six, and he called her into the library and shut the door.

'I want to know where you've been,' he said.

'Do you?' she retorted, mocking his assumption that she was willing to be questioned in such a hectoring manner.

'What's going on, Beatrice?'

'What indeed! What's the matter with you?'

'I want to know who that Goldsworth man is and why you let him into the house and what he was doing here.'

'Goldsworthy, Ivo, not Goldsworth.'

'Oh for God's sake! Where have you been with him?'

She laughed.

'Mr Goldsworthy is not capable of making me a pair of shoes,' she said. 'I went to my shoemaker's and other shops. And now I'm going upstairs to rest before getting ready for dinner.'

'Wait a minute, Beatrice! What's this letter Goldsworthy talked of writing? Who is Goldsworthy?'

'Nothing to do with you.'

'It damn well is!'

'Don't threaten me, Ivo! He's interested in art.'

'What do you mean — a dealer?'

'Yes.'

'He deals in pictures?'

'Yes — and furniture.'

'Have you been trying to sell things out of this house?'

'No — they're not mine to sell — of course not.'

'Thank God for small mercies! Well, what was he doing here?'

'Getting an idea of values for the letter he's writing me.'

'What do you want a valuation for? I hope to God Walter never hears of this. How much is it costing, this valuation?'

[107]

'Nothing. Mr Goldsworthy's doing it as a favour and in return for being allowed into the house – he was dying to see the Grevill collection. That's all. I'm going up. I'll see you later.'

'No – wait! Walter would have a fit if he found out you were valuing his possessions. You put me in a more and more embarrassing position with every day that passes. You refuse to move out of my brother's house. You take advantage of his hospitality. There's bound to be the most unholy row. We'll finish in the law courts more than likely. I've decided to buy us somewhere else to live. We must get out of Walter's way before it's too late.'

'You amaze me, Ivo. Are you on the side of your brother, who's treated you disgracefully, or the side of your wife, who's rescued you from sinking and drowning financially? Wake up! You can hardly buy anything, let alone a house, unless I agree. And the only proposition I agree with is that we're probably heading for a row with Walter or his henchman Reed. That's why I want a valuation – in order to draw a comparison between our expenses here of some hundreds of pounds and the tens of thousands the contents are worth. I won't use the valuation unless I'm forced to. And I won't move out of Castile House ditto. One question for you before I go: did you think I was having an affair with Mr Goldsworthy?'

'I never know what you're doing.'

'Poor Ivo! My sights are set higher than the Goldsworthys of this world. And you're my unfinished business.'

'Who's coming to dinner, Beatrice?'

'Graves will have put the seating-plan in the drawing-room by now. You can study it.'

Ivo, alone, paced the floor of the library. For the moment he was too agitated to stop by the tray that bore a decanter of whisky, a soda-siphon, a flask of water and two cut-glass tumblers. He opened the door into the drawing-room and strode across to the table on which reposed the contraption in the shape of the dining-room table: it was red leather-bound, coroneted, had slots for the cards bearing the names of guests to be slipped into, and would contract or extend telescopically to suit the size of the party. Twelve cards now showed, indicating a party of twelve, and the three that caught his eye referred to Mr Max Kirby and Mr and Mrs Brian McDonald.

He cursed, returned to the library, poured out whisky and water with a shaky hand, drained the glass, poured another and began to smoke cigarettes.

It was the second time Beatrice had invited Max Kirby to dinner. She had done so this evening in spite of having been warned by Ivo that he and Max together always had played and probably always would play games of chance. She had invited another of the old gaming cronies whom Ivo had been at pains to avoid, Buck McDonald. Thus she was putting temptation in his way while telling him not to be tempted. Was she testing him somehow – his good resolutions, his promises not to fool about with their money? Or was she just trying to tie him in tighter knots?

He drank whisky until seven, and upstairs changed his clothes in morose silence, answering Zeals' inquiries with monosyllables.

He drank more at dinner. The guests other than Max Kirby and the McDonalds were Lord and Lady Dunedin and some distant elderly Grevill cousins called Oswald and Letty Baynes with the trio of middle-aged Baynes offspring, short-sighted spinster Patience, widowed Amelia, and sprightly Marcia whose husband was in the Indian Civil Service. Ivo sat between Millicent Dunedin and Letty Baynes, responded to their pointless chatter tersely, and kept on glancing down the table, past the Spanish silver, as if to measure the widening emotional gulf between himself and the woman he was married to. Beatrice looked good – he was in receipt of another batch of compliments confirming it; but she was bad or crazy. She had asked to dinner not only gamblers who with help from himself might be his and her own undoing, but also relations quite likely to write a full account of this evening's slap-up entertainment to absent Walter, who would be righteously wrathful. She was overstepping boundaries: why should he not do the same?

When the ladies left the dining-room he asked Max to join him at the top end of the table. The decanter of port and bottle of brandy circulated. He helped himself to both, and arranged to meet Max and Buck McDonald for a game of cards at the Club of Clubs the following afternoon.

Ivo Grevill duly kept this appointment.

He had decided after all not to play, not to break his vow to Beatrice and co., not to risk losing money and having to confess his crime and being punished for ever and a day; yet had felt obliged to come along and inform his friends, who should be able easily to find others to play with.

He arrived at the club at three-fifteen, a quarter of an hour early, and ran into Jack Haspell, who insisted on standing him a drink. Ivo had a hangover, he accepted the offer of a hair of the dog, ordered a port and brandy mixture, the fashionable remedy for his condition, and sat down in one of the quieter rooms with Jack. He then cut through some small talk to ask for an answer to a question that had been troubling him: what had happened to Beatrice's first husband.

Jack's reply was guarded.

'He died in a shooting accident. He was a professional big-game hunter.'

'I'm aware of that. Were you acquainted with Smythe?'

'I never met him, no.'

'My wife's extremely reserved. She prefers not to mention her bad experience in Africa, and I wouldn't want to upset her by probing into the matter. Please regard our present conversation as confidential.'

'Strictly, Lord Ivo. Robert Smythe was an adventurous man, I gather, and not too reliable.'

'Did the accident happen on safari?'

'I believe so – a safari of sorts – they were on a shooting expedition alone – which was unfortunate.'

'In what way?'

'There was no witness. Consequently Beatrice found herself in difficulties.'

'Oh yes?'

'Robert Smythe was discovered lying dead at some distance from the camp where she waited for him for many hours. He had been shot through the heart. His death was eventually called accidental, but he must have committed suicide – he was mixed up with another woman. The shock made Beatrice ill, and landed her in rather hot water. That's all I know – she's never spoken to me of her trials and tribulations – I've only gleaned information from my South African business associates.'

'Trials, you say – in court?'

'Good gracious no! My meaning was that Beatrice required legal representation at the inquest, and again in connection with a libel action, and spent more or less every penny she possessed. She also fell seriously ill. But she emerged from her difficulties with flying colours, I do assure you. Apart from gossip and malice, her reputation was unblemished. All the same she was wise to begin again over here. She wrote to remind me of our distant cousinship, and luckily I was able to offer her employment and she wasn't shy about turning her hand to remunerative work for the first time in her life. She's a remarkable person, and now she's coming into her own happily married to your good self.'

[110]

Ivo downed his drink and stood.

Jack, also standing, asked in a worried way: 'I hope I've said nothing to displease you, Lord Ivo?'

'Not at all.'

'Have you had much shooting lately?'

'No. Excuse me, I'm expected elsewhere. Good afternoon.'

Ivo Grevill made for the Card Room. He had again changed his mind. Beatrice should have informed him that she had left South Africa under a cloud. In view of her history he never should have been invited to meet her at Sweirdale. He was not saying, he would not and could not say, that his wife was guilty of anything; but his suspicion that he was the victim of a conspiracy gained another degree of credibility, he inwardly and angrily declined to behave better than she had and she did, and in that spirit played cards with Max and Buck and a fourth club member, Alastair Green, until seven in the evening.

He had to hurry back to Castile House to be ready to receive the younger party invited to dine by Beatrice, Gregory du Sten, Marian McDonald, and Lady Hewes, Lady Raleigh and Mrs Abe Wiberg along with their respective husbands — the three ladies bought their hats from Frère Jacques.

The guests arrived and eventually departed at the hour ordained by society: carriages at ten-thirty in town, ten o'clock in the country.

As soon as they were out of the drawing-room the hostess turned to the host, her smile faded, she stared at him and said: 'You're tipsy.'

'Nonsense,' he replied.

'Where were you before dinner?'

'That's none of your business.'

'Oh but it is. You talked stupidly all evening. You disgraced me in front of my friends.'

'Your friends? You haven't got any friends, except for that disreputable little squirt Haspell. The women tonight didn't come here because you made their hats — they would have steered clear of you because you once made their hats — they came because you're married to me, because they're acquaintances of mine and wanted to have a free dinner and see the sights of my home — one of my old homes. They came to Castile House in spite of you, not because — don't fool yourself. I'm tired. I'm sick of everything. We're doing everything wrong — you are — and getting everything wrong — and I'm sick of it. Good night.'

[111]

He lurched towards the door.

'Ivo, Mr Reed's calling tomorrow morning.'

'What?'

'A note was delivered by hand this afternoon. It was from Reed and addressed to me as his co-trustee. He wanted to meet me urgently. I sent a note back telling him to call at eleven tomorrow.'

'What's it about?'

'He's had my bill for clothes.'

'Not that — he wouldn't need an urgent meeting to discuss a trivial bill — he's acting for Walter — he's going to turn us out.'

'Let him try.'

'You're being stupid — you're the stupid one. You can dig in your toes till you're blue in the face — not that I agree with what you're doing — it's not fair, it's crooked — but you can't get the better of Walter — he has the power to make you and everyone else do as he pleases — he'll have us out in the street in next to no time — and with nowhere to lay our heads unless you stop playing at being a lady and find us a decent billet.'

'You should trust me.'

'That's exactly what I don't do. I want to go to bed.'

'Well, I'm not stopping you. You're not worth talking to until you sober up.'

He left her. Upstairs in his dressing-room he locked his door. The next morning he felt ill. Although his memory of the previous evening was hazy, he remembered that Horace Reed was calling at Castile House at eleven o'clock. At nine-thirty, therefore, he escaped across the garden, collected Topper, walked the dog and repeatedly checked the time, and joined his wife and his solicitor in the library at ten past eleven.

He shook hands with Horace, told him to sit down, and, positioning himself in front of the fire, his eyes bloodshot and his shorn beard still looking black against the blotchy pallor of his cheeks, announced: 'I gather this is a meeting of my trustees. So I left you two to get on with it in my absence. But I've something to say before I again remove myself. I need seven and a half thousand pounds without delay.'

Beatrice stared at him and Horace cleared his throat.

Ivo said: 'All right?'

'You're not to go away,' Beatrice rapped out.

He sat abruptly in a chair by the fire.

[112]

Horace pronounced in his voice that sounded like walnuts being cracked: 'I'm here at the Duke's behest. However, it seems we should discuss your affairs before we discuss his. I now have two requests to release money from your trust, Lord Ivo, two thousand pounds for Lady Ivo's trousseau and the seven and a half you have just mentioned. You will recall that, at the time the trust was being set up, various debts of yours were paid and money was put in your bank account to provide for you in the interim before you received interest on the capital sum. Three thousand five hundred pounds were disbursed and, I assume, have been spent; added to the nine thousand five hundred now being asked for, the total is thirteen thousand. In other words, if my mental arithmetic is correct, you are speaking of expenditure in a few months of five percent of the two hundred and fifty thousand pounds in your trust, which has to last your lifetimes.'

Ivo growled at Beatrice: 'How the hell did you manage to spend two thousand on clothes?'

She retorted: 'I can guess how you've spent seven and a half.'

Horace grated: 'May I continue? The Duke is determined not to replenish the trust in any circumstances, and has no legal, or, in my opinion, moral obligation to do so. I therefore feel duty-bound to warn you about the ruinous level of your expenditure. And in view of the agreements you entered into with his grace, which I was privy to and helped to negotiate, I cannot undertake to confine these matters to discussion only with my co-trustee and the beneficiary of the trust.'

'You mean you'll sneak to my brother,' Ivo said. 'I won't stand for that, I really won't. It's nothing whatsoever to do with Walter any more.'

'Be quiet, Ivo' Beatrice said. 'Mr Reed, I'm sure it's not your intention to threaten us. No, it isn't, is it? Before we go any further, would you like to explain why you wanted this urgent meeting?'

'The reason again relates to expenditure, I'm sorry to say, Lady Ivo.'

'Oh dear! Haven't you scolded us enough about our expenses? Money's such a boring subject.'

'The particular expenditure I would refer to is yours at Castile House, Lady Ivo.'

'Surely the Duke didn't send you along to talk about our having to buy an extra pat of butter? Must we waste our time worrying about a few little drops in the ocean of my brother-in-law's finances?'

[113]

'I regret to say there are principles at stake. His grace invited you to stay for at most a few weeks in his London home and you've stayed four and a half months so far, and the costs of your visit have been significant. I am not parti/san, Lady Ivo, I've served your husband's family for many years, and I'm here not only to do the Duke's bidding but also, if possible, to pour oil on troubled waters. No doubt you believe that since Castile House is not often used by its owner you might as well live in it, and that the odd thousand pounds makes no difference to the Duke's budget. In fact the Duke keeps this place going largely for traditional and sentimental reasons, although, perhaps despite appearances, he has devoted his life to the task of making relative economies in every department of the estate. He has no money to spare – to be precise no more money for you to spend without his agreement or permission at Castile House – and he wishes to regain control of his property.'

Beatrice turned to Ivo. 'Are you convinced that your brother's hard up?'

Ivo addressed the solicitor: 'Stop talking rot, Horace.'

'I'm sorry you should think it rot, Lord Ivo. I'm afraid you're wrong to think so. I must ask you when you're moving into alternative accommoda/tion.'

Beatrice said: 'And we must ask you when you'll let us have the ten thou/sand pounds we need.'

'Quite right,' Ivo echoed.

Horace Reed replied: 'The two matters are indivisible. As I have not received co/operation with one, I am not able to co/operate with the other. The Duke foresaw the possibility of our failure to reach agreement. He therefore instructed me to inform you that he will be travelling south and arriving at Castile House next Monday morning.'

Following Horace Reed's somewhat huffy goodbyes, as the library door closed, Beatrice reproached her lord and master thus: 'You fool!'

He retorted: 'I've been unlucky – but how could you have put two damn thousand pounds on your back? And if you hadn't been so pig/headed about overstaying our welcome here, Walter wouldn't have wanted to poke his nose into our business, and you and Horace could have signed on the dotted line, and we'd be in the clear.'

'Where were you gambling? Who were you gambling with?'

'Max mainly – I warned you not to get Max and me together – he wouldn't let me off the hook of a game – it's your fault.'

'You say you don't trust me. I trusted you.'

'Well, you push me too damn far sometimes.'

'I've pushed you from nowhere in the right direction. Haven't I, Ivo?'

'Maybe, but God knows where we'll find ourselves on Monday.'

'I'm not afraid of your brother.'

'Don't fall out with him for ever, I do beg you, Beatrice.'

'What's this? You were the one who was always quarrelling with him – I never have.'

'He and I know the form. I'm not sure how destructive you're going to be.'

'You dare to call me destructive, when you've just destroyed a good part of everything I've built up?'

'I'm sorry I lost money – you should be sorry too for spending it. I wouldn't have played cards if I hadn't been feeling low – but we'll be all right in the end – don't worry.'

'Oh yes, we'll get the money or what's left of it in the end. It's ours – they can't stop us getting it. But you've broken your promise to me, and made me break my promise to Walter that you wouldn't ever gamble any more. Thanks to you, he's not going to be pleased with me or do me any favours in respect of where and how we live.'

'Don't rub it in so!'

'What did you have to be low about? You were low because you were or had been drunk.'

'No – it wasn't that at all – I had my reasons, I can tell you or rather I can't tell you! And I can't stick waging war on my brother, tricking him, stealing from him really, living where we're not wanted, and hardly being free to leave the house in case somebody locks the door while our backs are turned. I'm not able to go to Gelts, I haven't earned my wage for looking after Gelts, and I've had damn-all shooting this winter, and I don't see why we can't get a place of our own and establish our independence.'

'Patience is a virtue. Let's have a little more patience, Ivo, and less of your vices.'

'Thanks very much. I'm not listening to stuff like that.'

'Don't go, Ivo – I'm expecting you to lunch – one o'clock without fail. Do you hear me?'

[115]

He stalked out of the library.

But he reappeared in the drawing-room as requested before the arrival of his or her guests: Lord and Lady Gerald Kilpatrick, Lord Gerald being the younger son of another duke, the Duke of Kilmore, Sir Patrick and Lady Deane, and the French Chargé d'affaires and Madame Elias.

Ivo Grevill did his social duty not least because it was the Friday before the Monday referred to by Horace Reed, and he was unwilling to face his brother without the full support of his wife. Probably for a similar reason, to aim to secure a spouse's loyalty in the coming crisis, Beatrice enticed her husband into her bedroom late that evening and at length won from him the signs, sounds and grudging admissions suggesting that he was still her creature.

On the Saturday morning Ivo mounted the stairs to the nursery and spoke briefly to Nanny Campion.

'Have you heard that Walter's condescending to visit us?' he asked.

'Oh yes, dearie, the whole house is full of it.'

'I can't imagine why.'

'Everybody thinks highly of your brother. They're bound to, aren't they? He's been good to us.'

'Yes, by making himself scarce, which is a pretty easy way to be popular.'

'He pays our wages, dear. And it's thanks to him that I've seen something of you. We're all grateful – and now I'm looking forward to catching a glimpse of his grace.'

The response of Ivo, who had been standing in the doorway, was to exit and slam the door.

Twenty-four hours later, on the Sunday, he knocked on another door and received permission to enter.

'Yes?' Beatrice inquired, regarding his reflection in the mirror on her dress-ing-table, at which she sat as Mary brushed her black hair.

'Have we got people coming in tomorrow?'

'A few.'

'Who are they?'

'Lord and Lady Deveraux and the Bullingers for lunch, and Miss Paull and Brigadier Dimmick and the Melvilles for dinner.'

'We'll have to put them off. My brother won't feel like entertaining after a night on the train.'

'But we'll be doing the entertaining. I asked his friends in on purpose to meet him. And we'll be giving him a chance to see them and enjoy himself.'

'Enjoyment isn't what he's here for. He wants to talk to us, not to a lot of outsiders.'

'Exactly — I mean I've taken that into consideration. There'll be time enough for us to talk.'

'Do you know how long he's staying.'

'No, but —' Beatrice shot a warning glance at Ivo to remind him of the presence of Mary; 'but I'm sure he'll find reasons to return to Brougham as soon as possible. He's always busy there, isn't he?'

Ivo pondered for a moment and agreed.

The rest of that Sunday proceeded slowly. Beatrice appeared to be as unapprehensive as ever. But the servants could not altogether repress signs of a certain excitement, and Ivo was dreadfully restless and started smoking and drinking long before six o'clock.

At nine-thirty the following morning Walter stepped out of the town coach, thanked coachman Harris, greeted Graves and nodded at the footmen, and entered his house, in the hall of which Ivo, emerging from the dining-room napkin in hand, said that he was still having breakfast and he hoped his brother would join him.

Mrs Tighe, lurking in the background, stepped forward and bobbed a curtsey to the Duke.

'We are glad indeed to see your grace,' she declared.

Walter replied in equally polite terms, and turned to Graves, who acted as his valet in London just as Cox did in Cumberland: 'I'll be having a bath and changing my clothes in a little while.'

'Lady Ivo has arranged for you to be in the Blue Bedroom, your grace.'

'The Blue Bedroom, is it? That's something new. Where's Lady Ivo sleeping?'

Ivo cut in: 'We're in your rooms, Walter. But we'll remove ourselves if you're staying more than a night or two.'

Walter commented drily: 'I see. Thank you, Graves,' and walked into the dining-room ahead of his brother.

He refused Ivo's further offers of sustenance and inquired, warming his hands in front of the fire: 'Beatrice is well?'

'Yes, thanks. Are you all right?'

'I've asked Horace to be here at noon.'

[117]

'Again? We had the law laid down by Horace only a day or two ago.'

'I'm aware of that. It's why I decided to come south.'

'We don't want to quarrel, Walter.'

'You have no cause to quarrel with me.'

'Don't let's quarrel.'

'No – I sincerely hope it won't be necessary.'

'Walter . . . How's Billy?'

'Billy's as well as can be expected.'

'I'd like to see the boy again.'

'That's up to you.'

'Are you staying long in London?'

'It depends. I'll stay as long as I need to. I think I'll have my bath, Ivo. I didn't sleep much in the train, and I must speak to the servants this morning and I've got business to arrange with Horace this afternoon. I take it that Beatrice has breakfast upstairs?'

'She'll be down in good time for our meeting.'

'What? I would prefer her not to be present.'

'Sorry – I wouldn't be able to persuade her to stay away – sorry, Walter.'

'In that case, shall we meet in the library just before twelve?'

'Very well. Don't forget to say hullo to Nanny.'

'Thanks for your valuable advice.'

While Walter bathed, Ivo wrote a note for Beatrice, escaped from the house, walked Topper, and joined his brother and Horace Reed just as the clocks struck midday.

Walter's looks were noticeably blacker than before, that is to say he looked more displeased, and displeasure and tiredness combined to accentuate the family complexion. He sat at the famous piece of furniture known as the Brougham Desk, a large square marquetry table with drawers rather than a conventional desk, sternly authoritative despite his small build and pinched features, with Horace on his left and Ivo – now – opposite.

He said to his brother: 'Is your wife likely to be late?'

'I shouldn't think so.'

'Well, I shall try to say my say before she gets involved. This can't go on, Ivo. I gave you an inch and you're taking a mile. Your household expenses for three months are more than mine at Brougham for nearly a year. Your bill for flowers alone is more than my annual garden budget for Castile House. You've

[118]

called me ungenerous: see what happens when I'm generous! You exploit me. You exploit and exhaust my servants. And you've neglected Gelts, you haven't been near Gelts. And I hear you've started gambling again, notwithstanding all the assurances that persuaded me to part with a quarter of a million pounds. Not another brass farthing, Ivo! And I want my house back. The question is: how soon can I have it?'

As if by way of an answer, and a negative answer at that, Beatrice entered the room, swept in, it might be said, glittering gem-like in comparison with the dark metal of the brothers, confident and brisk, and greeted the Duke with the warmth of a close relation and the manner of his hostess.

'Walter, forgive me,' she pleaded, kissing him. 'You must think me rude not to have been up and about to welcome you. I'm afraid I've got into lazy ways since becoming a member of your family. Is your room all right? Please sit down. Everyone, please sit down. Good morning, Mr Reed. Shall I sit here, beside my husband and facing my brother-in-law? How formal we are! Ivo, you'll have to tell me what you've been saying, so that I can follow the discussion.'

Ivo growled: 'Walter's got a whole string of grievances against us.'

'Really, Walter?'

'I'm afraid the discussion you mention, and I must say I'd hoped for, won't be possible as I understand you've invited people to lunch and to dinner. We won't have time to talk things over at leisure.'

'Yes, the Deveraux and the Bullingers are coming to lunch – they're much looking forward to seeing you, and I knew you'd be pleased to see such old friends – and the Melvilles and Brigadier Dimmick and Betty Paull are dining.'

'I'd be more pleased to see them if I hadn't travelled overnight.'

'Why didn't I think of that? How tactless of me! I beg your pardon. Shall I send them notes to explain your feelings?'

'No – please do nothing of the sort.'

'Anyway, Walter, my hope is that you'll stay on here and we can talk to our hearts' content on other days.'

'May I remind you that I have many commitments?'

'Of course you do – which is sad for us – we'll just have to try to make you so comfortable and happy that you won't wish to leave.'

'I suggest we get down to brass tacks. We haven't long now, and I'm engaged all afternoon.'

[119]

'And I promise to keep very quiet. But surely Ivo's exaggerating, as usual? I mean grievances are awful. There – I won't say another word.'

Walter cleared his throat and said: 'Beatrice, I shall take the opportunity to mention a matter that concerns you personally. The tiara that was being mended: can you tell me what the damage was, and if it's ready for me to replace in safe keeping?'

'The damage was slight. But the jewellers are slow and still working on it. I must remember to inquire how they're getting on. Meanwhile I have a tiny query for you, Walter. Isn't that tiara, and aren't some other jewels, family heir-looms?'

'I believe they are. Why do you ask?'

'Heirlooms for the use of the family?'

'Possibly – but I'm responsible for their safety.'

'Doesn't Ivo share the responsibility and everything?'

'No – Ivo has no responsibilities or rights in connection with any family property.'

'What a shame! I'm sorry – it just seems a shame that a beautiful object like that tiara should never see the light of day. I suppose my ideas of waste are bound to differ from yours. That's all! I'll let you have our heirloom to hide in your strong-room as soon as possible. And apologies for the delay – I didn't realize you'd have the energy to fret about such a minor item. By the way, Mr Reed, are you lunching anywhere? Shouldn't we invite Mr Reed to lunch, Ivo?'

'Thank you, Lady Ivo, I'm already engaged,' Horace Reed replied in a hurry and almost blushing: he did not want his employer to think him guilty of social presumption.

Ivo growled again: 'Let Walter speak, Beatrice.'

'Oh dear, have I been talking too much? I'll be silent from now on.'

'Ivo's trust fund,' Walter began: 'I can't stop the trustees paying out the capital that apparently more or less belongs to the beneficiary. But I'm shocked by the squandering of so large a sum in such a short space of time, and disap-pointed that undertakings given to me have not been adhered to, and my old fears for the future of my brother have revived with a vengeance. I've therefore asked Horace to see if he can alter the terms of the trust, so that only the income, not capital, no more capital, except for one purpose, could be released. A revised trust deed would enable Ivo to be declared bankrupt, or the equivalent of bankrupt, and I'm prepared to publish a statement to the effect that I shall not pay his debts. He should be able to live and support his wife on the income from investment of the remaining capital, which would no longer in any sense be his. Apologies, Ivo – but a plan of that sort might save you from yourself.'

'You couldn't do it to me, Walter.'

'Why not?'

'You'd be putting me on an allowance like a damned schoolboy. I'd be as good as bankrupt from the word go. And do you want to be named in notices in the papers proving how mean you are?'

Beatrice chimed in: 'Can I say something after all?' She proceeded: 'Mr Reed, wouldn't I as your co-trustee have to agree to any tampering with the document we signed?'

'That is correct, Lady Ivo. But my impression is that his grace does not rule out litigation in order to achieve his object.'

Walter also addressed the solicitor: 'Am I right in thinking and saying that my brother would be much worse off than he is at present if he tried to fight me through the courts, and even if he were to win the action I'm prepared to bring?'

'Quite right, your grace.'

'On the other hand, money could be made available without delay, if my brother would agree to buy a house and move there, and my sister-in-law agreed to scrap the old trust deed and sign a new one. Isn't that so?'

'Precisely, your grace.'

'Beatrice,' the Duke continued, 'I must insist on you leaving Castile House. Why, Ivo knows perfectly well, even if you don't. Appearances here and at Brougham may have given you the idea that I or rather the estate has money to burn. The reality is that I've struggled for many years to remedy the effects of my father's extravagance. Your level of expenditure makes nonsense of my attempts to economize, and robs the other houses of money set aside for their upkeep. There are extra good reasons, which I needn't go into, for me to reclaim my property.'

'Oh but you should go into them, Walter,' she argued smoothly, 'because, to be frank with you, poverty isn't a very good excuse for resorting to threats to get rid of us. Perhaps you're not aware of the value of your possessions. You couldn't be telling us how poor you are if you knew of the tens of thousands, the hundreds of thousands of pounds plastered on the walls of your residences. We may have cost you more than you like to spend. Well, one of those pictures

[121]

on the wall of the stairs going up to the nursery, if sold, would bring you in a tidy sum. There are pictures that nobody notices worth thousands, and the Gainsborough behind me, over the mantelpiece, is worth a fortune. I've had them professionally valued.'

'What did you say?'

'We've had them valued. Wait a minute, please, Walter! I admit we've stayed longer than expected at Castile House. But we haven't kept you out of it, and we've warmed it up and breathed a bit of life into the place. Many problems would be solved if you let us live in it permanently. We'd be willing to contribute to the expenses.'

The Duke pushed back his chair and rose to his feet. His face was dark red, and the papers he gripped in his hand shook.

He interrupted her to snap and splutter: 'No! As guests in my house you should not have had my pictures valued. They belong to me and my son. No – you are not going to sell or force sales of our property, or occupy it for that matter. Ivo's contracted a debt of honour, I gather. The trust will not pay it until you're out of Castile House.'

Ivo now weighed in, turning to Beatrice and saying: 'Look what you've gone and done!' He spoke to his brother. 'Walter, I can't keep my creditors waiting – you must see that – I've got to have seven and a half thousand straight away.'

'You'll have it when you leave Castile House.'

'But you're not my trustee. You have no right to tell me what I will and won't have.'

'Horace has the right. Horace will do as I say.'

'Is that true, Horace?'

'Lord Ivo, I warned you that I was bound to be guided by the Duke.'

'It's blackmail and bullying. Beatrice, I must have that money. Help me!'

'You see, Ivo,' she returned, 'it's not what I've done, it's what you've done that loses the game, as you would say.'

'Oh hell! Beatrice, please!'

'We must make a virtue of necessity. You get your money when Horace agrees to pay it, and Horace agrees to pay it when we leave here. Your brother says so. We'd better pack our bags.'

'Are you serious, Walter?'

'I am – and don't try to put the blame on me – if you'd behaved properly

[122]

this unpleasantness would have been avoided.'

'How long are you giving us to get out?'

'That's up to you. How long before you have to pay your creditors?'

'Ten more days.'

'You'd better leave before you welsh on your debt.'

'Oh God! I'll never speak to you again, Walter.'

The front doorbell rang.

Beatrice stood and said: 'Gentlemen, our guests have arrived. Goodbye, Mr Reed. Walter, shall we adjourn to the drawing-room?'

4

THE Duke of Brougham left London quietly the next morning, and Lord and Lady Ivo Grevill prepared to leave Castile House rather less so.

Beatrice had put forward a new plan of action, and Ivo had ceased to disagree with it. She promised seductively to take care of everything. She made it all sound easy, and not like revenge. He read the newspapers, walked with Topper, called in at the Cumbria Club, played the host at luncheon and dinner parties, and pretended hardly to know what was going on. He was drinking more whiskies with less water in them and smoking innumerable Turkish cigarettes.

The invitation cards to the ball at Castile House were printed in a rush and posted by the evening of the day of Walter's departure. The schedule was tight; but Beatrice seemed to have anticipated the turn of events. The pleasure of the company of some two hundred guests, every person in society on the list drawn up by the Grevills when they arrived in London, was requested at ten o'clock in eight days' time. The band was to be engaged and the flowers were to be ordered, but on a confidential basis. The staff at Castile House would be given only four days' notice of the ball, when acceptances would have been received and Walter would not be able to cancel it without a public scandal. On the morning after, that is on the day before the Grevills had to remove themselves in order to qualify for the essential cash, they would decide where they were going to live in future.

Ivo did protest about the mere forty-eight hours they were allowing themselves in which to find a home. But Beatrice retorted that it would be temporary lodgings, that she might need months to settle for somewhere permanent, that there were lots of properties for leasing on the market and if the worst came to the worst they could spend a few days in a hotel, and finally that you never knew – anything might happen between now and then – they must wait and see.

She overruled Ivo's nervous queries with unanswerable questions of her own: 'Why not – why shouldn't we – what damage would it actually do – what have we to lose now anyway?' The principle she invoked seemed to be that the realization of one of her social ambitions took precedence over her brother-in-law's wishes, feelings and bank balance.

Besides, she said, Castile House existed not to be dust-sheeted and shut-tered, nor to have its front door locked and its servants left to twiddle their thumbs, but to be admired and enjoyed, and have the ghosts frightened off by music and laughter.

He was persuaded at least not to interfere. He refrained from visiting Nanny, who might be nosey. When Mrs Tighe and Graves sought him out to say they would have to have more help with all the extra work, he referred them to her ladyship. His one positive or pacific contribution to the project was to inform Zeals that the ball was by way of being their farewell to Castile House, knowing that his manservant would relay the information below stairs, where it would sound like glad tidings.

As the tempo of Beatrice's preparations, and the activities of the household, rose to a climax, his speculative instinct took over. The odds were now against Walter hearing of the ball in time to wreck it. Ivo would have bet that Horace Reed was not going to appear like a skeleton at the feast.

At six o'clock in the evening of the night of the ball, he was summoned from the library to inspect Beatrice's arrangements. The drawing-room was transformed. In place of the furniture and rugs, which had been stored in spare bedrooms, banks of flowers in moss and lines of gilded chairs edged the parquet floor. On the dais at one end a grand piano, music stands and so on awaited the band. The candles in the chandeliers had not yet been lit, but the open french windows admitted the roseate April sunset, which cast a warm glow on the red silk brocade and the old masters covering the walls. Fresh garden scents combined with those of the imported flowers, of beeswax polish and french chalk. The weather was mild and dry enough to promise that guests would be able to stroll out of doors and along the garden paths illuminated by Chinese lanterns in the trees.

Ivo was led by his wife, and ushered by Graves, through the high mahogany and ebony connecting doors into the diningroom. The breakfast table in the window had been removed, and the main whiteclothed table extended by means of leaves to its fullest limit in order to accommodate the forty guests invited to dine. The gold dinner service, its arboreal centrepiece bearing crystal bowls of comfits, the quartet of sixarmed candelabra, the shellshaped salts and crested plate, were on display. Napkins were folded to resemble bishops' mitres and the sets of three wine glasses added their own rich gleam to the array.

He congratulated his wife, and said in rallying accents to the butler: 'It's like the old days, Graves.'

'I'm glad your lordship's pleased,' Graves replied in a voice telling a different story, that he was not glad to have worked his fingers to the bone for an interloping lordling and a pernickety slavedriver of a socalled lady.

An hour later the Grevills had changed into their finery, and were rechecking that all was in order for the evening's entertainment. She wore a new Frère Jacques creation of green satin, which showed off her tiny waist and flawless shoulders and neck. Her jewels were her wedding and engagement rings, and on her head of wavy black hair the disputed tiara. Ivo was not altogether happy about the tiara, began to speak of the annoyance it could cause in a certain quarter, but changed his mind, seemed to remember that it was much less annoying than many other things, and commented on her appearance with a glint in his eye: 'Not bad.' He himself was relieved to think that in a matter of hours he might be out of debt and out of Walter's way. The diamond and sapphire studs in his white shirtfront matched the buttons of his white waistcoat and the links in the shirtcuffs projecting from the sleeves of his tailcoat.

At eight the dinner guests arrived, were seated in the diningroom by a quarter past, and served with clear soup and sherry, lobster thermidor with white wine, duckling and then a crown of cutlets with claret, syllabub with champagne, fruit and coffee with port, brandy, crème de menthe or kümmel.

At ninefortyfive Beatrice conducted the female contingent upstairs, while Ivo directed some gentlemen to the lavatories and led others into the library and offered them cigars.

By ten o'clock, when carriages began to drop their loads of grandees under

[126]

the portico, both Ivo and Beatrice, standing in the hall to greet these guests, evinced a complacent, not to say triumphant, air: Horace had not put a stop to the proceedings, and his master, the owner of Castile House, who would soon have to foot the last but not the least bill for lending it to his brother and sister-in-law, had missed his chance to interfere.

The musicians struck up, couples took to the floor in the drawing-room, people began to circulate, strolling into the garden, sitting out here and there, and before long the dining-room doors were thrown open to reveal yet another transformation – every sign of the recent dinner party removed, and the great table converted into a sort of buffet dispensing ices and liquid refreshments.

Compliments were showered upon the host and hostess. He was told by men that his wife was beautiful and he was lucky, and by women that she was clever and doing him credit, and asked by both male and female persons where he had found her. The bright lights in his family house seemed to shed reflected glory on Ivo's dark head; and Beatrice won praise too for being the consort of the brother of the proud possessor of such a grand London residence, almost another palace, chock-full of works of art and history. Men of all ages crowded round her to plead for dances; and Ivo's hand was squeezed with gratitude by the white-gloved hands of younger dancing partners, while the older ones thanked him wholeheartedly for the privilege of a peep at treasures beyond compare.

They danced together just after eleven o'clock. She demanded it, and he had the feeling that they could celebrate a sort of success, or at any rate having got away with something. She said to him with satisfaction as they whirled and twisted: 'Everyone's here, Ivo, everyone,' and he returned: 'I suppose I owe you a vote of thanks.' When the music stopped she was claimed by the next partner on her full dance-card, and he stepped out for a breath of fresh air, to cool down and to smoke.

He was discovered there by Graves.

'This telegram has just arrived, milord,' the butler said, proffering a small yellow envelope on a silver salver. 'I thought you would wish to see it.'

The stamp of the Post Office, Carlisle, was clearly legible on the envelope. Graves must have seen it and guessed that it meant trouble for his temporary taskmasters.

Ivo's hand trembled as he opened up the telegram, cursing himself for having counted his chickens prematurely.

[127]

The text ran: 'Sad to inform you that the Duke suffered a mortal road accident this p.m. and expired at eight thirty-five stop awaiting instructions stop Macmurray.'

Ivo re-read the words, or rather gazed at them for a minute or two.

Graves inquired: 'Will that be all, milord?'

Ivo replied thickly: 'Send Zeals to my dressing-room,' then, instead of re-entering the house, he almost pushed past Graves and strode — insofar as his unsteady legs allowed — farther into the garden.

Pairs of guests, groups of guests, recognized and greeted him, but he paid no attention. He reached the walled end of the illuminated pleasure grounds and passed through a gateway into the kitchen garden. He shut the gate and leant against the rough old wall in his spotless tailcoat in the blackness of the night. Horses stamped and whinnied in the stables, and he could just hear sounds of horses' hooves and vehicles' wheels on roads, and footsteps on public pavements.

How was he to get back into the house and hide upstairs without causing a commotion? How was he to summon his wife, call a halt to the festivities, break the news? Walter dead — and almost the last prophetic words he had addressed to his brother were: 'I'll never speak to you again.' He regretted them, he was sorry for everything, and especially that it was too late to be sorry. Poor orphan Billy! Ivo swore at fate.

Some time elapsed. He dropped the glowing end of his cigarette, trod on it, retraced his steps, was relieved to discover that the tradesmen's door was unlocked, and via the back door and servants' stairs reached his dressing-room.

Zeals was there — he had been lending a hand with the pantry work — and said: 'I was told you needed me.'

'Have you been waiting long?'

'Nothing to speak of. All well, milord?'

Ivo sat down on a chair by the stoked and flaring coal fire.

'My brother's dead.'

'When did that happen?'

'Today — tonight — somewhere up north — I know no details. Fetch my wife, Zeals! We'll have to cut the party short.'

'Shall I ask Mr Graves to make the announcement, milord?'

'No — not Graves — her ladyship will know. Come back here! We'll have to catch the Carlisle train in the morning – I'll tell you what to pack – and a telegram will have to be sent to Brougham.'

'My condolences, milord.'

'Yes – hurry!'

Soon Beatrice arrived, saying, after making the briefest inquiries, while Zeals stayed out in the passage: 'Does anybody else have to be told tonight?'

'What on earth do you mean?'

'Can't we keep the secret till the party finishes?'

'What – carry on dancing? Haven't you made enough trouble?'

'Don't be angry – I'm trying to think of the best way to cope – I'm just as shocked as you are, though I can't say I'm suffering unbearably. The party will be over in an hour or two – why spoil it?'

'Graves brought me the telegram, and Zeals is fully informed.'

'That's different. We can't have the staff knowing what the guests don't know. Walter found a way of stopping us having fun after all – I was afraid he would – it's typical.'

'Don't go on like that, for God's sake!'

'Well, don't you be such a humbug – I'm not impressed by crocodile tears. We'd better break the news.'

'I'm not breaking it – we can't break it – we'd only embarrass everybody – somebody else will have to do it – the question is who.'

She put forward the name of Sir Arthur Bullinger. Zeals was called in and instructed to find and fetch Sir Arthur, and the Grevills resumed their jerky dialogue.

'I'll be travelling up to Brougham on the morning train.'

'Yes.'

'Will you come with me?'

'That depends. Is Horace Reed going to insist on evicting us from Castile House now? I don't want him meddling here in our absence.'

'He wouldn't be able to. I've no inside information about Walter's will. But surely I'll have a say in things in the future. Castile House can't be left empty till Billy's grown up.'

'Does it all belong to that little boy?'

'He's the Duke – I suppose so.'

'Your brother dead! We never expected it, did we, Ivo?'

'No – it changes a lot.'

[129]

'It changes everything,' she said, and then in a lighter tone of voice: 'Will there be hordes of Grevills turning up to grab a bit of this and that?'

'Not that I know of. We had no close relations. People like the Bayneses have no legal claim on anything.'

'Fancy Billy being a duke and having so much!'

'He's an orphan, poor chap.'

'We'll have to take care of him.'

'Yes. He's a good boy really. I never agreed with Walter about his upbringing. Walter tried to keep him in cotton wool.'

'I can see that wouldn't be right. We'll do whatever's best. By the way, Ivo, do you think Walter will have made any provision for you?'

'God knows! I can't go into it at this stage, Beatrice – it's not the moment.'

'I only wondered. My mind's in a spin. I never dreamed Walter would die like this – I mean so soon.'

'Will you come to Brougham?'

'Are you sure Mr Reed won't act on some posthumous instruction of your brother's, and try to repossess this house?'

'Sure enough.'

'All right – I'll have to be at Brougham sooner or later – for the funeral, I mean, and to get to know Billy.'

'I'm very glad to hear you're willing to take an interest in the boy – though whether or not we'll be appointed his guardians remains to be seen.'

'I'm interested anyway,' she said.

Sir Arthur Bullinger was ushered into the dressing-room by Zeals.

Explanations followed, and help was volunteered. Sir Arthur, having called for and consumed a glass of consoling brandy, went downstairs to address the company. Ivo and Beatrice Grevill heard the band break off, the music stop, voices, then carriages driving in and out of the gravel sweep. Zeals informed them when the guests had gone and when the staff, including stables and garden staff, some with wives and children in tow, were assembled on the former dancing floor. Ivo spoke to them from the bandstand, saying it was a tragic day for everyone; he would do all he could to ensure security of employment; there was certain to be a memorial service in London; and he and his wife appreciated all the expressions of sympathy, which eased their grief, and they reciprocated.

Upstairs again, he knocked on the door of Beatrice's bedroom and was

[130]

allowed to enter. What was unpredictable, or unexpected by Ivo as he gave her an account of his speech, was her extinction of one lamp after another. In the dark, except for the glow of the fire, she approached him in her silken night-dress, put her finger on his lips, helped him out of his tailcoat, and so on. Their intercourse in the firelight was unusually excited and peremptory on her side, and had the charm of licentiousness on his. Afterwards he mumbled regrets and said something about a peculiar way to mourn his brother, and she hustled him out of her room, saying he never knew when he was lucky.

In the morning they, together with Mary who had become Beatrice's official lady's-maid, Zeals and Topper, travelled north, and were met at Carlisle Station by a deputation consisting of the stationmaster, Ian Macmurray and Saddlecombe. Two carriages awaited: Mary, Zeals, the dog and the luggage followed along in the second.

In the other carriage the conversation included the following snatches.

'I'm glad you received my telegram.'

'It arrived first thing this morning, Lord Ivo,' Ian Macmurray said.

'We got yours in the middle of a party we were giving last night.'

'I'm sorry, but it seemed essential to let you know without delay.'

'Quite right – I'm not complaining. Tell me what happened.'

'The Duke – the late Duke – was driving himself back from Gelts Abbey.'

'What was he doing at Gelts?'

'He told me there were matters to attend to in your absence.'

'Oh. I suppose the accident happened at Garrack Spur. Why was no one with him?'

'He said that I and everybody else on the estate had our own allotted work to do, and . . .'

'Yes – what else did he say?'

'He was not going to pay two men to do the same job, Lord Ivo.'

'I hope you're not blaming me. I can't help it if my brother chose to put his oar into what was my business. I was coming up to sort things out at Gelts in the very near future.'

'In the Estate Office we did suggest that Gelts could look after itself until you returned. But the Duke had his own ideas.'

'Was it Garrack Spur?'

'He must have been thrown out of the pony-trap on that dangerous corner on the Spur. The pony dragged the trap on its side down to the forester's

[131]

cottage, where Wickens lives. Wickens caught it, and he climbed up the hill and then into the valley and found the Duke almost in Garrack Tarn. The road belongs to the estate, you'll remember, Lord Ivo, and it's extremely rough, and the drop from the Spur is sheer.'

'That road has needed remaking for years.'

'It would have been a big expense to remake it.'

'Yes – so my brother said – well, he's paid still more heavily. Was his death instantaneous?'

'Yes, according to Dr Bennett . . .'

Beatrice, dressed in deep mourning clothes, spoke to Saddlecombe through her black veil.

'What rooms have you put us in?'

'We thought you might like to be in the Duchess Lily Suite, milady, as before, with his lordship using that dressing-room.'

'Oh no – much has changed since my previous visits to Brougham – I would prefer another room. My husband and I must have the best rooms from now on.'

'Not a state room, milady? The state rooms wouldn't be fit to sleep in without considerable preparation.'

'Why not the Duke's Apartments?'

'The Duke's Apartments haven't been occupied for many years, as your lordship will recall.'

Ivo explained to Beatrice: 'Walter was furious with our grandfather for spending so much money on the decoration of those rooms.'

Beatrice said to Ivo: 'I know – you've told me – your brother disapproved of your grandfather's folly, and kept the doors permanently locked. But that's over and done with. We're living in the present, aren't we?'

'The rooms are fancy with painted ceilings and a gilded bed.'

'So much the better.' Beatrice turned back to Saddlecombe. 'The Duke's Apartments will suit, thank you.'

'Excuse me, milady, but I'm not sure we'll be able to get them ready for you at such short notice.'

'Well, I am sure, Mr Saddlecombe, bearing in mind the army of staff you can call upon to do as we wish.'

'Everybody will be studying your ladyship's comfort – they'll be doing their best, believe me.'

[132]

'It's a question of orders, Mr Saddlecombe. One of the changes brought about by the Duke's death is that Brougham is again in charge of someone with experience of how to run a house.'

'I was trying to please your ladyship.'

'No doubt . . .'

Ivo spoke: 'Saddlecombe, Mr Reed will be arriving tomorrow or the next day, and Mrs Tighe and Graves will be coming up for the funeral.'

'Very good, milord . . .'

Ian Macmurray volunteered that he had taken the liberty of asking Mr Pibbs the chaplain to look in at seven o'clock that evening to discuss funerary matters.

Ivo asked where the mortal remains of his brother were for the moment.

'At the undertaker's,' Ian Macmurray replied. 'We imagined you'd like a period of lying in state in the chapel, Lord Ivo; but decisions were postponed until you arrived. We understand there will have to be a coroner's inquest before the interment . . .'

Another protracted speechless pause ensued. The carriage trundled swaying along the empty road, through the darkening landscape, in the deeper shade of humped hills, and past winking lights in the small windows of occasional cottages. The pure air seemed to have a cutting edge.

Eventually the lodges on either side of the gates to the mile and a half of drive through the Brougham park came into view.

Then the horses' hooves rang less metallically on the softer surface of the grassy driveway.

Beatrice broke the silence within the carriage: 'I wonder how Lord Medringham feels about becoming the Duke of Brougham.'

To this semi-rhetorical question, the full answer was provided when the carriage reached its destination, stopped, and the great front door of Brougham opened, the seventeenth Duke of Brougham and fifth of Castile ran out across the terrace and down the steps, pursued by Cox, his butler, and threw thin arms round the waist of the tall top-hatted gentleman in the long black overcoat, exclaiming in his boy's treble: 'Oh Uncle Ivo!'

'Hullo, Billy – hullo, old boy – yes, we're here – you'll be all right now,' Ivo said.

[133]

'Good evening, Billy – don't you recognize me through my veil?' Beatrice asked.

'Oh – yes – Aunt Beatrice.'

'You must kiss me, Billy.'

'Oh – yes.' He did so. 'Please come in,' he added in an almost ducal manner.

Ivo exchanged greetings with Cox and led the way into the house with his arm round the boy's shoulders. Beatrice, Ian Macmurray, Saddlecombe, and Zeals with Topper and Mary carrying some of the luggage, followed into the hall, where, amongst the footmen relieving the travellers of articles of clothing and bustling about with trunks and suitcases, Nurse Tucker stood in her uniform, grey dress with starched white collar and cuffs and blue silver-buckled belt, and fixed her anxious regard on her young charge.

Ivo spoke to her: 'Evening, Nurse.'

She replied: 'I hope his lordship – I mean the Duke – didn't catch cold out there with no coat on – he was so determined to see you. But he shouldn't get excited, milord. It's really his supper-time, too.'

'Don't worry. I'll see he comes to no harm. I'll bring him upstairs in ten minutes.'

Billy pleaded reproachfully: 'Oh, longer than that, Uncle!'

'Well – a quarter of an hour. You know my wife, don't you?'

Beatrice, in the act of passing by, nodded at Nurse, who bobbed a curtsey and said: 'We met at your wedding, madam.'

Beatrice halted.

'The name is Lady Ivo Grevill,' she said with emphasis on the title.

'Oh – my mistake – milady.'

'Thank you.'

Nurse Tucker withdrew, flustered, while Beatrice continued up the stairs to inspect the Duke's Apartments, Saddlecombe having gone ahead to unlock doors and mobilize housemaids. Ivo escorted his nephew into the drawing-room.

'Are you going to have a drink, Uncle?' Billy inquired.

'I wouldn't mind one, I must say.'

'Can I do your soda-water?'

'If you like. You pour out my whisky – I'll tell you when to stop – that's it – you're never too young to learn how to pour a drink. I'll have soda water this

[134]

evening to amuse you – my usual tipple is tap water, you know, just flavoured with alcohol.'

'You're teasing, Uncle,' Billy laughed.

'The point is, remember, always keep your whisky weak.'

'Will you smoke?'

'I smoke too much nowadays. But who cares? A little of what you fancy does you good – so a lot may be better for you.'

'Can I light your cigarette?

'Nurse wouldn't be pleased with me – I'm getting you into wicked ways.'

'When I'm grown up I'll drink and smoke in spite of her and Father.'

Billy stopped, putting his hand to his mouth and looking uncomfortable, if not sad.

'Come and sit down,' Ivo growled, moving over to a sofa by the fire and indicating a nearby armchair for Billy, who perched on the edge.

'About your father, my brother – it's rotten luck – but there it is – least said, soonest mended.' He drank some whisky and puffed and exhaled a cloud of scented smoke. 'I'll help you with your inheritance.'

'Will you, Uncle?'

'Of course. And I've got Pibbs calling in this evening – I promise you we'll arrange a suitable funeral for your father.'

'Do I have to be at the funeral?'

'Oh yes. You've inherited a lot of responsibilities along with all the money in the world. You have to do the right thing now and behave like a duke. Have you got a morning coat?'

'What's that?'

'The sort of tailcoat to wear at a funeral. You'd better go into Carlisle tomorrow and get the clothes you'll be needing.'

'Can we go together?'

'I'll be too busy – I'll be working for you here. You go with Zeals – he knows the score. You like him, don't you?'

'Would Nurse have to come?'

'No – not if you don't want her to.'

'I don't.'

'Well, tell her that I said you could go alone with Zeals. I don't see why you shouldn't do as you please within reason.'

'Because I'm so rich, Uncle Ivo?'

[135]

'Partly.'

'But all the money in the world isn't mine, is it?'

'No, I was gilding the lily – exaggerating – you mustn't take me too seriously.'

'Are you rich, Uncle?'

'That's a leading question.'

'What? Are you?'

'No. You're the rich man in his castle, I'm the poor man at your gate. Don't worry, Billy, I'm joking.'

'You're not really poor?'

'Let's change the subject, shall we?'

'But I wouldn't be pleased if you were poor and I was rich, Uncle – it wouldn't be fair.'

'No – I agree, though some wouldn't. Anyway, Horace Reed's arriving soon – he'll tell us what's what and read your father's will and possibly look after my interests as well as yours. We'll see. But I won't forget your ideas of fairness and unfairness. Come along – your supper's served, Billy.'

'Will you take me shooting, Uncle?'

'Yes, after the funeral, if you come quietly now.'

'And fishing?'

'Yes, as soon as possible. Come on – we'd better not let Aunt Beatrice catch us here.'

The boy immediately stood up. In the hall and on the stairs be began play-fully to cling on to his uncle's arm, and tug at it and bump into him. He was giggling by the time they reached the nursery.

Nurse Tucker, showing disapproval of the merriment, rebuked both of them, saying to Billy: 'I don't think that noise is fitting,' and aside to Ivo: 'He'll be too excited to eat or sleep, milord.'

Ivo replied: 'Don't check the boy – I want him to have his head.' To Billy he added, after they had wished each other good night: 'You can tell Nurse what I want you to do tomorrow.'

On the way downstairs he collected Beatrice, who was supervising the work in the Duke's Apartments, having the mattresses in the bedroom and dressing-room swapped with properly aired ones, and seeing to it that the beds were made with the best linen. He opined that Nurse Tucker was as much use as a sick headache, and together in the drawing-room they received the Reverend Pibbs.

In the next twenty-four hours they both had to take innumerable decisions, social, organizational, respecting the funeral and the part Billy should play in it, about memorial services in Carlisle and possibly in London and the dignitaries who would have to attend, and notices in newspapers and the condition of the mausoleum in the park, and so on.

Horace Reed arrived the following evening; was introduced to his new employer, who was then removed to the nursery to be put to bed; was shown to his room in the Bachelor Wing by a footman who unpacked for him; changed into his evening clothes and at seven-thirty, by appointment, presented himself bearing his black leather attaché case in the drawing-room and was offered a glass of pre-prandial sherry by Lord and Lady Ivo Grevill.

He declined it, but agreed to sit on a straight-backed chair with his attaché case on his knees.

Ivo, standing in front of the fire, said: 'Sir Arthur Bullinger's joining us for dinner, also the two Miss Colquhouns and the Ian Macmurrays. They'll be here shortly. But we'd like to have an outline of my brother's will, then we'll be able to discuss it in the next few days while you're on the spot, and with luck see our future a bit more clearly. Isn't that right, Beatrice?'

She assented, reclining on one of the two William Kent settees at right angles to the fireplace. She was elaborately dressed, held an ornamental fan in her raised white hand, and bent her head in a mildly encouraging gesture in the direction of the solicitor, who as usual looked as if he needed a closer shave.

Having cleared his throat and opened the case and paused, Horace began: 'I hope I have fully conveyed my sympathies, and those of my colleagues at Slater, Gregan and Reed, to both of you in such melancholy circumstances.'

'Thank you, yes,' Ivo acknowledged.

'I myself shall greatly miss the late duke. I respected his prudence and his fairness, and appreciated his courtesy. He salvaged the estate he inherited, and has left it on a firmer financial footing than for many years.'

'Certainly, yes.'

'He was intending to alter his testamentary dispositions before he died. But perhaps that's neither here nor there. As it is, his will of some four years ago stands.'

Horace opened the case and produced the document, complete with pink string and appended red sealing-wax seals.

'The Duke's will is visibly short,' he continued, exhibiting it. 'He left

[137]

bequests and gratuities amounting to approximately half a million pounds. His residences, lands, chattels and the residue of the fortune he bequeathed to his son, to be held in trust until Lord Medringham – as he was – attains his majority, twenty-one years of age. The chosen trustees are Lord Deveraux and Brigadier Dimmick.'

'Yes? Go on.'

'That is all, Lord Ivo, apart from a note referring to yourself and the customary legal provisions.'

'What's the note?'

'May I read it to you?'

'Yes!'

'The Duke's own words were as follows: "With apologies to my brother Lord Ivo Grevill, I hereby state that in my opinion as temporary guardian of the family's treasure I can leave him nothing. He has already received very much more money than the conventional younger son's portion, and he long ago sold the furniture and works of art he inherited from our mother. My hope is that he, on reflection, will agree with my reluctance to deplete and to some extent divide the estate of the dukedom, or, rather, my determination to keep what little remains of the estate intact. I also hope that he will soon find steady and remunerative employment."'

'What's he talking about, "the little that remains of the estate"?'

'In the last four years, since the Duke drew up his will, the estate has flourished remarkably, Lord Ivo. Partly for that reason, his grace thought of redrafting the will itself, his list of wishes and I daresay the note too. He had an access of wealth at his disposal. But of course even today the estate is neither large nor rich in comparison with what it used to be.'

'It's a damned sight richer than I am, I can tell you that!'

'I was speaking relatively, Lord Ivo.'

'How dare my brother cut me out – I'll take this will to law, you know – you shouldn't have let him do it – you were meant to be acting for me as well as for him! But you lawyers are only interested in your damn notes of fee.'

'I'm sorry that you should think so ill of me, Lord Ivo.'

'Well, I damn well do! I've never been treated so shabbily in my whole life!'

'Mr Reed,' Beatrice interposed. 'Mr Reed, may I call you Horace?'

'Please.'

'Horace, then, will you tell us if our existing financial arrangements and agreements are affected by the death of my brother-in-law?'

'They are not and yet they are, Lady Ivo. Such a contradiction happens to be an accurate comment on the state of your affairs. Financially, all is as it was before you were bereaved. But to the best of my knowledge you are no longer required to vacate Castile House. Brougham, Gelts Abbey and Castile House are at your disposal until the present Duke comes of age. Lord Ivo did not give me a chance to explain: inasmuch as you will have no household expenses for the next dozen or so years, you will be very much better off than you might have been.'

Ivo weighed in: 'Are we Billy's appointed guardians?'

'Not exactly,' Horace replied, shifting in his chair. 'The guardianship will devolve upon you as the Duke's next of kin.'

'Did Walter want me to look after Billy?'

'He left no instruction to the contrary.'

'Horace,' Beatrice began again, 'you said my brother-in-law intended to redraft his will partly because he found himself a wealthier man. What other reason or reasons did he have to redraft it? Was he meaning to appoint a guardian?'

'The answer to your question is no longer relevant, Lady Ivo.'

'Oh but I insist. It would be nice for my husband to know that his brother trusted him to that extent.'

'Certainly I recall the late Duke speaking of Lord Medringham's particular affection for his uncle.'

'My God,' Ivo exclaimed, 'how you lawyers do beat about the bush! Speak up, Horace: was my brother or was he not going to make me Billy's legal guardian?'

'He had finally decided that his son should be a ward of court. I'm sorry, Lord Ivo.'

'Well . . . Well,' Ivo repeated in a thick voice, 'I can't say I am. If only for the boy's sake, I can't be sorry my brother didn't survive to make that bloomer – Billy won't be ruled by the members of your profession, and we'll be able to live in the style we're accustomed to until he kicks us out.'

The door opened and Cox announced: 'Miss Judith Colquhoun and Miss Alethea Colquhoun.'

Ivo stepped forward to welcome the homely middle-aged neighbours.

[139]

Beatrice arose, saying in a brusque undertone to her fellow-trustee of her husband's trust fund, who was also on his feet: 'There's nobody to stop us having the money we asked for now. Please release it immediately – otherwise Lord Ivo's cheques to his creditors may not be honoured.'

Sir Arthur Bullinger arrived without his wife Mildred, who was 'confined to barracks' by her arthritis, and Ian Macmurray with his wife Delia.

The evening passed. Ivo drank heavily. But after the guests had gone Beatrice persuaded him not to air his grievances against his brother or quarrel with Horace Reed, and upstairs she put her hands over her ears when he started cursing, then packed him off to his dressing-room beyond the reception rooms in the Duke's Apartments.

The next two days were increasingly hectic. The house filled up almost to overflowing with relations and family connections, the five Bayneses, the two Deveraux, the High Sheriff and his lady, Brigadier Dimmick with three Dimmick cousins, the Hazzlewoods and others, while present members of the staff of Castile House and Gelts Abbey together with former retainers occupied available servants' bedrooms or camped in some of the halls below stairs and in outhouses. Ivo and Beatrice scarcely saw each other, except across the ever lengthening dining-table in the so-called Grand Dining-room, and were either too preoccupied or too tired to talk much when they had the opportunity. Horace Reed lost himself from early in the morning until late at night in sets of household account books, which he was determined to present in an audited state to the interested parties gathered together, the new Duke's trustees and agents of one sort and another. The boy who was the living focus of all this activity had none of the fun and games with his uncle that he had anticipated; instead he was forced to be polite to countless strangers, summoned hither and thither to be kissed and hugged and patted and petted and pitied, and had to pretend he was sadder to have lost his father than he actually felt. Although spared the ordeal of the inquest, he had bad dreams of injury and death when or if he slept, grew paler with darker shading round his eyes, and his breathing threatened another of his asthmatic crises.

The evening before the funeral, Cox knocked on the door of Ivo's dressing-room, was admitted by Zeals and delivered a message from Nurse Tucker to the effect that she wondered whether the Duke might be excused attendance at the obsequies, and could just appear at the subsequent social gathering.

Ivo's reply was negative.

[140]

To Cox and Zeals he grumbled: 'The boy must learn to do his duty. I won't have him mollycoddled by that woman.'

He would not have broken the rule of never slanging one servant to other servants if he had not again partaken of a couple of whiskies and water too many.

At ten-thirty on the morning of the funeral the house-party assembled in the drawing-room, ante-room and gallery, the connecting doors having been thrown open. The trio of chief mourners joined the rest and a respectful hush descended. Billy in stick-up collar and black tails looked ill and had to take a strange heaving breath every so often. Ivo's appearance was contradictory, at once smart and hungover, his countenance saturnine and liverish and his bearing haughtily upright. Beatrice wore a black picture-hat with stretched veil, a dress with lace round her neck, a double row of the famous Grevill pearls which she had extracted from the strong-room, a belt that accentuated her shapeliness, and the prettiest buttoned and buckled boots peeping out from under her sweeping skirts.

Ivo soon announced: 'We should be going. Remember that the chapel's always cold, and we're walking up to the mausoleum after the service. I hope you'll be warm enough. The weather's not bad, thank God.'

They drifted into the hall. Lady's-maid Mary helped Beatrice into her overcoat and handed her gloves and feather boa and a stylish furled umbrella. Zeals had coats, top-hats and sticks ready for his master and his master's nephew. Cox, footmen and maids assisted visiting ladies and gentlemen to find and to don their outer garments. A procession formed, led by the Duke walking between Lord and Lady Ivo, and advanced through the outer hall, the business room of the deceased, the orangery and up the steps into the gallery of the chapel, where a fine burned in the grate. Extra chairs had been introduced into this place reserved for the family's worship, and now seventeen people crammed into it.

Valentine Deveraux and Ronald Dimmick, who were reading the lessons, and Sir Cedric Byrch, High Sheriff, who had offered to pronounce the eulogy, were in the right-hand front pew down below. A number of pews behind them had been reserved for gentry, and a similar number of pews on the left-hand side of the aisle for senior estate staff. Lower orders of workers and members of the public sat and stood at the back of the church. Ian Macmurray and Saddlecombe, the two ushers, were marshalling latecomers in the area

[141]

beneath the gallery. Bolder members of the congregation stared over their shoulders and up at the important narrow-shouldered boy behind and in all senses above them, while the organ played lugubrious music.

The coffin of the late Duke had lain in state in the chapel overnight, but had been removed before the funeral, leaving only the catafalque in the area between the choir-stalls. The solid wooden construction, reserved for the usage of defunct Grevills, whereas the coffins of commoner parishioners rested on a pair of trestles, had been draped in the traditional deep blue velvet coverlet embroidered with the tiger's head crest and mottos of the family in gold and silver thread. Wreaths and bunches of flowers placed around the base, and great displays of flowers on the altar and alongside it, culled from the gardens and glass-houses of Brougham and Castile House by order of Lady Ivo, who had also bought from the florists of Carlisle and London, wafted their scents like incense on the mote-filled air.

The music changed. Mr Mays, organist and schoolmaster, launched into a still gloomier march. The children of the choir in their high-necked surplices, then the sopranos, tenors and basses, the verger and Mr Pibbs paraded up the aisle ahead of the four beefy undertakers shouldering the oak coffin with best brass handles. By the sweat of their brows, in a basic manner of speaking, the undertakers lowered the coffin on to the catafalque, placed and somehow fixed one particular wreath on the lid, and as discreetly as their rustic bulk allowed withdrew to sit on chairs in a cubby-hole under the pulpit.

Billy had not seen the coffin – any coffin – before. He had not been required to pay his respects to the deceased father who had frighteningly spent last night in the chapel. Now the sight of the wooden box and the idea of its contents shocked him into breathing with more difficulty. He gasped and rattled and sat down or collapsed on his chair. Ivo and Beatrice exchanged a glance, his indicating with a scowl a refusal to take any notice of the boy's distress, hers indicating with a resigned gesture of her head that one of them had to try to be helpful; whereupon she sat on her chair next to Billy's and patted him on the back in a gingerly manner.

'Do you want to go back to the house?' she hissed in his ear.

He shook or flapped his hand as if to say no.

'Are you all right, will you be all right?'

He nodded.

'How long do your attacks last?'

[142]

He could not answer.

She urged him to remain seated, and he, if more because the flesh was weak than the spirit was willing to obey her, did so throughout the service. It was embarrassing and pitiable, the rattling sound that accompanied the prayers and addresses and filled the sacramental silences.

But during the singing of the final hymn, 'He who would valiant be,' Billy raised his head and seemed to breathe more easily. After the blessing, when the undertakers reappeared and clumsily manhandled the coffin on to their shoulders, Ivo, standing, bent down and asked him if he would rather not walk up to the mausoleum.

'No – yes – I want to,' he wheezed.

They descended from the gallery to the public porch of the chapel. Mr Pibbs was waiting for them there, and, after greetings were abbreviated by the verger's warning that the exodus of congregation could no longer be restrained, set off on the path through the graveyard. Billy by himself, top-hat on the back of his head, white-faced and black-clothed, stumbled along behind the vicar, in front of his uncle and aunt and the mass of mourners, and between the lines of people who had not been able to squeeze into the chapel or had come to see the sight or represented newspapers. Sympathetic cries were uttered; hands reached out to the small lonely figure; a cheeky photographer behind a tripod shouted out a request for him to stop still; the regimental band of the Grevill Rifles struck up in the roadway; and the horses in the shafts of the hearse, startled by the noise, attempted to rear and bolt, stamping and neighing.

The coffin with its single wreath still in place was already in position in the extraordinary vehicle known as the Grevill Quadriga. It was antiquated, more than a hundred years old, drawn Roman-style by four horses abreast, open-sided, having a shiny black-painted tin canopy crowned by nodding black ostrich plumes and supported by brass pillars at the corners; and was used only for the funerals of the dukes of Brougham and Castile and their issue, otherwise being stored under dust-sheets in one of the coach-houses. The coffin on a black velvet platform was held in place by brass arms ending in creepily sculpted miniature hands.

The band marched off; the four excited carriage horses with more ostrich feathers on their heads jerked the swaying hearse forward until checked by black-clad coachman Bailey and a couple of stable lads hanging on to their

[143]

bridles; Mr Pibbs, Billy and the Ivo Grevills pursued; and a crowd of perhaps two hundred brought up the rear, silently straggling and straying, some bearing tributes of flowers.

The way was past the front of the house, along the drive, then branching on to the steep grassy track that led to the circular copper-domed seventeenth-century folly on a hill, in which lay the mortal remains of the Grevills of yesteryear.

The procession took a quarter of an hour to reach the steps of the mausoleum, from which Mr Pibbs, having waited for everyone to gather round in an approximate semi-circle, spoke the somewhat inapplicable words of the usual grave-side prayers. The undertakers again shouldered the coffin and bore it up the steps and through the high mausoleum doorway. The chief mourners, following, entered the cold windowless dim round chamber, most of the shelved spaces in the wall of which housed leaden caskets of different sizes. The coffin was shoved into an empty space, a last prayer was said, and the ceremony ended.

Ivo said to Billy: 'You did well.'

The boy managed to smile up at him.

'Did you like the look of the wreath we got you?' his uncle asked, pointing at it.

Billy nodded.

'We wrote on the card "With sorrow from your affectionate son". That was about right, wasn't it?'

'What did you write on yours, Uncle Ivo?' the boy inquired as if in hope of finding a resemblance between himself and his hero.

'There was no wreath of mine,' Ivo growled, adding in a softer voice: 'Thank Mr Pibbs and the undertakers!'

Billy duly did as he was told.

An undertaker promised to make a nice lead casket for the Duke his father to rest in.

'Have all these boxes got bodies inside?' Billy asked the man.

'Oh yes, your grace, though probably not what we might call bodies by now,' the man replied.

Billy took this information badly: he was overcome by a mixture of surprise, horror, exhaustion and asthma. The facts of death, the things he had not known about this morgue-like building, the possibility that his uncle was cross with him for unknown reasons, combined together to cause him to cough and retch. Beatrice with assistance from Mr Pibbs helped him out of the mausoleum and down through the crowd to where vehicles were lined along the drive to return mourners to the house for luncheon. He was bundled into one, and Nurse Tucker turned up and got in with him and gave urgent instructions to the driver. Ivo came swinging downhill and joined his wife.

She said: 'He's very poorly, you know.'

Ivo glanced at her, but could not see her eyes or her expression through the veil.

Spring seemed to have respectfully held itself back until the Duke of Brougham and Castile was laid to rest in his mausoleum. In the days following the funeral the temperature rose, and most of winter's traces were chased away by sunshine and gentle zephyrs. The greens of new grass and burgeoning leaves replaced the ochre tints in the park, and early blossoming trees splashed the landscape with white and pink. Although the great spread of snowdrops on the wooded slopes beyond the lake had withered, an equivalent expanse of daffodils now showed on the ground reaching down to the water's edge. Within the house, the lower sashes of particular windows in the drawing-room, the library and the Chinese dining-room were raised to their full six-foot extent, thus giving access to the West Front terrace. The sounds of spring were audible in these suddenly airy rooms, birdsongs, the echoing tap of woodpeckers, the clapping of the wings of amorous pigeons, the hilarious quacking of duck and weird cries of waterfowl, and the buzz of reviving insects.

Billy, the Billy Medringham whose health had suffered from his transmogrification into Billy Brougham, was no doubt helped to recover from his asthmatic attack by the pleasant weather. He had an incentive to be out and about, reunited, engaged in sporting activity and having unwonted fun with his Uncle Ivo. Moreover, he had never liked the room with sealed windows and double doors along the nursery passage, reserved for his bouts of illness and the prescribed treatment thereof, the permanently boiling kettle, for instance, which was supposed to steam open his constricted breathing apparatus.

Neither his uncle nor his aunt visited him there. Ivo announced flatly that he could not abide a sickroom, and Beatrice excused herself on the grounds

[145]

that she might infect the invalid with some germ. They confined their attention to sending a few messages upstairs and, in spite of their busy schedules, to waiting to speak to Dr Bennett after his various visits.

The doctor had first reported to them in the privacy of the business room in the late afternoon of the day of the funeral. He was in his sixties, countrified and bluff, and had attended the bedsides of Grevills for years.

Having been introduced to Lady Ivo, he congratulated her husband on marrying such a handsome creature, uttered his customary pleasantry to the effect that he thanked the good God all his patients were not so healthy as Lord Ivo Grevill had been in youth, and apologized for having failed through pressure of work to pay his respects to the late Duke.

'I was also sorry to miss the splendid wake I hear you laid on,' he added.

'The occasion was rendered doubly sad for us by Billy being taken ill,' Beatrice said, switching the subject from the frivolous to the serious aspects of the day.

'Of course,' Dr Bennett agreed in a contrite manner. 'Asthma's an alarming disease for all concerned. I'm afraid the young Duke has inherited his mother's lungs. The hope is that he'll grow out of his weakness.'

'What about now?' Ivo asked.

'He'll pull through. He's not so ill as he may have seemed. His constitution's quite tough, and he's well looked after. I'll call in tomorrow. You have no cause to worry, I assure you both.'

Dr Bennett referred to medication which Nurse Tucker understood and would administer, and mentioned other professional visits he still had to make.

'Dukes take precedence,' he joked. 'My common or garden patients will be wondering what's become of me.'

The Grevills let him go.

The next day Dr Bennett reported a marked improvement in Billy's condition.

'He's on the mend, just as I expected, I'm glad to say. No damage done, though I'd like him to stay in bed and continue the treatment for another forty-eight hours at least. Poor fellow, he can't wait to be out in the sun, and I don't blame him.'

'Is he likely to have another attack, Doctor?' Beatrice inquired.

'Oh yes – some time – his condition's chronic, I'm afraid.'

'What should we do if or when he's ill?'

[146]

'Rest in a warm room with an even temperature is my prescription. Shield him from draughts and night air. But Tucker will be remaining in charge for the time being, I trust. She's a good nurse and is fully equipped with medicines. In my opinion the Duke isn't fit enough for school as yet, or for that matter to be far from home.'

Dr Bennett continued to call at Brougham until Billy was back in the nurseries. His final report to the Grevills was optimistic.

'You can see him now without worrying that he'll pick up an infection, Lady Ivo. He's no more likely to contract an infection than any of us are – he's warded off the germs that I may have been carrying round with me, after all; and I do believe he must be allowed to live his life dangerously. He's lucky to have such a conscientious aunt, but I don't see why normal business shouldn't be resumed immediately. Perhaps try to keep him indoors if the weather should change for the worse.'

'Oh yes,' Beatrice chimed in gratefully. 'You've been such a comfort, Doctor. But I think we have another question, haven't we, Ivo? Is darling Billy in real danger?'

'Frankly, we know too little about asthma, Lady Ivo. My answer would have to be: perhaps. I'm sorry – don't be alarmed. He's not in danger provided a steady tenor of existence is maintained. Shocks and emotional upsets are bound to be bad for him. Moderation is his lifeline; extreme experience of any kind, exceptional pressure, could conceivably be fatal. Losing his mother was a severe blow, the more so as his father was such a self-sufficient man. But I have the feeling he's struck lucky – he has yourself and Lord Ivo to care for him – I'm looking foward to his maiden speech in the House of Lords.'

While Dr Bennett came and went, and the invalid wheezingly chafed at his isolation in what his nurse called the sanatorium, members of the house-party for the funeral, including Horace Reed, departed; but Lord Deveraux and his lady and Brigadier Dimmick extended their stay.

Important engagements in London were cancelled by the two executors and trustees of the late duke's estate, and then more cancellations were telegraphed through daily, as these gentlemen marked time until a nine-year-old boy was deemed to be capable of granting them an audience.

The Grevills were not slow to seize their opportunity: Ivo and Beatrice by tacit agreement, or rather Beatrice and Ivo in that order, concentrated on and courted the appointed arbiters of at least the next twelve years of their destiny.

They took trouble to please Valentine Deveraux and deaf old Ronald Dimmick, arranging a night's stay at Gelts, shoots of vermin there and again at Brougham, and the loan of guns to the visitors and fishing-rods. They made expeditions, they had picnics out and invited people in to meals to amuse them; and Beatrice deigned to spend time alone with Augusta Deveraux, who was as strait-laced and sanctimonious as her husband.

The trip to Gelts proved the value of what they were doing. Passing Garrack Spur and stopping to peer down at Garrack Tarn, where Walter had met his end, they were able to express their affection for a brother, a brother-in-law and his trustees' dear friend, in whose memory they promised to pursue the same modest policies in respect of the expense of living in his houses. When Valentine and especially Augusta Deveraux raised their eyebrows at the resident butler, cook, kitchen staff and housemaids of Gelts, and at Thark and the other gamekeepers, Ivo explained that Walter had been dead set on maintaining the reputation of the house and the shooting, on keeping the place in a state of permanent readiness to receive his guests, also to provide Billy with a sporting education, not to mention the fact that it continued to offer the only employment in the area.

Valentine passed the remark that it might be considered extravagant to run so luxurious an outpost of empire for the benefit of a young boy who had two other homes with a total of some hundred and fifty rooms.

Ivo repeated: 'I've told you what Walter wanted, and we want for his sake.' He turned for corroboration to Beatrice: 'Isn't that so?'

She agreed and added: 'Speaking personally, I don't think I could manage Gelts as well as the other two houses, if I had to open it up and warm it and get servants here every time Billy felt like paying a visit. You know that Walter employed his brother in a supervisory capacity? I suppose that Ivo, now he can count on my assistance, might waive the fee he has always received, if strict penny-pinching is going to be the rule in future.'

Ivo addressed himself directly to the trustees: 'We're thinking of Billy. But you may choose to do without my services, and take the blame if or when Gelts falls to pieces.'

The polite and almost inevitable answer was negative, which enabled Beatrice to say to Ivo: 'There! I was sure the trustees would be sensible and decide in your favour – remember to tell Horace!'

Such efforts to influence the new holders of the strings of the ducal purse were a strain. Common ground between hosts and guests was hard to find; and the Grevills were keen to be left alone and in possession of the estate – in that possession which might be nominal and temporary but was nine-tenths of the law.

Perhaps a sort of tension was the reason why Ivo did not attempt to exercise his marital rights, and was subliminally relieved that Beatrice left him in peace in his dressing-room in the Duke's Apartments. Even as they worked together with the same end in view, namely to make the most of not having Walter to boss them about and complicate their lives, a new barrier formed between them – they were unusually reserved and restrained, and the more their minds seemed to meet the less they looked straight at each other.

On Billy's first afternoon on his feet and fully dressed, they went to the nursery to fetch him down to drawing-room tea.

Nurse Tucker protested, and a few hard words were exchanged.

'I don't think the Duke's ready for a social occasion, milord,' she said.

'Mind your own business,' Ivo retorted savagely, as if to relieve pent-up feelings.

'The Duke's ever so delicate, milady,' Nurse persisted.

Beatrice stared at her, then stated: 'We are in the position of the Duke's parents, and not to be obstructed. Do you understand?'

Nurse bowed her head.

'Come on, Billy,' Ivo summoned, and the boy skipped across and followed him out of the room.

Beatrice rubbed it in: 'Never, Nurse – do you understand?'

'Yes, milady.'

On the stairs Billy said to Ivo: 'You gave her what-for, didn't you, Uncle?'

Ivo grunted in answer to this boyish sally, but Beatrice asked: 'Why – aren't we fond of Nurse Tucker, Billy?'

'I don't like having to sleep in the night-nursery,' he mumbled cryptically.

'Do you mean you and Nurse still sleep in the same bedroom?'

'Yes, when I'm not ill – and she snores.'

Ivo now interjected: 'It's only because of his asthma, Beatrice. She may snore and be annoying, but she's good at her job.'

Beatrice spoke to Billy: 'Aren't you too old to sleep in the same room as a woman?'

'Yes, I am. But Father made me.'

[149]

'We can change that. We're in charge now. Aren't we, Ivo?'

Ivo instead of responding to her query spoke to Billy: 'You know who you're going to meet this afternoon, don't you?' – and proceeded to explain.

They arrived in the drawing-room where tea at Brougham was usually served. Billy's trustees were soon asking him questions more or less unanswerable by someone of his age – would he abide by their rulings; what were his interests and aspirations; would he object to carrying on with tutors at home; did he realize how great his expectations were, and that he had become a public figure obliged to set an example; and would he be prepared to regard his uncle and aunt as his new father and mother?

He was breathing so badly by the time Augusta Deveraux prescribed a supplement to his diet of raw beef sandwiches, and Ronald Dimmick launched into a recommendation of a career in the army, that Ivo interrupted and told Billy to say goodbye to everyone.

Out in the staircase hall, alone with Billy, he said: 'Sorry – that wasn't quite the thing.'

'It'll be nice now, won't it, Uncle?'

'Don't you miss your father?'

'Do you, Uncle Ivo?'

'You go and get better as quickly as you can!'

The boy pulled himself up the first flight of stone stairs by means of his hands on the gilded banister rail.

Where the stairs divided he turned and smiled down at his uncle, who called in an echoing voice: 'We'll make you better – good night!' – and turned abruptly to rejoin the guests.

The next day Lord and Lady Deveraux and the Brigadier left Brougham, and in the afternoon Billy spent an hour fishing with his uncle. The day after that they went shooting with the four-ten and Billy bagged a rabbit. And in the next fortnight, as the weather continued to favour life out of doors, Ivo was prevailed upon to give instruction in sportsmanship. Gradually Billy's brown eyes fringed with black lashes regained the pellucid sparkle of childhood, and his pallor was modified by a light and faintly freckled tan. No doubt, thanks to written orders conveyed by Zeals to Nurse Tucker, he also benefited from sleeping on his own.

But now people seeking favours from the young duke or from the representative of the old one – the duke in all but name – beat a path to the doors of

Brougham. Neither guests in the ordinary sense, nor necessarily gentry, they were the leaders of deputations, the presidents of charities, the chair-persons of committees, the managing directors of businesses, and so on. They had received assistance of one sort and another from Walter, and were hoping to continue to receive it from or through the medium of his brother. The period of mourning was almost rudely interrupted. Perhaps the bigwigs of Carlisle could not postpone discussion of the Service of Remembrance they were plan-ning, and had to insist on talking to a member of the family as soon as they decently could. But the pleaders of causes and the grinders of axes did not delay for much longer.

To start with Ivo was pleased to be the centre of the attention of so many strangers. He welcomed them, he insisted on their joining himself and his wife for meals: they filled the present communicative vacuum between himself and Beatrice. It flattered him to replace Walter in the post of president of a variety of institutions, and to sit at the desk in Walter's business room, pretending he had the power to do more than refer petitioners for finance to Horace Reed.

They repaid his favour unknowingly in another way. They rescued him from having to play with his nephew on every single afternoon. He liked to be loved by Billy. There had been enormous satisfaction in being more loved by Billy than Billy's own father was. He had enjoyed his role of occasional avun-cular hero, the dashing horseman, crack shot, general sport and dandy who put Walter in the shade, and was obviously worshipped by the latter's son. And he intended to carry on as before when he had to switch from being just an uncle to being in the position of a father – he meant to be better at it than Walter. But second and third thoughts brought home to him the changes in their relationship. He was less at ease with Billy, and more bored by having to stand and watch while the boy fished inexpertly and missed sitting rabbits with the four-ten. His visitors therefore gave him an excuse to delegate his paternalistic duties to Zeals or to one of Thark's gamekeepers summoned over from Gelts.

Even so, restlessness asserted itself. After six weeks, after two months, he was well aware that he had never stayed put in one place in the country for so long. He himself was doing none of the sporting things he was accustomed to and excelled at, and on some days hardly got out into the open air. He was fed up with what he called pen-pushing. The excitement of finding the three grand seats of the family were at his disposal, the relief of never again being cross-

examined, judged and sentenced by Walter, had evaporated, and an unspeci-
fied frustration, combined with novel anxieties, darkened the back of his mind.

His consumption of alcohol had not moderated. He was drinking not only
more whiskies and water, but, breaking with habit and flouting self-discipline,
wines and brandy in the middle of the day. He may have felt that he required
relaxation however obtained. The patience he had to exercise in attempting to
emulate Walter did not come naturally. Concealing his impotence in a worldly
sense was to go against the grain. His peppery temper grew hotter, not depend-
able, and apt to flash out at servants. He would sit scowling and brooding at
the head of the dining-room table, in moods as black as his looks, until his
guests forced him to remember his manners and he would talk and laugh
louder than he had in his soberer past.

Occasionally he would be forthcoming to Beatrice inasmuch as he fired
impersonal exclamations at her. He would see visitors off and say to his wife:
'God, how deadly!' He had noticed her aloof attitude to Billy and Billy's nervy
reactions, and in throwaway sentences offered her a mixture of criticism and
threat: 'It wouldn't hurt to kiss him good-night!' or 'He'll hate you if you're
not careful.' He revealed the direction of his thoughts or his wishes by saying:
'I'm getting out of here – let's go to London.' And again: 'How Walter put
up with this sort of life, God alone knows!'

She did not answer back. Possibly they both were, or had been, too busy to
indulge in inessential confabulation. She was also sought after by local wor-
thies, who would come to Brougham to beg her to preside over the Women's
Knitting Circle and suchlike. And any hours she had to spare she spent going
through the contents of the strong-room and discussing the redecoration of the
house and alterations to the gardens with Saddlecombe. Judging by appearances, life after Walter's death – in a manner of speaking – suited her quite
well. She had scope for her grasp of practical matters, and her facial contours
lost some of their sharpness and acquired a smoother authority.

She made no amorous move in her husband's direction. Although history
proved that she was not deterred by any form of Ivo's resistance to her charms,
and that she was capable of reversing his deepest disinclination, she seemed to
have decided to wait. It was definitely not that either of them had ceased to be
interested in the other. They may not have touched, but they watched as well
as waited, they watched each other nonetheless closely if out of the corners of
their eyes, and exchanged emotion covertly, he by his volcanic statements

[152]

which told only a fraction of the story, she by her provocative stares and unhelpful silences.

The crisis they could have been waiting for shared the same abrupt and incomplete character as the rest of their recent exchanges.

They had entertained to dinner the Mayor of Carlisle and Mrs Peters and four members of the board of the Chamber of Commerce plus wives, who were keen to hold a garden party at Brougham in the summer and had come to seek permission. Since the guests needed to get home that evening in order to be in their offices on the next day, the Grevills had arranged to eat early, at seven-thirty, and had said their goodbyes by nine. The evening was balmy, and Ivo returned to the drawing-room, which was empty, Beatrice apparently having gone upstairs without bothering to bid him good night. He poured himself one of his whiskies, although he had been drinking brandy a quarter of an hour before, lit yet another Turkish cigarette, and bending his head stepped through the open lower half of one of the drawing-room windows on to the terrace. Night had fallen, but the lights from the house shed a radi-ance, and a certain luminosity was reflected from the shimmering surface of the lake. The hoot of an owl and cry of a waterbird accentuated the quiet-ness.

'Ivo,' Beatrice said.

He jumped. He had not seen her. She was standing by the balustrading, half hidden by one of the statues, and wearing a dark red dress.

His irritable response was: 'You gave me a start.'

She took no notice of his irritation, slowly turned to him, so that her brooch of diamonds scintillated, and announced flatly: 'It's time to go to Castile House.'

'What? Really!'

He was taken aback and annoyed with her for laying down the law.

'We'll take Billy.'

A long pause ensued. He did not look at her.

Then he burst out in his cursing vein: 'I won't have you doing that!'

After another unexpected silence she returned without raising her voice: 'I've sacked Nurse Tucker. Nanny Campion at Castile House can look after him.'

'Nanny Campion's years past it,' he almost shouted at her.

She said: 'Everybody'll hear you.'

[153]

'You shouldn't have done it, Beatrice,' he reproached her, adding inconsequently: 'No – no!'

She was brisk in reply: 'Don't be stupid. I had every justification. Nurse Tucker's a maddening female, and holds Billy back in my opinion. Good night,' and she walked straight past him and into the house.

He remained on the terrace for half an hour. Then he had yet another whisky. At ten-thirty he told Cox to lock up and repaired to the Duke's Apartments.

When he entered Beatrice's bedroom she was instantly ready for him.

In the morning, Zeals, knowing his master well enough not to speak too soon, waited until his lordship had shaved, bathed, dressed and was ready to go down to breakfast before imparting the news that Nurse wanted a word.

Ivo frowned, took a last look at his reflection in the cheval-glass, and muttered: 'I can do nothing for her.'

'It's to say goodbye, milord, and she'd be grateful.'

'Oh – very well – ten-thirty in the business room.'

'I'll tell her, milord.'

At the appointed hour Nurse Tucker duly knocked on the door of the business room and was asked to come in.

She wore a dress, not her nursing attire, and her face was red, her grey hair disarrayed, and her eyes behind her spectacles watery and angry.

She shut the door and stood by it, while Ivo sat in Walter's desk-chair.

'Milord, her ladyship gave me my notice,' she began.

'I can't interfere in these matters,' he replied.

'The late Duke was pleased with my work, he was always saying how pleased he was.'

'Saddlecombe will acknowledge that in your reference and see you get the right amount of money.'

'I'm not one for money, milord. I've my savings and a house of my own to go to, thank heaven. It's Billy – it's the present Duke that worries me.'

'He's better, isn't he?'

'I can't see that London's the place for him, milord. The dust and the fogs couldn't do him any good. He won't grow stronger in London – and I was determined to let you know what I think, though her ladyship said I shouldn't.'

'What you shouldn't have done is displease my wife. By quarrelling with her you've left me no alternative except to take Billy down to Castile House. We couldn't leave him here. He may not be long in London and Nanny Campion will keep an eye on him.'

'Beg pardon, milord, my disagreement with her ladyship arose because she was so set on taking him to town. She sacked me for saying it would be a mistake. Her idea about London came first, not after I displeased or disagreed with her.'

'Is that true?'

'I always tell the truth. I do, whatever anyone else may say.'

'Oh – well – I'll talk to her ladyship – but it makes no difference.'

'I still can't see why she's determined to have Billy in London. She could have left him here with me, like the late Duke did. He would have been safe.'

'Goodbye, Nurse. When are you leaving us?'

'This evening – by the night train. Her ladyship wished me to go as soon as possible.'

'Did she? Well – thank you – I'm sorry.'

'It's mutual, milord. Goodbye.'

A quarter of an hour after this interview ended, Ivo rang the bell and instructed a footman to find and send along Zeals. He then paced the floor.

Zeals, entering the business room, inquired: 'Milord?'

Ivo stopped and seemed to remember something and said: 'Oh – Zeals – Nurse Tucker won't be on duty in the nursery later today and tonight. I think the Duke should have somebody within range to call upon in emergency.'

'That's right, milord.'

'You two get on together, don't you?'

'We do. He's a good lad.'

'Would you mind sleeping in a room near his nursery?'

'How long would it be for?'

'Not long. We're going south. We'll be at Castile House tomorrow or the day after. I can't leave him unprotected.'

'Who'll be seeing to the Duke in London, milord?'

'Well – Nanny Campion temporarily – that's the idea.'

'Is she up to it?'

[155]

'Until we find a replacement.'

'I wouldn't want the Duke to come to harm.'

'No – of course not. Will you do as I ask, Zeals?'

'What happens if the Duke's taken ill?'

'You could come to me or her ladyship.'

'Yes, milord.'

'Does that mean you will sleep along the nursery passage?'

'Just in the meanwhile, milord. Shall I pack for London?'

'Thank you – yes.'

'Shall we be taking Topper to London?'

'Stop asking questions, Zeals! I'll give you my instructions in due course. I've too damn much on my mind at present. That'll be all.'

Zeals withdrew.

Ivo hesitated indecisively, then marched out of the business room, crossed the hall and the staircase hall, and mounted the white stone stairs with the centred red carpet two at a time and almost ran into Beatrice descending on the half-way landing.

'I was coming to talk to you,' he said in his almost threatening tone of voice.

'Not here,' she replied, proceeding downstairs with her husband following.

They entered the octagonal ante-room between the library and the morning-room.

Beatrice said: 'Shut the door,' and when he had done so: 'What is it?'

'You engineered this whole business with Tucker. She was bound to be against Billy living in London. When she protested you were able to sack her.'

'But Ivo, you've been every bit as irritated by her as I have. Anyway, what does it matter? We can find another nurse, if that's what Billy needs – and a better one in London than in Carlisle.'

'You've got it neatly worked out, haven't you?'

'Why are you complaining?'

'I've arranged for Zeals to sleep in a room near Billy tonight.'

'What on earth for?'

'In case the boy should be frightened on his own.'

'I don't think Zeals would be much of a comfort, except maybe for horses.'

'It's no joke, Beatrice.'

'Well, stop contradicting youself – you've always said that fussing over Billy

[156]

isn't good for him. Putting first things first, Castile House must be warned of our arrival, and our engagements cancelled.'

'When are you thinking of travelling?'

'When are you? Tomorrow? We can go whenever we feel like it. We can do as we please now.'

'It's such a rush. I'm expected at some function in Carlisle tomorrow – one of Walter's charities has organized a sale of work to raise money.'

'That's beside the point, Ivo. Don't you want to go to London?'

'You know I have wanted to.'

'Everything's ready for Billy at Castile House, and for ourselves – a change of scene couldn't do him any harm, and we need to get away. You'd make Nanny Campion happy by letting her look after the boy. I don't mind decid-ing if you won't: we'll catch the morning train tomorrow. I'll ring for Saddlecombe, shall I?'

He raised no further objections. He gave the requisite orders and retired to the business room to write out telegrams and excusatory letters. Then he went up to the nursery and, interrupting the lesson Mr Pibbs was giving his grace, broke the news. His tentative manner of doing so was in contrast to Billy's excited reaction to the prospect of Zeals acting as nursemaid and a holiday in the metropolis.

In the afternoon he disappointed Billy by breaking a sort of promise to take him shooting – he said he had too much to do; on the other hand he promised to grant Billy's wish not to leave Topper behind at Brougham. Ian Macmurray appeared at tea-time and stayed on to discuss estate business until Ivo had to change for dinner, at which a final group of guests was enter-tained.

The Grevills and their ward spent most of the next day in the first-class compartment reserved for them in the southward-bound train.

Ivo and Billy sat together on one side of the compartment, Beatrice oppo-site and alone. The uncle and nephew whiled away some of the time by chat-ting and making plans. Beatrice's only contributions to the amusement of Billy were to send him along to see her husband's valet and her own lady's-maid in the third class, or to keep Topper company in the luggage van. Otherwise she gazed out of the window, toyed with newspapers, wrote in a notebook, closed her eyes as if sleeping, but opened them disconcertingly to stare across at her fellow-passengers.

[157]

At one moment, after more humdrum topics had been exhausted, Billy asked: 'Uncle Ivo, why aren't you the Duke?'

'Because I'm a younger son,' Ivo replied, 'and younger sons don't count for much in families like ours.'

'But you were Father's brother.'

'Yes!' Ivo's agreement was exclamatory and harsh. 'A lot of good it did me,' he continued, but, relenting somewhat, explained: 'Titles go from father to eldest son – the eldest surviving son of a duke inherits, that's the rule. Brothers only come into the picture if there are no duke's sons or if all the sons have died or disappeared – and if there are no brothers, cousins are next in line.'

'Would you be the Duke if I died or disappeared?'

'You ask some funny questions.'

'But would you?'

'I suppose I would.'

'You'd be better at it than me.'

'Who knows? You haven't shown your paces yet. I expect you'll do well enough.'

'Uncle, if you and I had both disappeared, who'd be the Duke?'

'Nobody – there aren't any male Grevills left, so far as anyone knows. Your father used to discuss the subject with me. The family doesn't seem to breed as it did in olden days – we decided that over the years Grevills have grown tired of procreating, and sick of the whole business.'

'What's procreating?'

'Having children.'

'Won't you have children, Uncle?'

'No.'

'What happens if there aren't any more Dukes of Brougham and Castile?'

'Nothing – the world won't fall apart – dukedoms just cease to be – it's happened often.'

'Isn't it sad?'

'If you think so, you'd better hurry up and stop it happening.'

'Hurry how?'

Ivo shrugged his shoulders.

Beatrice made a startling intervention: 'Can't you talk about something less morbid?' – a question which effectively finished this conversation.

At twelve-forty-five Zeals arrived to lay out the contents of the picnic

[158]

hamper, and at two o'clock he returned to clear up and repack it.

In the course of the afternoon Billy broached the subject of his future.

'How long are we staying at Castile House, Uncle?'

'It depends.'

'Depends on what?'

'Nanny Campion to some extent. She was your father's nanny and mine, you know. She's very old now, perhaps she won't be able to manage you.'

'Would we go back to Brougham if she can't?'

'Yes, probably, provided we've found another, younger nurse to take with us.'

'When can I start school?'

'Is that what you're after?'

'Oh yes.'

'I don't see why you shouldn't start as soon as your health improves. The trouble is that school might be difficult for you with your name – some nasty little so-and-sos might be down on a duke. My grandfather, your great-grandfather, was alive when Walter and I went to preparatory school: Grandfather was Duke, Father hadn't inherited and was Marquess of Medringham, and Walter – your father – was little Lord Grevill, which wasn't too much of a mouthful for the other boys to swallow. You might be happier to be educated at home.'

'I hate being in the nursery, Uncle.'

'It can't be helped at present. We don't want you getting ill. But you'll like Nanny Campion. She's a good old soul. And the nurseries at Castile House are a bit of fun.'

'What do you mean?'

'You can walk out of the day-nursery on to the roof and look down on the people in the street. That part of the roof's flat, it's covered with lead, and it's safe because of the parapet – like a wall at the edge – though your father and I dared each other to stand on top and balance there.'

'How high above the ground is it?'

'Fifty feet or sixty. We'd have been strawberry jam if we'd fallen. The parapet has a pediment in the middle, one of those raised triangular things – it must be ten feet higher than the parapet at its topmost point – and I'd run up and down that. If I hadn't done it at a run, if I'd gone slow and given myself time to think where I was, I would have lost my nerve and my bearings for sure. I don't believe your father ever tackled the pediment. He was always more cautious than me, or more sensible.'

'What did Nanny Campion say when she saw you on the pediment, Uncle?'

'She never did see me. I'd wait until she couldn't see me do it. If she'd caught me in the act, and squeaked and distracted me, I'd have come to grief probably. It was stupid really, but I never could resist a challenge and a risk. There are better occupations in London, I promise you. I spent hours in museums when I was your age. Firearms and natural history were my crazes – which may explain my interest in sport, particularly shooting.'

In the slight pause following this last speech Beatrice directed a prolonged stare at Ivo, which caused him to shift uncomfortably in his seat.

Billy began to ask another question, but Ivo interrupted him.

'Look here, you're not to clamber about on the roof of Castile House, that's an order, understand? Learn from my mistakes, don't do what I did, and you won't go far wrong. Is that clear?'

Billy said yes vaguely, and admitted that he was puzzled by the various family names and titles, and did not see why his being a duke should make his schooling problematical.

Ivo explained as best he could, then packed Billy off to spend more time with Zeals.

Beatrice kept her eyes closed and the train puffed and pulled through the changing landscape.

Eventually they arrived at Euston Station and were met by two conveyances, the coach in charge of Harris for the Duke and the Grevills, and a workaday equipage for servants, dog and luggage.

Introductions of Billy to this crowd of urban employees took place in the hall of Castile House. Beatrice let Ivo shepherd the boy up to the day-nursery, where Nanny Campion embraced her new young charge, shedding a joyful tear and telling him she had a nice hot supper waiting for him, and scolded her old one for having the idea that she was still equal to the task which he had been so optimistic as to expect her to perform.

'I'm too ancient – your telegram gave me such a shock. I would have run off somewhere but for my curiosity – and if I hadn't been silly about every member of your family – and this little lad especially. I'll do it while I can, dearie, and count it an honour, rest assured.' She turned to Billy. 'There there, my dear – we'll be friends, won't we? – as I always have been with this naughty uncle of yours, and I once was with your poor dear father.' To Ivo she added: 'I trust her ladyship's well. Please give her my respects.'

That evening Ivo and Beatrice dined alone for the first time for months. They sat in formal attire at either end of the main dining-room table, which even in its most contracted form put considerable distance between them, and peered at each other through the branches of a pair of the Spanish candelabra. They spoke little. Graves remained in the room for the duration of the meal, and the footmen Albert and Charles carried the food in and out. In fact most of the talk was between Graves, whose length of service entitled him to fill silences with queries appertaining to family matters, and Ivo who was quite pleased to provide answers. When Beatrice rose to leave, her husband stayed to drink port and smoke. A quarter of an hour later he received the message that her ladyship was tired and with apologies had retired for the night.

Beatrice's understandable tiredness after the journey from Cumberland developed into some sort of indisposition, though neither her looks nor her appetite seemed to suffer from it. She complained of feeling achingly limp. She came downstairs late in the morning and for several evenings had her dinner served in her bedroom. She informed Ivo that she would have to refuse invitations from all the people who had been their guests in the period before Walter's death. Her reaction to his stated wish to ask a few old friends to dine was negative: she said she would rather he did not entertain without her, and reminded him that they were still officially in mourning and ought to give purely social entertainment a miss. She saw Billy at lunch-time and tea-time; but never exactly conversed with him; she cross-questioned and ticked him off, and stared at him until he dropped his eyes.

Ivo's restlessness now began to develop into almost another sort of indisposition. Perhaps he and she were indisposed in their different ways for similar reasons. They no longer expressed their feelings in the form of argument and quarrel. He evaded the challenge of her unblinking regard, which seemed to bore into his skull, trying either to extract his thoughts or insinuate her own.

Metropolitan temptations did not help him to relax. He slept at night with the aid of alcohol, but morning again rendered him the quarry of impatience. His leisurely routine became a rush: he hurried through his breakfast, paced the rooms, chain-smoking cigarettes, and bounded up the stairs to greet Billy and excuse himself from further avuncular duties by saying how busy he was.

[161]

He did not like to disappoint the boy, the strain of doing so tightened the screw of his agitation; on the other hand he feared he would be almost physically incapable of walking at Billy's pace, hanging about in museums, answering endless juvenile questions, maintaining a show of unflagging interest and affection. His inclination was not to be too much involved with Billy.

'Sorry, old chap,' he repeated.

'Another day,' he would add to compensate for not being as good an uncle as he had promised to be. 'I'm working on your behalf, doing the work your father did and you'll have to do before long,' he explained inaccurately. 'Zeals will take you and Topper for a walk in Hyde Park. You can go wherever you please with Zeals.'

And bracing himself to withstand first the wistful look on Billy's pale face, secondly Nanny's fond yet forthright grousing to the effect that she and her little Duke were beginning to feel neglected, and thirdly an interview with his wife, he would approach Beatrice's bedroom and knock with self-controlled soft-ness.

They bade each other good-morning, inquired after each other's health, and he would say he had a few important things to deal with and was then going out and would be back to lunch, to which her response would be a dismissive goodbye: their dialogues were becoming ever briefer, and more fraught with undertones of hostility the more they were polite.

The work that kept Ivo and Billy apart, the important things that extricated him from Beatrice's bedroom, were soon done. He armed himself with hat, stick and gloves, and if need be put on his light spring overcoat, and joined the purposeful bustle of the town: it seemed to alleviate his fevered sense of wasting time. He called in at his clubs, not the Cumbria Club any more, he shunned the dimness and dullness of the Cumbria, nor the Club of Clubs, which was out of bounds, but White's or the St James's. He looked for and met his pre-marital cronies, with whom he could talk sport and play billiards or cards for stakes low enough never to have to be revealed to anyone, win or lose.

One day he dared to have a message delivered to Castile House to say he was detained and would not be home for luncheon: he had jibbed at the ordeal of yet another meal for three, at which Billy would talk too much and Beatrice not enough, and the atmosphere was certain to be thick with unpleasant emo-tions.

On returning in the early evening he was informed that her ladyship had

[162]

had her lunch and tea in her bedroom and Billy his in the nursery, and that her ladyship would be grateful if his lordship would leave her undisturbed for the rest of the day.

Ivo ate dinner alone, drawing comparisons between his pointless solitude and the companionship of his fellow-members of clubs, and resenting other facts of his life.

In the morning the Grevills were more conversational than usual.

Ivo demanded in the doorway of Beatrice's bedroom: 'Were you ill yesterday?'

'I'm better today,' she replied.

'You avoided Billy – was that necessary? Why do you avoid him? You might have had lunch with him at least, when I couldn't. I don't believe you've been up to the nursery since we've had him here.'

'He's your nephew – and you can't be bothered with him – why should I?'

'Oh for God's sake! Will you go up and see him soon, and say a word to Nanny?'

She opened her amber eyes wide and stared at her husband, who said as if surrendering or simply to escape: 'I'll be back for lunch today.'

Forty-eight more hours of neither peace nor war elapsed, and Ivo converted his discontent into characteristic action.

He decided not to dine at home. He acted not so much decisively as on an impulse partly rebellious, partly self-indulgent. He did not want to spend the evening with Beatrice, he wanted to continue to play billiards, and eat, drink and be at any rate merrier, with his friendly acquaintance Tommy Ryland at White's. At about six-thirty he therefore despatched a messenger to Castile House bearing news of his intentions.

At nine o'clock his conscience smote him. He felt as if he were betraying his wife for the first time – and was afraid she really might be ill, and that he might be taking unfair advantage of her illness. Yet he was even less willing to face her in recriminatory mood, with some degree of right on her side, and to be beaten metaphorically with the stick of his truancy. He played a last game with Tommy, having instructed the night-porter to find him a cab at ten. When he walked through the portals of Castile House he hoped it was too late for Beatrice to pick a quarrel.

Albert, who had opened the front door, greeted him thus: 'Milord, her ladyship's in the library and wishes to see you.'

[163]

Ivo handed Albert his outdoor accoutrements, crossed the hall with measured and indeed reluctant tread, and was ushered by Albert through the library door.

Beatrice in her evening dress and jewels sat on the small chair beside and beyond the fireplace, in which a hot coal fire burned although the weather was temperate and the room not cold. The lighting of the library was localized, lamps mostly illuminating the reading and writing areas while the merely social seating was left in the relative dark; yet Beatrice's eyes glittered moistly, perhaps reflecting the nearby flames.

Her fiery stare alarmed Ivo, who headed for the whisky decanter to conceal his agitation and gain time, saying: 'Good evening.'

She returned as expected: 'Where were you?' – but in a surprising tone of voice, without rancour, as if absent-mindedly.

'White's,' he replied. 'Sorry – I had to give Tommy Ryland the chance to win back the money he'd lost at billiards.'

'Who won in the end? And what money, Ivo?'

'I did – and it wasn't much money – just chicken-feed. You've been waiting to see me?'

'Yes.'

She stopped. She seemed to try to concentrate. She might be stopping in order to pick the right words.

'What's wrong?' he asked.

'Nothing. Well, not exactly anything. I obeyed your orders.'

She spoke the last sentence with a touch of satire.

'What have you done?' he demanded.

'What have I done? You've done it, not I. You should give me the benefit of the doubt.'

'What the hell is this about?'

'I went up to the nursery this evening.'

'And?'

'Nanny Campion was dozing – asleep – she didn't hear me or know I was there. Nor did Billy.'

'Where was he?'

'Outside – balancing on the parapet – getting half-way to the top of the pediment.'

'What did you do, Beatrice?'

[164]

'The right thing – withdrew – retreated slowly so as not to catch his eye or distract him.'

'He's safe, isn't he?'

'Oh yes. He froze at the half-way mark – I'm sure he lost his nerve – he might have had vertigo or started his attack of asthma – but he overbalanced in the direction of safety or jumped down – I heard him land on the leads, and re-enter the nursery wheezing, and waking Nanny.'

'Did you go in then?'

'No. I would have had to accuse both Nanny and Billy of misconduct, not to say crimes. I was upset by what I'd witnessed and needed to calm down. I crept away. It was such a narrow squeak, Ivo.'

'Shall I tell them off?'

'Nanny will resign if you do. And she suits very well, don't you think?'

'She's too old, I've told you all along.'

'But she has other advantages.'

'True.'

'If you scold Billy, he'll assume I was spying on him, which again wouldn't be good.'

'Are we going to do damn all and let him risk his neck?'

'You shouldn't have put ideas into his head, Ivo.'

'Well, you shouldn't have sacked Nurse Tucker and insisted on bringing Billy to London. I knew it was a mistake.'

'It's too soon to say that.'

'Maybe, yes.

'You want Billy to be a sportsman, don't you? You used to complain of Walter turning him into a namby-pamby. We all have to live dangerously, Doctor Bennett said so.'

'I know.'

'Let's sleep on it, shall we?'

'That might be best,' he conceded.

'There! We're agreed. Now I'll go to bed.'

'Good night.'

'I'll say good night to you upstairs,' she replied.

5

THE asthma that had attacked Billy on the foot-wide steeply sloping pediment crowning the front of Castile House took a turn for the worse.

On the morning following his uncle and aunt's agreement, which, meta-phorically speaking, was sealed in her bedroom, Zeals called his master with the news. He knocked gently and, without waiting to be told to come in, entered the dressing-room, drew the curtains, began to collect yesterday's clothes and shoes for laundering and valeting and to lay out clean silk under-wear, and spoke in a lowered voice.

'Seven-thirty, milord. Are you awake?'

Ivo grunted affirmatively.

'Nanny Campion's been on to me, milord. His grace isn't all that grand.'

'What?'

'It seems to be his grace's breathing, milord. He has trouble that way, I know. Nanny Campion's asking if we should have the doctor.'

'How bad is he? I'd better see for myself.'

'Shall I go for the doctor meanwhile?'

'Yes – it couldn't do any harm – Dr Aubrey Willson in Harley Street – Graves will give you the extact address. If Dr Willson isn't able to return with you, tell him to get here as soon as he can.'

'Very well, milord. What suit will you be wearing?'

'Don't worry about that.'

'Yes, milord.'

Zeals departed. Ivo arose and entered the bathroom, donned his red dressing-gown and slippers, hurried into the passage and hesitated. He turned back and approached his wife's bedroom door, knocked and spoke his name and said it was an emergency, and was asked in.

'What's happened?'

Beatrice sounded sleepy and annoyed.

'Billy's ill. I've sent Zeals for Dr Willson.'

'Is that necessary? It's only asthma, isn't it?'

'Yes. But Nanny's worried apparently. I'm just going to investigate.'

'It's happened before, Ivo. Servants always work one another into a frenzy. Billy's illness is chronic – everybody might as well get used to it. Doctors can't do much for him.'

'I'm going to see him nonetheless, Beatrice.'

'Do as you please,' she retorted. 'But I won't be ready to talk to Dr Willson for at least two hours,' she called after her husband.

Up in the day-nursery, Ivo found Nanny wringing her hands.

'Oh thank goodness, dearie, thank the Lord you're here! Oh it has given me a fright, hearing the boy straining to catch his breath this morning! He wasn't so bad yesterday, or didn't seem to be. But I've never come across asthma, though I did see your mother suffer with her TB. I don't know what to do or where to be. And I'm too old for it, dearie.'

'I've summoned Dr Willson, Nan.'

'Yes, Mr Zeals just popped up to tell me.'

'Shall I look in on Billy?'

'Trying to talk makes him worse – he waved me out of his room – but it might be different with you – he does think the world of you, dearie.'

'I don't want to make him worse.'

'Of course you don't. What a pity! He was getting on so well, we were getting on so well together. But he does have everything to live for, and he's such a brave boy. He aims to be as brave as his uncle, that's what he says – he was saying it yesterday evening.'

'When exactly did he say that?'

'Well – I must have dropped off for a moment, and he came through the french window, he'd been out there on the leads, and I woke with him gasping and saying to me that he wanted to be brave like you are, dearie. He was so determined! It must have been before his supper-time, seven o'clock or there-

[167]

abouts. I was worried by his breathing then. But he promised me it would soon be better. I can't imagine what might have brought on this horrid asthma of his.'

'I'd better shave and dress before Dr Willson arrives.'

'Yes, dearie.'

'If you should see Billy, tell him I was here, but kept out of the way on purpose, so as not to add to his difficulties.'

'I have taken good care of the boy — you'd know if you'd seen more of him. I'm sure I haven't done anything wrong, not knowingly — it's just that I was given no advice.'

'We've been busy, Nan. I'll have to leave you now.'

'Yes, dearie.'

Ivo, back in his dressing-room, managed to make himself presentable even without the assistance of Zeals.

He was eating his breakfast at the smaller table in the dining-room when Dr Willson was admitted into the hall and shown upstairs by Graves.

A quarter of an hour later the London doctor of generations of Grevills, an elderly brisk little man in a tailcoat and striped trousers, reported to Ivo that the patient, largely thanks to medicaments just administered and prescribed, should soon be on his feet again.

Dr Willson corroborated the opinions of Dr Bennett, from whom he had recently heard, and advocated a period of rest in a warm atmosphere for the Duke, and no undue excitement. He accepted the offer of a cup of coffee; referred with regret to the loss recently suffered by Lord Ivo and his family; hoped to have the honour of meeting Lady Ivo in the not too distant future; and left the house, promising to return in forty-eight hours or so, unless required urgently in the meanwhile.

Ivo adjourned to the library and tried in vain to settle to reading the newspapers. He wanted to go out, but was waiting for Beatrice, and in two minds as to whether or not to pay Billy a visit. He paced and smoked, walked across to the stables and back again, and yearned to be elsewhere.

At ten-forty-five the carriage drove round to the front door, and at eleven o'clock Beatrice appeared, smartly dressed for outdoors, although still in mourning.

Ivo called her into the library.

She complied reluctantly, saying: 'What do you want? I'm late already.'

[168]

'Where are you going?'

'Out. Isn't that obvious?'

'I asked you where?'

'Shopping.'

'Answer my question, Beatrice.'

'You don't tell me where you're going, I don't ask you where. Oh all right, I'm going to Frère Jacques to fit clothes.'

'The doctor was here.'

'Oh yes?'

'You're not interested, are you?'

'What do you think? What did he say, Ivo?'

'He wasn't too worried.'

'I told you it was nothing much.'

'Is that the sum of your sympathy for Billy?'

'Don't be stupid. Anyway, what have you done for your nephew today? Have you seen him?'

'I mean to later on.'

'In other words you're in no position to criticize me. And you seem to be missing the point, Ivo. Remember whose side I'm on. Are you lunching in?'

'No.'

'Where will you be?'

'I don't know.'

'Oh well – I'll see you this evening.'

They parted.

Ivo smoked another cigarette indecisively, collected his hat, stick and gloves, and marched out into the dry and intermittently sunny spring day.

At some stage he realized he was walking by a roundabout route in the direction of St James's and his clubs in that area. He therefore changed direction, he was not in the mood to associate with smug successful superior men, he headed for the district north of the Marble Arch in which the Club of Clubs was situated.

He had steered clear of the Club of Clubs for months. Now, gripped by irresolution, he could not resist it. The cheekily warm greeting of the doorman Joe in his grubby uniform, the exclusion of daylight within, suited him. He refreshed himself with drinks before luncheon.

In the dining-room Max Kirby was sitting alone at a table for two. Ivo by

[169]

invitation joined him, and was pleased to have to concentrate exclusively on the sort of conversation he preferred and had been used to in his bachelor days, waggish banter and gossip referring to sport, speculation, good and bad luck, flukes and fraud. He was prevailed upon without much difficulty to share a bottle of wine and then a decanter of port.

Max said he was sorry that Ivo's brother had kicked the bucket, and followed up with the uninhibited query: 'I hope he remembered you in his last will and testament?'

Ivo replied: 'My brother believed that charity begins at home, worst luck.'

'I know there was a son and heir,' Max persisted, 'but he must still be a whipper-snapper. Won't you be in charge of the ducal money-bags in the meanwhile?'

'Unfortunately no.'

'A case of so near and yet so far, is it?'

'Right!'

At half-past-two Max inquired: 'Do you think we might indulge in a game of cards?'

Ivo signalled agreement; Max mobilized two other club members on the way to the Card Room, namely Ian Whitaker and Sean Baydell; the foursome played poker until six o'clock; Ivo lost two thousand pounds, and pleaded with the others to give him a chance to win it back on the following afternoon.

He returned by cab to Castile House via the offices of Slater, Gregan and Reed, through the letter-box of which firm he delivered a note to Horace Reed to say he would be calling in at eleven o'clock sharp the next morning on urgent business.

In the hall of Castile House he asked Albert, who had opened the door for him: 'Where's her ladyship?'

Albert believed her ladyship had already gone up to change for dinner.

Ivo mounted the stairs two at a time to the nursery floor.

Billy in pyjamas and dressing-gown was sitting at the round table in the day-nursery, and eating his supper or trying to in the company of Nanny and Zeals.

When Zeals had excused himself, and Nanny had taken dishes that needed washing up into her little pantry, Ivo said: 'I'm glad you're better.'

'Yes, Uncle – and Mr Zeals is going to give me riding lessons on your old rocking-horse,' Billy replied.

[170]

Ivo stood by the french windows looking across the six feet of flat leaded roof at the waist-high parapet and the slope of the pediment.

'Don't take any risks, will you?'

'No. Uncle, when I've learnt to ride can we go back to Brougham?'

'You'd like that, would you?'

'We can go shooting and fishing at Brougham, and I might begin to ride on a proper pony, mightn't I?'

'I don't see why not. Perhaps we ought to go tomorrow or as soon as you're fit to travel.'

'Oh – not yet, Uncle.'

'I suppose we'll have to wait until we've found someone to watch over you and keep you healthy.'

'Please not another nanny. I want to be at school.'

'You can't have objections to my old Nan.'

'No – I don't – she tells me all the things you used to do when you were my age. But I still want to be at school.'

'You're not in any hurry to get away from London?'

'Well – Mr Zeals is giving me lessons – and he was a jockey, wasn't he? And the rocking-horse doesn't buck or shy, he says. Besides, you had fun in London, didn't you, Uncle? Will you take me to look at guns one day?'

'Don't copy me – I'm the last person you should copy.'

'No, you're not. Do you think I'll ever be like you, Uncle, and as good at things?'

'I sincerely hope you'll be very different – I'm not good at anything much, Billy – you get well and be yourself. I'll have to go and get ready for dinner now.'

'Will I see you again?'

'What? Yes! Yes, of course. Billy, you haven't done anything stupid, have you? You're not planning anything stupid?'

'What do yo mean, Uncle?'

'No – well – never mind.'

They said good night to each other.

Ivo in his dressing-room had the following snatch at conversation with Zeals:

'I hear you're teaching his grace how to ride.'

'No objections, milord?'

'Watch out for the boy.'

'Yes, milord. It's a great old rocking-horse.'

'In store, isn't it?'

'In the second night-nursery with a load of furniture, milord.'

Ivo postponed his reunion with his wife until a minute or two before dinner was announced: he did not relish the prospect of being alone with her.

He could hardly bring himself to eat any of the succession of elaborate courses, or to speak while they were served. He squashed Beatrice's efforts to make conversation with his discouraging answers, drank wine morosely, and remained in the dining-room with his port long after she had left the room.

Eventually he joined her.

She sat in the centre of one of the settees in the drawing-room, facing the door, with newspapers and books open beside her, and stared at him and asked in her angry voice, at once level and cutting: 'What's the matter with you?'

'The matter with me?' He had emphasized the last word, and he barked out a sarcastic laugh. 'Nothing's the matter with me,' he lied in reply.

'You accuse me of avoiding your nephew when you avoid your wife. It's true, you've been avoiding me for days, weeks, and especially this evening. Why?'

'I'm doing nothing of the sort.'

'Look at the clock, Ivo!'

'I don't know what you've got to complain about.'

'If you don't, it's because you're drunk.'

'Drunk? Nonsense! You can go too far, Beatrice. I'm warning you.'

'There's no point in talking.' She stood up. 'But I'll expect an answer in the morning. Here!' She reached for a piece of paper on the settee and thrust it at him as she passed by. 'Here's something to keep you happy overnight.' And she swept out.

The paper was a bill from Frère Jacques for three thousand pounds.

He read it again, began to sweat, then lurched into the hall in pursuit of her, and, ignoring the footman Charles on duty by the front door, shouted up the stairs which she mounted steadily with one hand raising the skirt of her dress: 'It's wrong – you can't have spent that much money – you can't have run up another bill for that much – for God's sake, Beatrice!'

She did not stop or answer.

He re-entered the drawing-room, immediately returned to the hall, said to

Charles: 'Find me a cab,' and following him out of the house strode to and fro under the portico. When the cab arrived, he ignored Charles' offers to fetch his hat and coat, gave the address of the Club of Clubs and climbed in. He reached his destination at ten o'clock at night and left at two in the morning, by which time he had lost another five thousand pounds in round numbers.

At Castile House he mumbled an apology to Charles, who was still on duty and opened the front door to him. For the next few hours he slept as heavily as alcohol and despair allowed, woke with a bad hangover, a physical and moral double hangover, as it were, but got himself up, breakfasted on black coffee and again escaped from the house. He walked to Hyde Park, he tried to walk off at least his physical sickness, and kept on taking big breaths to calm his nerves and control his panicky feelings. The sun shone, the day seemed to be too hot for him, and he yearned for the chill mists and wilder winds of the hills of Gelts.

At ten to eleven he reached the offices of Slater, Gregan and Reed in Bedford Terrace, and was admitted without delay into Horace's murky office.

He interrupted Horace's inquiries into the health of himself, his wife and his nephew by saying in his gruffest voice: 'I'm afraid I need money badly.'

Horace hid his surprise behind a whiskery smile and the oddly phrased question: 'How is that, Lord Ivo?'

'I need ten thousand give or take a few pounds.'

'That's a considerable sum.'

'I'm well aware of it.'

'May I ask what it's needed for?'

'To pay bills – what do you think!'

'Which bills would they be, Lord Ivo?'

'Does it matter? My wife's an extravagant woman. But she has to dress well in her position, and she's run up another bill for suitable clothes. And I've hit an unlucky streak at cards.'

'Your brother gave you the trust fund on condition that you ceased altogether to gamble, Lord Ivo.'

'My brother's dead and buried, Horace. Let's stick to the damn point. When can I have the money?'

'Please don't raise your voice – I am not yet deaf, Lord Ivo. There are difficulties. I was about to write you a letter, which would have explained that Lord Deveraux, as one of the two trustees of your brother's estate, is refusing

[173]

to sanction payment of the household expenses of Castile House in the period between your marriage and the death of the Duke. He is particularly adamant about the cost of champagne consumed, and a band employed, on the day or the night your brother died.'

'How dare he? We had no idea there was anything wrong with Walter when we gave our ball at Castile House. I received the telegram in the middle of it – ask anybody! How dare you suggest we were swigging champagne and dancing after we knew Walter was dead!'

'I never suggested such a thing, Lord Ivo. I was merely dating the ball you gave, which Lord Deveraux refuses to pay for.'

'Oh for God's sake, what's the damage – it can't be all that serious?'

'The costs in dispute come to something over five hundred pounds.'

'To hell with it! Add it to my bill. You'll have to release ten thousand five hundred instead of ten. But I need the money in a hurry.'

'The difficulties extend further, I'm sorry to say. If I were to agree such a release of capital, you would have spent another worrying proportion of your capital, which, I must remind you, has to last the lifetimes of yourself and Lady Ivo, in a matter of months. Lord Deveraux is already aghast at the amount of money drawn out of the trust, and would be much more so if I were to accede to your request. With apologies, Lord Ivo, I have to pay strict attention to the view of Lord Deveraux, who, with Brigadier Dimmick, now employs me and my firm.'

'You had no right to let Valentine Deveraux poke his nose into my affairs, Horace.'

'No, sir, I had no alternative. Lord Deveraux carries conscientiousness to extremes, and considers himself honour-bound by his position of trust to protect the interests of his friend the late Duke's son and heir. He therefore demanded details of your finances in order to ascertain whether or not they were ever likely to impinge upon the Brougham estate. As a result, and in short, he has instructed me to inform you that he will stand by the late Duke's decision to advance you no more money in any circumstances, and advised me to think very carefully indeed before again depleting your own trust fund.'

'I see – what it boils down to is that I'm still at the mercy of the late damned Duke – and I'm sick of it, Horace, I'm warning everyone! Now you listen to me! If Walter hadn't kicked us out of Castile House we wouldn't have had a farewell ball, so Walter and his blasted estate can damn well pay for what he was responsible for. It's not my fault that Walter's dead, and that my wife and I are going to have to live in three enormous houses and behave as if we're as rich as Walter was. I can't help it if Walter appointed Valentine Deveraux, who's holier-than-thou, to muck up my life and everything. You could say, or I could, that Walter's responsible for my having to come here today to crawl to you for money. His representatives in fairness should be falling over themselves to repair the damage he himself has done by dying.'

'The late Duke was not a gambler.'

'True enough – he was a skinflint. Listen, Horace, I'm asking you one more time – will you help to get me the money I owe? You sign your name, and Beatrice signs hers, and it's mine – and Valentine Deveraux can stew in his own juice. It's a debt of honour, Horace – I can't welsh on it – there'd be a scandal, and a slur on the family, and a bad mark against Billy – and I'd be ruined and ostracized. Won't you give me the money? Please do this for me.'

'Lord Ivo, may I remind you that you've been in equally dire straits before? I would suggest that you look for a postponement of the payment of your debts. It would be stupid of your creditors to insist on getting paid nil now, when they might get paid in full later on.'

'Listen – you don't know the half of it. I haven't told my wife, that's the danger. You don't know what you may be doing. Oh God! Well, I'm not getting down on my knees to anybody. Goodbye – and don't blame me, Horace!'

The solicitor tried to persuade his client not to walk out of the office, but in vain. He pursued Ivo through the front door of the building and into the street, and presumed to pluck at the sleeve of his coat, but was shaken off.

Ivo hailed a cab and directed it to the Club of Clubs. Arriving there at getting on for noon, he ordered and drank brandy; met Max Kirby and the other two members of yesterday's foursome, Ian Whitaker, the middle-aged cool-headed professional gambler, and young Sean Baydell, the Irish adventurer and noted amateur jockey; toyed with some lunch impatiently in their company; and by two o'clock was again playing poker in the Card Room.

To begin with he won. At three o'clock he was up on all his debts. But at five, when Max and Ian Whitaker said they would call it a day, the reckoning showed he was down by approximately another four thousand, in other words he owed eleven thousand pounds to his fellow-card-players and a grand total of fourteen and a half. He said he would pay within seven days, an offer accepted by Ian Whitaker and Max, the latter commenting that most of Cumberland was the sort of collateral he liked. Sean Baydell, however, asked if he could be paid at once.

Ivo, alone with Sean in the Card Room, suggested they should play a last game for double or quits. Sean agreed and won it. Ivo called for more brandy, pleaded for another game, insisted on other games after Sean cast interrogative aspersions on whether or not he could afford them, and lost disastrously.

At five-forty-five Sean stood up, having refused to continue. He was richer on paper by some two hundred thousand pounds. He agreed unwillingly to wait for his money for forty-eight hours.

Ivo returned to Castile House and found Beatrice in the drawing-room.

He stopped at the sight of her, reaching out for the edge of the coromandel screen that shielded the doorway as if to support himself, and she stared at him speechlessly before asking: 'Are you ill?'

He wiped the sweat from his forehead, ran his fingers through his disarrayed hair, rubbed his markedly blue chin, averted his eyes and said: 'We're bank-rupt.'

They were far apart in the great room, separated by the gilded furniture and the priceless knick-knacks on the occasional tables.

'You've gambled our money away,' she remarked, she assumed, with conviction, and explained his recent behaviour by repeating: 'You've been gambling our money away.'

He slightly, helplessly, shrugged his shoulders.

The evening sun slanted in at the windows and gleamed on the faceted glass drops of the chandeliers.

'You can't be bankrupt,' she said. 'It's absurd.'

'Well, I've told you,' he replied.

'But they'll have to release more money – I'll talk to them . . .'

He cut in, shouting, hoarse with rage: 'I've done that – you think I'm a fool – but I tried everything – and it was no good. Now there's not enough money to save us, there's not enough, I'm telling you!'

'Ivo . . .'

'No!' he exclaimed: 'No!' – and retreated behind the screen and out into the hall and through the front door and across the gravel sweep and into the street.

He headed for Belgrave Square and round into Eaton Square, but without really knowing where he was. He halted as an idea struck him, and began to walk ever more quickly and then to run back along Belgrave Place and into Castile Street.

He was too late.

He joined Graves, Albert, Charles, Zeals supporting Nanny Campion who was crying, Mrs Tighe also in tears, and several strangers, passers-by no doubt, who were crowding round a particular part of the curved and spiked iron bars across the basement windows.

Beatrice emerged through the open front door.

Ivo was about to restrain her, but Graves called out in a quavering voice: 'No, milady – don't look, please – go indoors, go indoors – oh beg pardon, I should say your grace!'

Both Beatrice and Ivo were momentarily arrested by this speech. Then Ivo strode towards his wife and lent force to the butler's plea by pushing her roughly in the desired direction. She made an attempt, so far as dignity allowed, not to be pushed, and in the hall snapped at him under her breath in protest: 'I know what happened.'

He retorted with stressful haste: 'I bet – later, later!' – and hurrying back to the scene of the accident he told Mrs Tighe to take Nanny indoors at once and attend to her, and issued other authoritative orders: the strangers must clear out and the gates across the driveway be closed; Zeals was to go on to the stables and mobilize transport and find and fetch Dr Willson; Charles was to call upon the services of available grooms and gardeners, Albert to summon the police; Graves would have to inform the rest of the staff of the situation and calm everyone down; and the body was not to be disturbed until the professionals, medical and official, arrived.

The Duke of Brougham and Castile, formerly Lord Ivo Grevill, remained out there with his nephew for a good two hours in spite of feeling and looking ill. He managed to deal with practical matters, for instance the composition of telegrams to Horace Reed, breaking the sad news and requiring Horace's attendance at Castile House first thing in the morning, and to Saddlecombe. One of the two police constables who turned up had gone to Scotland Yard and returned with a senior officer, Superintendent Bowles, a smart and respectful man, to whom Ivo gave an account of the little he knew of the

[177]

circumstances of the fatal fall. He explained ruefully that his nephew had been caught only yesterday climbing on the parapet of the front elevation and the central pediment, and pointed out these architectural features immediately above the basement railings, regretting the fact that the french window in the nursery allowing access to them had not been locked. Zeals was instructed to show the policemen the area of the roof under discussion, and to help Nanny to answer the questions she was bound to be asked.

After Billy had been removed by a team of hospital orderlies and undertakers overseen by Dr Willson, Ivo suggested that the Doctor should look in on his wife, who, he had been informed, was broken-hearted and had retired to bed.

He received innumerable expressions of sympathy. To a gentleman so grand as well as grief-stricken the police were especially deferential, and the undertakers carried discretion to extremes; while members of his staff told him with varying degrees of emotion how sorry they were, because the little duke had been a general favourite and he and his uncle such great friends. Several of the servants thanked heaven that Lord Ivo, or rather his grace, happened to be in residence: they said they would have felt even worse if this catastrophe had occurred while he and her ladyship had been at Brougham, for instance.

To the new Duke in the library, Dr Willson had two reports to make. First, he had administered a sedative to Lady Ivo – he apologized to her husband for not yet feeling capable of calling her the Duchess of Brougham – and advised that she should be left in peace, at least until he had examined her again in the morning. Secondly, he had communicated his opinion to Superintendent Bowles that, since death was clearly the consequence of yet another boyish prank which had gone wrong, and could therefore be called natural, an inquest would be superfluous.

Ivo's response was to clear his throat and mutter: 'An inquest – that's the last thing in the world we want.'

Dr Willson reassured him: the Superintendent was reasonable, and the Coroner likewise, and between them they were likely to draw the correct conclusion.

At this point Graves knocked on the library door, entered and said that the police were leaving and the officer in charge wondered whether his grace had a moment to spare; Ivo signalled a positive answer; the doctor seized his chance to withdraw; and Superintendent Bowles marched in.

[178]

'My nephew, who was also my ward,' Ivo said, 'will be buried in Cumberland in the family tomb in the park of our home. How soon will we be free to travel north?'

'Yes, sir – I shall be speaking to the Coroner – and hope to be able to give you clearance by eleven o'clock tomorrow, if that would be convenient.'

'I can't believe an inquest's necessary. All it would do is upset a lot of people.'

'Yes, sir,' the Superintendent repeated. 'I'm sorry I'm not in a position to decide.'

'Would it help if I talked to your superiors?'

'Better leave it to me, sir. I'm hopeful there won't be any trouble.'

'Well – I was out of the house at the time of my nephew's death. My wife was in – but she won't have any information to contribute – and she's so cut up that she needed the doctor – who told me a moment ago that she's not to be disturbed. My nephew wasn't too well, and was being looked after by my old nurse.'

'We have interviewed Miss Campion, sir. She says she was returning to the nursery from the Duke's bedroom when she was informed of the accident by Mr Zeals, your valet.'

'Have you spoken to Zeals?'

'Yes, sir. He admits he was up on the nursery floor, making for another room there, a storeroom with a rocking-horse in it. He claims he was going to give the young gentleman a riding lesson. But he heard the commotion in the street, he says, and ran into the nursery and out on to the leads and looked over the top of the parapet. Miss Campion and Mr Zeals both believe that the Duke must have slipped through the french window in the day-nursery while his nanny's back was turned, and tried to walk up and down the slopes of the pediment – apparently he regarded it as a challenge, getting to the top of the pediment, and a test of nerve. May I ask you a question, sir? Is Mr Zeals truthful?'

'Yes – so far as I know. It's true that he's been teaching Billy how to sit on a horse – and he's been in my employment for a good few years and I've never caught him lying. Why do you ask?'

'Your nephew died a nasty death, if I may say so, sir – it's been a shock for all concerned. Miss Campion was too distressed to tell me much, and Mr Zeals seemed to be in a bad state. I shall have to check through their statements with them when they're more composed.'

[179]

'My nephew got on well with Zeals.'

'I understand the Duke was determined to be as like his uncle – yourself, sir – as possible. When he climbed the pediment, might he have been following in your footsteps in a manner of speaking?'

'Where did you get that idea?'

'From talking to Miss Campion, sir.'

'God knows if he was copying me. I hope not.'

'Would I be right in thinking the Duke's health was not equal to dangerous escapades?'

'His father took that view. Billy wanted to be a normal boy.'

'Did you encourage him?'

'To some extent, naturally.'

'May I offer my condolences, sir?'

'Thank you. Look here, my wife can't be involved in an inquest. She has no relevant information, I've told you.'

'Again, whether or not she's called will depend on the Coroner, sir. If she has a doctor's note, it would make a difference.'

'I'll have a word with Dr Willson when he returns. I can guarantee to have such a note ready for you tomorrow. Goodbye, officer.'

It was getting on for eight o'clock, and Ivo ordered Albert to lock the front door and Charles to send Zeals to his dressing-room.

Upstairs he thought of trying to talk to Beatrice, but decided against it. In his dressing-room he began to change out of his day clothes, and was joined by Zeals.

'Are you all right?' he asked.

'Not too bad, your grace. How's yourself?'

'It's a hell of a business.'

'That it is.'

'The policeman thought you weren't speaking the truth.'

'Did he now!'

'Is there anything you want to tell me?'

'Such as?'

'I'm asking you, Zeals.'

'It was the asthma that killed him.'

'What?'

'He had the asthma, he started coughing and that – he wasn't fit, not after his last attack – he shouldn't have been out there at all – and I blame myself for not remembering history repeats itself.'

'What are you getting at?'

'Nothing worth saying.'

'Come on, Zeals!'

'No, your grace, beg pardon.'

'Is it something to do with my wife?'

'You'll have to ask her.'

'Zeals! What's the matter with you? Don't you speak to me like that, and I won't be lied to!'

'There was yesterday and there's today – two different things, your grace.'

'Stop talking in riddles!'

'Her ladyship – the Duchess, that is – she spotted him climbing on the pediment yesterday.'

'I know, she informed me.'

'But yesterday she let him be. I saw her come and go from the room with the rocking-horse. Even so he was sick with his asthma. Today I was at the top of the servants' stairs.'

'What did you see?'

'Right into the day-nursery and through the french window.'

'Yes?'

'He got to the top, your grace, and was balancing down the other side. He did have guts, the Duke did, I will say.'

'Go on.'

'I'd rather not.'

'Do as you're told!'

'Her ladyship was in the nursery, and she stepped through the french window and frightened him with one of her looks.'

'Is that all?'

'He spotted her and started coughing and of course he couldn't keep upright and he fell off the wrong side.'

'She would have been trying to save him.'

'Yes, milord. The shock of her standing there took his breath away.'

'How can you be so sure he was breathless because he saw her? You've said he was breathless yesterday without seeing her. You're contradicting yourself – and I don't believe you.'

[181]

'It's the truth.'

'I think she was looking for him and caught him breaking the rules and hurried out to the rescue and stopped still when he started to cough and wobble.'

'It was all the other way round – she wasn't in no hurry – and she made him cough by standing there.'

'Do you know what you're saying? These are pretty serious allegations – and they're unfounded and unsupported – they're damn near slander. Have you been spreading them round?'

'No – I've kept mum till you started asking questions. I didn't say a word to the policeman.'

'Don't you ever dare gossip, Zeals! I won't employ servants who tell tales about their masters. I don't like mischief-makers.'

'That isn't fair, your grace.'

'Maybe not – but you listen to me – we can't bury the boy until the police are satisfied he died accidentally. They're coming back tomorrow to check your story that you saw nothing until it was all over. I'd like to travel north by tomorrow's night train, if possible. The people at Brougham will need time to get used to the idea that the Duke died in an accident like his father. You'd better think about packing for me. Is that understood?'

'Very well, your grace.'

Ivo had finished dressing in his informal green velvet smoking-suit. He descended to the dining-room, where Graves and Albert waited to serve his dinner.

'I'm late, Graves,' he said.

'No wonder, your grace,' the butler replied.

Then Ivo, feeling he had drunk enough earlier in the day and for some time past, also that he had to keep his wits about him, refused wine and asked for plain water: it was like a tribute of sorts to Billy.

As soon as he had eaten his last mouthful of savoury, he refused dessert, rose, dropped his napkin on the floor, left the room, mounted the flights of stairs to the nursery floor and opened the day-nursery door.

Nanny Campion in her dressing-gown was sitting on one side of the low coal fire and Mrs Tighe on the other side. They held teacups and saucers in their hands just beneath their chins, chalice-fashion.

Startled by his entry, by his visit, Mrs Tighe rose to her feet, while Nanny, also trying to, exclaimed: 'Oh good gracious me! What next?'

[182]

'Don't move, Nan,' he said.

He acknowledged Mrs Tighe's tearful sympathetic murmurings and let her leave the room.

'Oh dearie!'

As he sat down Nanny began to cry, averting her face and fumbling for the handkerchief in her sleeve.

He spoke words of conventional comfort, then said: 'Billy will be buried at Brougham. Will you want to come, Nan?'

'Oh I would love to be there and see Brougham once more – how good of you to think of me! But I can't, dearie – I'm past it – I was too old to take care of Billy, I always said it – and now you must blame me – I wasn't expecting you to have it all out with me just yet.'

She cried again, and he had to persuade her that his intentions were not to reproach or accuse her of anything.

She grew calmer and remarked: 'I blame myself, you'll never stop me blaming myself, and I shall till the day I die. Poor Billy! I should have refused to be responsible for him. But I did it for you and the family, dearie – and then he was so lovable.'

Ivo growled back, gazing into the fire: 'You had no choice in the matter.'

Nanny changed the subject: 'I haven't asked how you're feeling – you'll be thinking I've got very selfish in my old age. Are you bearing up, my dearie? How's your lady?'

'She had to go to bed.'

'So Mrs Tighe was saying.'

'She needed the doctor – and he's coming again tomorrow – she's taken it very hard.'

'Has she indeed?'

'Definitely, Nan.'

'I expect she's sorry she took so little notice of somebody. I'm sure she'll be sorry now.'

'What are you hinting at?'

'I wouldn't hint. I'm too old for that, too. I say things straight out to you as I always have. Your lady did put the fear into Billy. Perhaps she didn't see him if she could help it because she knew he was scared of her.'

'He never told me.'

'No, he wouldn't, would he? And he was a brave boy – more brave than he

[183]

should have been, as it turns out. He wanted to show you he was as brave as he thought you were, dearie.'

'I wish you hadn't said so to the police, Nan.'

'What's the harm in your being his hero? I said nothing wrong, I'm sure. All I could tell the man was that I had nothing to tell.'

'You mean you witnessed nothing?'

'That's right. Billy was in bed till tea-time. He put his clothes on to eat his tea – oh he was a gentleman! – and when he'd quite finished I went into his bedroom to straighten it up. He must have gone out on the roof then – and his bedroom window looks the other way, doesn't it? The first I heard of anything was Mr Zeals shouting blue murder and running down the servants' staircase.'

'What was he getting at?'

'Getting at, dearie? Why, that Billy had fallen and met his end, poor lamb.'

'You haven't spoken to Zeals since?'

'No – why should I? He was only ever in the nursery for Billy's sake.'

'You saw nothing and no one else, Nan?'

'No – apart from Dr Willson this morning.'

'When was the last time my wife came up?'

'I do believe she looked in yesterday afternoon. I'm afraid I was having forty winks, but I thought I saw her black dress disappearing behind the door. Why are you asking, dearie?'

'There may be an inquest. The police return tomorrow, and they'll be talking to you again, and I wouldn't want you to say things that could land you in the witness box.'

'Oh no – don't you frighten me! But whyever should there be an inquest? That's like a trial!'

'Forget it, Nan – nothing to worry about – I don't want you to be more upset than you are already – than we all are for that matter.'

'Thank you, dearie. But you did give me a start, almost putting me in a witness-box! Never mind – it's good of you to bother about me and try to cheer me up. You have forgiven me for not being where I should have been this after-noon, haven't you?'

'Yes, Nan – you couldn't be expected to watch over Billy every minute of the day.'

'Oh but I did know he'd be climbing out on the roof sooner or later.'

'How did you know?'

'He told me.'

'Really?'

'Well – you'd talked to him about it – how you used to climb that pediment – and he was determined to – he thought it was a dare.'

'You mustn't ever say that to anybody.'

'All right, dearie. Don't mind me – I won't get you into trouble – I'm dependent on you now as you were dependent on me once upon a time. Your brother was kind to give me house-room in my retirement, and I was and will be grateful to him; but you were always my best boy, and I can see a silver lining to the clouds over the family. Yes, you've lost two dear ones – on the other hand you've become what you wanted to be since you were small. I'll be happy to die with you king of the castle. Have I said something wrong?'

Ivo was standing up, frowning and as if agitated.

He said: 'I must go. Good night, Nan.'

'Shall I see you again, dearie?'

'Who knows? It depends on when we can get to Brougham. Nan, don't let your tongue run away with you. Good night.'

He retired to bed, but not to sleep much.

His next day was unusually busy.

Black-garbed and with black rings under his black eyes, at nine o'clock he received Horace Reed in the library and prefaced his list of instructions thus: 'Let me make something crystal clear for a start. I never again want to hear that I can't afford to do as I please. No more of your tut-tutting, Horace! And I won't be asked disagreeable questions.'

He instructed the solicitor to raise a quarter of a million pounds in cash or a cash equivalent by lunch-time, when he would be calling at the offices of Slater, Gregan and Reed; to scrap all bank accounts in the name of Ivo Grevill, and wind up trust funds; to notify the newspapers of Billy's death; and to book him an appointment at noon with the Stationmaster at Euston Station for the purpose of discussing travel arrangements to Carlisle.

As Horace Reed departed, Dr Willson arrived.

In due course the latter, having seen his patient, reported to Ivo that she was calmer and coming to terms with her bereavement, and would be fit to play her part in the obsequies.

'She shouldn't have to appear at an inquest, if they insist on holding one,'

[185]

Ivo said. 'And the same applies to Nanny – you remember Nanny Campion? – who's as old as the hills and senile nowadays.'

Accordingly, to please his grace, Dr Willson wrote out notes to the effect that in his opinion the general health of the Duchess of Brougham was not at present equal to speaking in public of the death of her beloved nephew, and that the age and mental condition of Miss Campion would cast doubt on any evidence she might be called to give to the Coroner.

Ivo's third visitor was Superintendent Bowles, to whom he presented Dr Willson's notes and proceeded to say: 'Do you want another word with Zeals? Yes – well – I've employed the man for quite a few years, and I've spoken to him at some length about yesterday. To the best of my knowledge and belief his story is nothing but the truth. I very much doubt that he'd dare to lie to me.' And he escorted the Superintendent across the hall, condescended to shake the hands of two other policemen waiting there, and showed them all into the dining-room, where by arrangement Zeals was ready to be interviewed.

Ivo returned to the library, permitted himself to smoke a couple of cigarettes, paced the floor, and ten minutes later was relieved to be informed by the Superintendent that he would be taking no further action, evidently foul play was not involved, and he had the authority vested in him by the Coroner to dispense with formalities and sanction the transportation of the late Duke of Brougham, and the interment.

Ivo got rid of the police, and spent the rest of the morning and until late afternoon registering Billy's death, then at Euston Station, then in Horace Reed's office, signing papers and getting his gambling debts paid, then at the undertaker's, and finally in the stables of Castile House, organizing the vehicles that would be needed later in the day for the first stage of the funeral procession northwards.

Beatrice had not yet emerged from her bedroom. He sent her a brusque missive that read like a telegram: 'No inquest – private sleeping car for our use will be attached to night train – supper ordered for seven o'clock – please be ready to leave at eight.'

He had brought home two folded sheets of papers on which Horace had jotted at his request details of the fortune he was heir to. He sat at the desk in the library and unfolded them, smoothed them and scanned the lines of multi-numbered sums of money. When he thought he heard somebody coming downstairs he covered his reading matter with a sheet of blotting-paper; but it was a false alarm, not his wife. Either the vertiginous view of his wealth, or the memory of how he had acquired it, or wondering how much he wanted it, or maybe straightforward exhaustion, caused him a sudden nausea. He stood up, strode towards the silver salver bearing the whisky decanter, soda-siphon and glasses, changed his mind, reached for his cigarette case, changed his mind again, and without drinking or smoking returned to the desk and tore the record of his altered status into little pieces and put them on the burning coal fire. Glumly he wandered from the library into the empty drawing-room, hands in pockets, staring out of the windows. He was glad when the chiming clocks gave him leave to prepare for the journey.

In his dressing-room he refused to let Zeals speak of his interrogation by the police. He raised his hand in a repressive gesture, said he was sick of that stuff, checked that the other members of staff who were travelling to Brougham would be ready by eight, and bathed and donned a different black suit.

Beatrice did not join him for supper. Her message that she was not hungry, conveyed to him by Graves, had an adverse effect on his own appetite, although he had not eaten since breakfast. A mixture of bad feelings made the food stick in his throat.

At seven-thirty the hearse began to manoeuvre into the driveway. It was a glass-sided waggon draped in black with pillars at the corners supporting a black canopy, and was drawn by two black horses in line, black-hooded. The small coffin rested on a sort of plinth which was covered with flowers. A youth dressed like a jockey, but all in black, rode the leading horse, and the two top-hatted coachmen wore huge black greatcoats with layered capes over the shoulders. The equipage had difficulty in turning into the driveway, but after a few minutes halted beneath the portico; and the undertaker and five of his men, who had arrived in a coach at present parked in the road, formed a guard of honour on either side of the front door.

Meanwhile the three Castile House conveyances were advancing into the street and queueing for admission into the driveway; a crowd of members of the public gathered out there, and another crowd of family retainers with their wives, husbands, children and relations congregated around the hearse. Albert and Charles carried pieces of luggage from the tradesmen's side-door towards one of the coaches, in which Topper was eventually stowed by Zeals; and in the front hall Ivo watched and waited, looking at his half-hunter and up the stairs, scowling darkly at the activities out of doors, then summoning a

[187]

smile for Graves and Mrs Tighe, who appeared prematurely in their travelling clothes.

At two minutes to eight Beatrice's maid Mary bustled through the green baize door in hat and overcoat to say that her grace would soon be ready. Ten minutes elapsed, and Ivo, by now top-hatted and with ebony stick in black-gloved hand, observed his heavily-veiled wife descending the stairs.

When she was close enough to hear it, he muttered: 'You've been a great help.'

She ignored him, walked straight through the front door opened by Albert, stood between the undertakers as if giving permission for Billy to start on his last journey, and was joined by Ivo doffing his hat. The chief undertaker went to walk ahead of the procession, the coachman flicked his black whip over the backs of the horses, the hearse jolted forwards and negotiated the gateway into Castile Street, the other undertakers following on foot and then climbing into their coach; and the first of the ducal vehicles with Harris on the box having pulled into the drive and under the portico, Charles opened the door and lowered the step, the Duke and Duchess entered, sat and had a rug spread over their knees, were shut in and driven almost in slow motion in the direction of Euston Station.

Ivo growled at Beatrice: 'I've bones to pick with you.'

Beatrice turned to look at him, to stare at him probably, although he could not see her eyes, and said: 'If you're determined to quarrel with me, I shall get out at once.'

He was silenced. He gazed through the window on his side, not registering the interest of onlookers or the passing scene. She sat on the edge of the seat, straight-backed and supporting herself by holding on to the strap. The noise of horses' hooves, of wheels on cobbles, of the creaking of the coachwork, was anyway not conducive to talk.

At about nine o'clock the Euston stationmaster met and led the procession towards a siding. The platform there was empty, except for some porters and a white-coated attendant. The Duke and Duchess, Mrs Tighe and Mary, Graves and Zeals, left their carriages. Billy in his coffin was removed from the hearse and placed with his flowers in the luggage van of the private sleeping-carriage. The attendant stepped forward to show the living members of the party the accommodation within, the pair of connecting compartments with single bunks for the gentry, the lounge area, and beyond it the two double-bunk

[188]

compartments, one for Mrs Tighe and Mary, the other for the male staff.

The stationmaster and the undertaker took their leave in the lounge, and handsome tips to boot. Ivo and Beatrice were alone when Zeals knocked on the lounge door and was told to come in.

He had Topper straining on a lead to reach his master.

'Where do you want him to be, your grace?' he asked.

'Not here,' Ivo returned dismissively.

Zeals indicated assent, and addressed Beatrice: 'Don't you worry too much, your grace – we got you off.'

And he winked at Ivo before bowing out.

The lounge was relatively large, long and luxurious, walled with panels of marquetry, thickly carpeted, and had a table to eat or work at and four chairs, and a pair of seats or small sofas, covered with red plush and antimacassars, facing each other on either side of a window. It must have been insulated: the hubbub of the station was excluded, except for the occasional muffled tooting of a train.

Beatrice asked Ivo in an ominously quiet voice: 'What was the meaning of that?'

He replied, removing his black kid gloves, pulling them from each finger in turn: 'Nothing, nothing.'

'I don't understand you.'

He turned on her, flushed and furious: 'You don't understand me? That's rich! I never have understood you, and never will.'

'You haven't answered my question. What did Zeals mean?'

'Nothing – I've told you.'

Deliberately she removed her veiled hat.

'Ivo,' she said, 'if you won't at least explain, I shall call Zeals in here and dismiss him on the spot.'

'You can't dismiss him – what are you thinking of? He's my servant – and he's done nothing wrong – he hasn't, that's the point.'

'Are you suggesting I have? Was he suggesting I was in the wrong?'

'There wasn't an inquest.'

'What's the connection?'

'Oh drop it, Beatrice! Things are bad without you making a scene.'

[189]

'Where's Zeals? I'm going to have him fetched.'

'All right – don't – I'll explain – although I was determined not to have a row with you tonight! But you push me so damn far, Beatrice, skulking upstairs and leaving me to clear up the mess and everything. All right! Zeals helped to put a stopper on the inquest.'

'Who wanted one?'

'It's the law – after sudden deaths – I'm not a lawyer.'

'But Billy's death was an accident.'

'Yes – I know – the police agreed in the end – and the Coroner luckily took the same view.'

'Luckily, Ivo?'

'Yes – and you needn't stare at me – you were damn lucky they all came round to agreeing there was no funny business.'

'Who thought there was? Who said so? Was it Zeals?'

'Come off it, Beatrice!'

'No – tell me!'

'What do you say you were doing just before Billy died? Where were you?'

'Strange to relate, I'm inclined to say nothing whatsoever. You'll believe your valet rather than your wife. Your facts of the matter are servants' gossip. How squalid! You're not the only one with bones to pick. On the evening of the accident you said something to me that I've taken exception to. I told you then that I knew what had happened. You replied in the nastiest possible way, "I bet".'

'It's water under the bridge – I was agitated – don't be touchy!'

'Touchy's an understatement. You meant that you'd jumped to the usual unfair conclusions. You've always unloaded your guilt on to my shoulders. Well, I wouldn't stoop to try to prove my innocence – why should I prove my innocence when you haven't proved my guilt? The result of your "bet" was that I preferred to keep my own counsel and out of harm's way – I stayed in my room as you stayed in yours – yes, Ivo, I might have been a leper for all the attention I got from you – and I'm still outraged by your behaviour, and even more so by your conspiring with Zeals against me.'

Ivo flung himself, or more accurately collapsed in a gesture of exasperation, on one of the sofas, exclaiming: 'You twist the whole bag of tricks out of recognition.'

'Very well,' she retorted, 'straighten things out! What did Zeals say about me? What did he do?'

[190]

'He saw you in the day-nursery.'

'Yes?'

'I talked to him, and he didn't tell the police.'

'What did he think he had to tell?'

'He saw you step through the french window on to the roof when Billy was climbing the pediment, and frighten him and give him asthma, which made him fall.'

'Zeals' words to me five minutes ago – you heard them – were "we got you off". Off what, Ivo?'

'I don't know – interrogation – scandal at least – scandal if nothing worse. I obtained a note from the doctor excusing you from having to face the police. It's all glossed over, thank God!'

'In other words you swallowed Zeals' story hook, line and sinker. Thank you. Your loyalty and trust are much appreciated.'

'Cut out the sarcasm, Beatrice.'

'Sarcasm's the least of it. Your disloyalty disgusts me. But your stupidity's worse. How could you – how can you – believe I gave Billy asthma? How does one person give another asthma?'

'Easily – that's the answer to that question – easily, if you stand and stare and put the fear of God into a boy who's balancing fifty feet above the ground! And easily, too, when you knew he was prone to asthma and got it the day before as a result of climbing on the roof – you knew the strain and the danger had made him ill, and you'd been warned by the doctors that any sort of shock would be bad for him. You think I'm stupid, but I can damn well see through you.'

'Oh yes? And what do you see or imagine you see? Think carefully before you say it, Ivo!'

'You asked for it – I'm not afraid of you – and I'm sick of all the lying – you were the death of Billy!'

Beatrice, who had been standing throughout this dialogue, now pulled forward and then sat on one of the four dining-chairs. The action was deliberate: she had not lost her characteristic composure; she possibly showed a flicker of relief that implications had been distilled into accusation; and staring at Ivo unblinkingly, she seemed to prepare with a certain zest to mount her defence.

'Indeed?' she inquired without raising her voice, and continued with even

[191]

a touch of satire. 'How do you make that out? Billy died of falling, not asthma.'

His reply was also pitched low – he had not shouted at her throughout – for obvious reasons he particularly wished not to be overheard, and perhaps he was merely repeating aloud sentences he had often said in more emotional accents to himself.

'Billy died of the sight of you,' he said, somewhat slumped on the sofa, not looking at her. 'And you were well aware of the effect you'd have on him by catching him red-handed. You told me twenty-four hours earlier that you'd seen him on the roof and had to take care not to let him see you in case he panicked. You knew what you were up to. You've been against Billy from the start – jealous of him – and especially since Walter's death – you've said threatening things to me. And you set the scene yourself – you premeditated it, that's the word – by sacking Nurse Tucker, who was able to protect Billy, and bringing him to London and handing him over to Nanny Campion, who's too old to protect anyone and no match for you. And why did you have us moved into the Duke's Apartments at Brougham? Why did you marry me, if it comes to that? You've been eaten up with ambition all along, envy and ambition – don't deny it! It's too late in the day, granted, but I've proved to my own satisfaction that you stop at nothing to get what you're after. Probably your first husband got the point as I have, when it was too late to save his skin. You're right at any rate to complain of my not trusting you. I don't, and never will again. I'll never feel sure you're not going to stick a knife in my back.'

'Have you quite finished, Ivo?'

'No,' he said. 'No – I'm not having any more to do with you. I wouldn't touch you if you paid me. After the funeral, you're out. That's definite, Beatrice. And I'll have a divorce. You think you're so clever, but what Zeals said is true, he and I between us rescued you from the pretty tight spot you'd got yourself into. You think you've been clever enough to polish off poor Billy and become a duchess. But your scheme's going to ricochet, because, thanks to your ruthless meddling, I want something I never wanted before, namely a son, an heir, and a wife who can bear me one. Are you smiling? I have the resources now to get exactly what I want by hook or by crook, so you'd better damn well take me seriously.'

Beatrice stood up. She walked to the door leading to the staff quarters, opened it, and asked the attendant, who was in his galley at the far end of the corridor, to send along her maid.

A few minutes later Mary entered, and Beatrice led the way towards her own sleeping compartment on the other side of the lounge, where she supervised the unpacking of her overnight case.

Zeals had followed Mary into the lounge and asked his master: 'Shall I unpack for you at the same time, your grace?'

Ivo said no, he could manage.

Zeals tried again to please. 'There's whisky and soda available, your grace. Shall I bring it in?'

Ivo's negative was terser.

Zeals withdrew. Ivo reached for his cigarette case, but once more changed his mind: apparently his elevation to the rank of a duke had reduced his dependence on alcohol and tobacco. The black-haired hand that might have smoked a cigarette shook slightly – his immobility on the sofa was deceptive, rather the outward sign of tension than relaxation. He was waiting apprehensively for his wife to come back and give him a piece of her mind.

The attendant knocked and entered. The car was about to be coupled to an engine, therefore his passengers should be seated in the interest of their safety and comfort, he explained.

Ivo said: 'Tell her grace, will you?'

The attendant did so. He then adjusted lamps to give more light in the lounge and drew the curtains. He together with Mary returned to their part of the car, closing the lounge door. Beatrice reappeared and sat on the sofa opposite Ivo. Loud clanking and a considerable bump ensued, and shortly afterwards with a great hiss of steam they moved.

'Ivo,' Beatrice began, 'can you hear me?'

As he only shrugged his shoulders she began again: 'Ivo, are you listening? Can you hear?'

'Yes,' he growled.

'That's good – because nobody else will be able to – and you're not the only one with a tale to tell – at least you'll have to listen to my version of your story. You think, you've often said or hinted, that I picked you out for worldly reasons of my own. You imply that I forced the pace of our courtship and somehow seduced you into marrying me. Well, I think you'd find it difficult to convince people that you, the brother of a duke, an experienced mature man, had no alternative except to marry a widow from the colonies, without any money, who made hats, and wasn't pregnant, and warned you that she couldn't bear

[193]

children. How could I have forced you to do anything you didn't want to do? The force, the power, was all on your side, everyone would agree. I never seduced you in any sense. It was the other way round, when I was driven half-mad by the phobia of thunderstorms that I've suffered from since childhood. I was really ill — it's true — I've got letters from doctors who were called in to cure me of my terror of thunder — you as good as raped me, people would be inclined to believe, if you ever made the mistake of trying to put me publicly in the wrong.'

Ivo interjected here with a groan: 'My God, how you talk! I won't be threatened, Beatrice.'

'Who threatened first?' she asked rhetorically, and carried on: 'You say it was ambition that made me marry you. Certainly you had a title to offer, and you might have raised me up into high society. But you didn't have the money it takes to be in society — you didn't have the necessary — and you're a spendthrift and gambler — you weren't much of a match from a worldly, materialistic point of view. No — you had no profession or career, no prospects in fact, and money in your hands slipped through your fingers, and you had the richest tastes into the bargain. What you offered a wife was insecurity, probably poverty and drudgery, and, not counting accidents, rapid descent of the social ladder. All that was soon clear to me: more than likely I'd be worse off married to you than I was on my own with my independence and without a grand gentleman to slave for. Besides, you were an adulterer, which wasn't encouraging for your possible wife. Do you seriously believe you could persuade anyone that I was doing well for myself by marrying you?'

He did not answer: instead, he raised a corner of the curtain and looked out at the passing scene of railway tracks and the lit windows of trains pulling in and out of the station.

Ignoring his show of indifference she continued: 'But you were like a king without a country. I don't pay compliments or go in for flattery. You call me heartless because I don't use endearments, which are so hackneyed they mean nothing. I won't change my spots: all the same I will admit that I pitied you. You convinced me you were a victim of your class system — born and brought up in one way, then expected to live in another, like a poor man — and I understood your resentment and why you were envious. Yes, Ivo, what you call my envy was only a reflection of yours — I joined in your rebellion against the injus-

[194]

tice of your situation – I thought you needed me and a little practical assistance, and therefore approached your brother.'

'Oh yes,' he sneered, 'you went to Walter behind my back and without my permission, and made a deal with him that was a hell of a lot better for you than for me.'

'I won you redress, a fortune, security for life, a total transformation of your circumstances.'

'Yes, on condition I married you – that's to say on condition you had control of my money and I put myself in your power. Naturally Walter was keen to agree – he was no fool, I will give him that – he saw how dangerous you were – he was prepared to pay up as he never had before in order to spite me.'

'But Ivo, this is persecution mania – your exaggerations go far beyond the bounds of credibility. Normal people don't complain of being handed a quarter of a million pounds on a plate – what's wrong with you?'

'What about having to marry you in order to get a penny?'

'The condition you object to was undertaking not to gamble away your quarter of a million and then to expect more – which was only fair and would have been good all round if you'd observed it and kept your word. Marrying me was your choice. You were at liberty to choose not to. You can't shift the blame for what you of your own free will chose to do. If I'm to blame by your topsy-turvy standards, it's simply because I wouldn't give in to you and grant you the advantages of marriage without the obligations.'

'Where did you learn such high-falutin' language, Beatrice? It's all nonsense. You couldn't wait to sleep with me at Sweirdale, when we scarcely knew each other – that stuff about thunderstorms is just lies, your taking refuge in my bedroom was a tricky way to get close to me – and then you used sex and money as bribes.'

'Poor Ivo, treated so badly by everyone, and not able to stand up for himself or say no!'

'Do shut up, Beatrice!'

'It seems to me you got exactly what you wanted, fun and games and more money than ever before, and I got precious little gratitude for providing them, and now I'm reproached for having caught you and practised on your innocence. If my influence was irresistible, and I could bend you to my will, why did you keep on gambling and losing money although I'd asked you, told you, begged you not to, and absolutely forbidden it? I was worried that you'd gamble and lose the roof over our heads – I was as alarmed as any wife would be. That's why I stayed on at Castile House – the alternative to overstaying our welcome might have been to have no home and no money to buy one.'

'It killed my brother.'

'What?'

'You kept me kicking my heels in London, you wouldn't let me go anywhere, consequently Walter had to drive from Brougham to Gelts to attend to duty I should have done, and he died of it.'

'How preposterous! You might as well say that I took a secret trip to Cumberland to whip Walter's horse over the cliff. I couldn't foresee his accident. But after it I did foresee Billy's.'

At this point the car in which they sat bumped into the regular LNW – London North Western – night train to Carlisle. Again there were metallic noises of uncoupling and coupling, the deafening drum of engines gathering momentum, shouts and the background hiss of steam.

Ivo parted the curtain to peep out at the people on the platform, and muttered almost under his breath: 'You foresaw it too damn well.'

'No,' she contradicted him, 'you foresaw it, that was the beginning and end of the trouble.'

'And that's more preposterous than anything I've said! I loved Billy – he was my flesh and blood – I didn't cold-shoulder him as you did – he had no reason to be frightened of me.'

'But I was the frightened one, Ivo.'

'You? How do you make that out?'

'Of course I was frightened you'd do something drastic. You were at last rid of Walter, who you believed had stolen your inheritance, who wouldn't share with you, who kept you short of cash and disapproved of you. Only Billy stood between you and all the money and the best estate and the dukedom. You'd always longed to be duke – you thought you were better fitted than your brother to be duke – isn't it true? And now you found yourself boating and shooting with the boy who was the last obstacle to the realization of your highest hopes. I was more frightened, with much more cause, than Billy ever was.'

'Well, you sacked Nurse Tucker. It was none of my doing. If Billy had remained at Brougham with Tucker in charge, he'd be alive today.'

'Sorry, Ivo, I beg to differ. Nurse Tucker didn't go shooting with you, she wasn't in charge when guns were being fired, nor was she in the boat at the far end of the lake which can't be seen from the house.'

'Good God! Are you accusing me of planning to murder Billy?'

'I'm defending myself from your accusation that I did so.'

'Beatrice, we shouldn't be saying these things to each other.'

'Oh? You mean you can say them but I shouldn't. You forget there are two sides to every question, and I'm explaining my side, my answer, which I believe legal and public opinion would find more believable than yours. No, don't move! You can't escape me here – you'll have to hear me out! I sacked Nurse Tucker and sent the telegram to Nanny Campion for Billy's sake, because I thought he'd be safer in London; and I took the law into my own hands, and made the arrangement without consulting you, because I hoped you wouldn't be prepared, you'd be embarrassed, to countermand my orders. And I was right. And I was wrong. How could you have told Billy you used to climb on the roof of Castile House? He was bound to try it – you must have known he'd try it. And then you went and gambled and lost all our money.'

'One can't stop boys climbing and taking risks – I never intended to harm Billy. As for my gambling, that's a separate issue.'

'I disagree. Don't pretend to be stupider than you are, Ivo. The more money you lost the greater the danger that Billy was in. It's obvious – you needed what belonged to him – you'd ruined yourself – you would have been penniless in the midst of plenty – no one could fail to perceive the potential solution of the problem. So I paid two visits to the nursery to check nothing bad was happening. The first time I saw Billy on the parapet, but kept out of sight in order not to surprise him, watched until he was down on the flat part of the roof, and informed you, warned you, that I was worrying about what became of him. The next day, in the afternoon, you returned to Castile House, said you'd lost the remainder of our fortune, and disappeared. I rushed up to the nursery – Billy was balancing on the pediment – I stepped through the french window to be sure nobody else was on the roof – far from frightening the child, my aim was to rescue him – I was so afraid that you might have decided to remedy your situation and improve your prospects once and for all – and he started breathing badly and he fell. Perhaps it was just as well you didn't let the policemen talk to me. I wouldn't have incriminated myself – quite the opposite – I would have been sympathized with – but your reputation at least would have been ruined good and proper. You wanted to avoid an inquest not because you

[197]

thought I was in danger of getting into trouble, but because you thought you were.'

'Talk, talk, talk! I might have guessed that you'd lie your way out of the whole business, and try to put the blame on me.'

'But you are to blame, Ivo, and you would have seemed even more so under cross-examination in the witness-box. How could you have answered those leading questions: who had a motive for murdering Billy, who gained most from his death, what did you expect to live on after spending your entire fortune, why did you remove your nephew from his customary safer situation in the country and expose him to a variety of risks in town, why did you urge him to live dangerously, why didn't you have locks fitted to the french window in the nursery?'

'You know it all, don't you, Beatrice?'

'Oh yes.'

'It's a pack of lies. If anyone's to blame, you are.'

'Well – what I know best is that you were fully aware of everything I did and never stopped me doing it. I could argue that I was unwittingly used by you as your cat's paw, pulling chestnuts out of the fire for you. Anyway, what you call my lies would be difficult to disprove. That's the point, Ivo.'

'You wouldn't speak against me – a wife can't give evidence against her husband.'

'Maybe not – but mud sticks – and I'm not so sure about the legal position of wives in divorce cases or when they've been divorced.'

'So that's it.'

'And I would speak against you, as you call it, if I had to. We've both got a lot to lose, you see.'

A knocking on the door of the lounge startled them.

Ivo, for some reason, almost as if they had been engaged in intimate or nefarious business, stood up before saying: 'Come in!'

It was the attendant, warning that the train would start in a minute or two.

'Oh – thank you. Don't disturb us again – I'll see to the lamps – good night.'

The door closed.

Ivo subsided heavily, hopelessly perhaps, on the sofa opposite the one on which Beatrice sat poised and straight-backed.

'Cards on the table,' he muttered.

[198]

'What did you say?'

'We might as well put our cards on the table.'

'That's what I thought you said. You have no cards, Ivo. If you were able to divorce me, which I doubt, the costs would be unacceptable – money and property would be the least of your losses – you'd never raise your head again when I was finished with you. Ivo, we're stuck with each other. All we need to discuss is how to make ourselves as comfortable as possible.'

'What are you driving at now?'

'Zeals must go.'

'Oh no you don't!'

'Zeals hates me, he's been against me from the day we were introduced, and I've had enough of his insolence, and won't keep a servant who thinks he's got grounds to blackmail me.'

'It can't be done.'

'In that case I shall call his bluff. I'll go the police before he does and speak my piece about you.'

'What else?'

'Nanny Campion must move out of Castile House. I want nobody round me who's too close to the recent past, or to you. And I've had more than enough of Graves pulling long faces.'

'You're the most heartless woman I've ever come across. Anything more?'

'I shall call myself the Duchess of Castile. Brougham's an unlucky name.'

'It's not on, Beatrice.'

'It is for me. Please yourself. We can both please ourselves – we must live for today rather than yesterday or tomorrow – because I'm afraid you'll be the last of your line.'

The train moved. The engine puffed rapidly and loudly in short bursts. Within the lounge of the private car the oil lamps swayed in their fittings and rocked the shadows, while the woodwork creaked.

Ivo Grevill, black-browed, sunk in an attitude of dejection on the sofa, grated out: 'I'm not accepting any of this.'

His wife, his duchess, stared at him with slanting amber eyes, at once blank and penetrating, and said: 'You will. Don't forget that you've always followed my lead, and remember where it's got you. As a gambler you ought to be able to recognize luck, and who changed yours. Life's going to be different from now on.'

[199]

'You terrify me, Beatrice.'

'Oh well, there's a price to pay for everything.'

'You shouldn't say that — you shouldn't have said half of what you have — with Billy lying in his coffin just through there. I'm not listening to any more. I'm turning in.'

He was on his feet, lurching in the direction of the two sleeping-compartments.

'What about the lamps?' she asked.

Without speaking or being spoken to, he extinguished the four lamps in question.

'Wait a moment!' She issued her order from the semi-darkness. 'Come here! No, come and sit beside me, Ivo. You see, we can't escape each other now — we're too involved — we'll have to make the best of it — we can still enjoy ourselves.'

'I'm not in the mood, I'm not ready, Beatrice.'

'You can leave all that to me. You know how nice I can be to you. We're all alone with our secrets. I feel like celebrating.'

'No!' he exclaimed, standing. 'You keep off! You think you've got it cut and dried. You think you've tied me up with your lying and your intimidation in a harmless bundle. If you're so damn clever, I'm surprised you haven't considered a pretty simple possibility. I've told you what I want. You've told me you won't give it to me. But I could take it. According to you I was capable of engineering Billy's death, if not of being its cause. Married to a man like me, you're missing a trick to count on our life together stretching far ahead. Good night.'

He turned and headed for the lit corridor.

In a voice he had never heard her use before, loudly furious and shrill, she shouted after him: 'My first husband tried that on and look what happened to him!'

Ivo entered his sleeping-compartment and audibly locked the door.

The train gathered speed on its journey north.